Praise for *How*

"Ebenbach explores science fiction f[ ] novel focused on a one-way trip to t[ ] [ ] by an eccentric billionaire with funding via reality television, six scientists emerge from a 'Survivors' gauntlet of seemingly meaningless tests . . . The poignancy of the impossible pregnancy is the Bradbury touch, the reality show framework carries fingerprints of Douglas Adams, and the handbook provides a Vonnegut-esque struggle with the paradoxes of the human condition. *How to Mars* is Andy Weir's *The Martian* (2014) infused with poetry in a superbly concise package."
—*Booklist*

"David Ebenbach's new novel wittily dismantles the classic space adventure story. In it, the first colonists on Mars struggle not only with the technical and existential challenges of living on another world, but also with much more familiar conundrums: boredom, cabin fever, a crazy coworker, an unplanned pregnancy, corporate incompetence. Funny and wonderfully inventive, *How to Mars* is equal parts an absurdist cautionary tale and a warm-hearted exploration of those things, good, bad and indifferent, that make us human."
—Emily Mitchell, author of *Viral Stories*

"Six Marsonauts must survive on the red planet after their reality TV show is canceled in this delightfully unconventional novel. Two years after having been chosen to receive one-way tickets to Mars for a lifetime of research—all while living under constant surveillance for TV—six scientists are finding life undeniably monotonous, especially since their show was canceled because of low ratings . . . But when Jenny, the astrophysicist, realizes she's pregnant after having begun a romantic relationship with Josh—although the *Destination Mars!* Handbook repeatedly stresses that sex is strictly forbidden—the small community must come together to resolve the looming issues associated with welcoming a newborn into their cramped habitat . . .The

story has a strong sense of whimsy, but Ebenbach also creates depth by exploring issues like engineer Stefan's feelings of estrangement and violence and Jenny's guilt over her sister's suicide years earlier. A poignant examination of what it means to be human."
—*Kirkus*

Praise for David Ebenbach

Praise for *The Guy We Didn't Invite to the Orgy*

"Ebenbach is more at home in the minefield of ambiguity than most of us are in our houses."
—Roy Kesey, author of *Any Deadly Thing* and *Pacazo*

"A brilliant, original, and illuminating book!"
—Stephen O'Connor, author of *Thomas Jefferson Dreams of Sally Hemings*

Praise for *Miss Portland*

"Ebenbach delivers an absorbing, suspenseful story of emotional depth and complexity."
—*Fiction Southeast*

"A complex, intimate, and deeply humane portrait of a person whose experience of the world is both alternate and poignantly familiar."
—*Foreword Reviews*

How To Mars
David Ebenbach

Also by David Ebenbach

Novels
Miss Portland (2017)

Collections
Between Camelots (2005)
Into the Wilderness (2012)
The Guy We Didn't Invite to the Orgy and Other Stories (2017)

Non-Fiction
The Artist's Torah (2012)

Poetry
Autogeography (2013)
We Were the People Who Moved (2015)
Some Unimaginable Animal (2019)

HOW TO
MARS

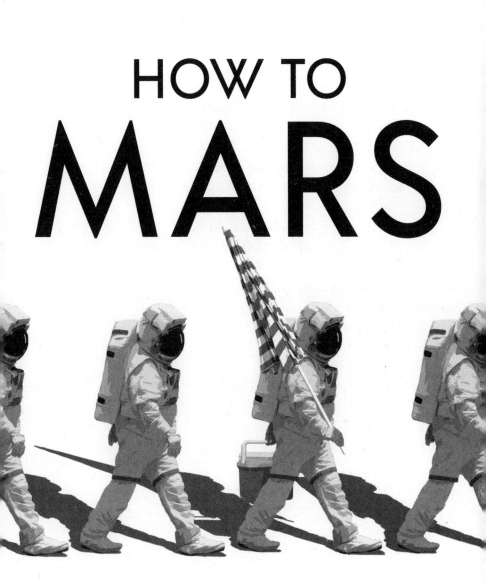

DAVID EBENBACH

TACHYON
SAN FRANCISCO

Cover and interior design by Elizabeth Story
Author photo copyright © 2021 by Rachel Gartner

Tachyon Publications LLC
1459 18th Street #139
San Francisco, CA 94107
415.285.5615
www.tachyonpublications.com
tachyon@tachyonpublications.com

Series Editor: Jacob Weisman
Editor: Jaymee Goh

Print ISBN: 978-1-61696-356-9
Digital ISBN: 978-1-61696-357-6

Printed in the United States by Versa Press, Inc.

9 8 7 6 5 4 3 2

To Rachel and Reuben,
the only stars I need.

Prakt Means Splendor

THIS IS HOW I find out Jenny is pregnant on Mars.

"Do you want to go outside?" Jenny says. It's just after lunch, which was freeze-dried Reubens. She doesn't say anything more specific than "outside," even though now we have names for this red ridge and that red valley and red-orange Mt. Nearby over there and the various piles of red rocks and even the various scattered dead landers and rovers from old missions, which are landmarks and which we call by the names of the missions, even though some of them had silly names like *Undertaking* and *Beagle* and *Optimism*. But Jenny just says "outside." In some sense, even after more than two years, this is still our schema of the planet: there's inside, which is where everybody is, and there's outside, which is where nobody is.

"Sure," I eventually say.

Jenny nods. It doesn't bother her that it has taken me a while to answer. We have two speeds here: Slow and Slooooooooooooow. Well, three speeds if you count Something is on Fire, but that's rare.

We put on the suits—one leg, two legs, et cetera. Roger and Nicole look up from their tablets and watch us get suited up, because us putting on the suits is the big game in town at the moment. Trixie is sleeping in the bunk dome. I think Stefan is on the toilet. Anyway, we put the suits on, including Jenny tucking her brown curls into her helmet, and then the audience goes back to its tablets and we go to the airlocks and out.

You know how they call Mars the red planet? Well, that's because it's red there. Like, you go outside and you see red. Red to the east, red to the west. Red north, red south. In fact, the dust gets everywhere, so inside is red, too. Though actually, we have a sort of simmering debate among us about just how red versus just how orange the planet is, but we try to keep it simmering rather than boiling over. You wouldn't believe how likely it is that someone gets their ass kicked for arguing one side or the other. Like, there was the night that Roger made mild fun of the orange crowd by saying, "You can't even rhyme anything with orange," and Stefan . . . well, Stefan squeezed and twisted two of Roger's fingers, twisted them until they broke—one and then the other. That actually happened. I still shudder when I think about it. Now, Stefan is more complicated than that episode suggests, and things have been a lot calmer since—but still, that was what you would call a pretty sobering moment. So, anyway, we just keep our opinions to ourselves, even though it's obviously red out here. Aside from the mountain, which is more complicated.

Anyway, I say to Jenny, through our radio system, "So."

We start walking, which is a way bouncier thing than it was on Earth, because of the much lower gravity, and so it's a little hard to have a serious conversation while walking. It makes you feel like everyone is partly balloon animal. You wouldn't want to tell someone they had a terminal disease, for example, while walking on Mars. But there aren't that many places to have conversations—inside and outside are the main two ones—so we do have some important conversations out here, and also some boring ones, and also there's a lot of not-talking, too.

Mars is a planet where the question "What's new?" doesn't come in very handy. It's great.

So we start bounce-walking under the old basically familiar sun. Jenny is taking us in the general direction of the *Prakt*, a big piece of not-working space equipment sent here by a consortium of Scandinavian corporations. It's about one o'clock, in Mars hours, which are technically only a little longer than Earth hours.

About halfway between Home Sweet and the *Prakt*, Jenny says, "Let's go to our channel." I hear the click that says that she's changed to channel nine hundred and forty-seven, which is where we go when we don't want to be overheard. I change my own radio to channel nine hundred and forty-seven. It's romantic.

After a few moments, she says, "Hey, Josh."

I think about the fact that we all call each other by our first names. I guess I originally expected that we'd wind up with cool nicknames, like Ace and Ratchet and Doc, or at least that we'd do last names, like baseball players. But no.

"Hey, Jenny," I say.

I can hear, through the radio, a long, long sigh. There's something about what we breathe here that makes sighs longer on Mars. Or at least it seems that way. Then Jenny says, "And hey, plus-one."

I take one more bounce-step and then bounce-stop. "Wait," I say. I can't see her face and she can't see mine, because the suits have these gold mirrory sunglass-fronts on them where our faces are. So you lose all the paralanguage for sure. "What?"

She sighs again, like the sound of the tide going all the way out, if there were an ocean. "I'm pregnant," she says.

I'm not sure how long we stand there thinking about that. I know I should be saying something, but mostly my mind is suddenly kind of shorting out and the things I *can* think of are not worth putting into words. I don't ask her if the baby's mine, for example, because the baby is mine. I don't express disbelief in the fundamental premise of pregnancy based on the fact that we both had operations before coming here, because I'm realizing right now that those operations sometimes don't work, which is something I should have considered before this. Because, statistically, Jenny and I have had a large amount of sex by now. I don't even ask what we're going to do, because I'm sure that we have no idea what we're going to do. The whole point was that pregnancy on Mars is supposed to be a bad idea a hundred different ways. That's why the people in charge told all of us not to have sex here, even after the operations.

I say, "Wow." I'm feeling a lot of things, but "Wow" is all I manage.

"Yes." Just from her voice, I can't tell what Jenny is feeling.

"I guess this is why they told us not to have sex here," I add.

"Yes," she says. "It is."

"I guess they're going to be mad at us." There's supposed to be a call home tonight. "They're going to say that we promised not to."

"That's right," she says.

A few minutes go by. We stare at each other's sunglass-faces. I feel like my blood is buzzing, like it has a small electrical current in it.

She adds, "And yet there's a whole drawer in the med closet that's full of pregnancy tests."

"Huh," I say.

The *Prakt* glints off in the distance. From under its coating of red dust.

When we get back to Home Sweet, there's a party, because there's no such thing as a private radio channel on a planet this bored. You can just scan all the channels until you find the conversation. So there's a party. We don't have any disco ball on Mars, or streamers, but everybody has written *CONGRATULATIONS* or *MAZEL TOV* or ¡*FELICIDADES*! on their tablets and they're holding their tablets up to show us. The *mazel tovs* are for me and the *felicidades* are for Jenny, even though she doesn't speak as much Spanish as you might expect from a person who has a Puerto Rican mother, not to mention an African American father who's partly Dominican. Anyway, the *congratulations* are for both of us. Also, someone has broken out the freeze-dried cake.

"You guys," Jenny says.

That night we get the communication request that we've been expecting. Earth wants to talk to us. We all hate talking to Earth, because it takes a radio signal about eleven minutes to travel from one planet to the other, and then eleven more for a response to get back, which means that a call is like,

Them: "Hello!"

[eleven minutes plus eleven minutes]

Us: "Hello! How are you?"

[eleven minutes plus eleven minutes]

Them: "Fine."

Even for us that's too slow.

Plus, we don't even really get to talk to Earth. We get to talk to some communications person at the *Destination Mars!* corporation. Not even the *Destination Mars!* founder, the person who thought this whole thing up originally and is supposed to be, well, a pretty eccentric person; we talk to communications people. A couple of times we've gotten a hearty virtual handshake from one world leader or another, and there was the one time that they put us on with the Cincinnati Bengals cheerleaders for some reason, but mostly it's corporate. We're not talking to a representative sample of the Earth population, is what I'm saying.

Still, it's necessary. We have to arrange for supplies to get sent and we have to tell them about our discoveries, even though we haven't had any discoveries for a long time. Most of us haven't even been trying. We were sent here for science, one-way tickets to Mars for a lifetime of Mars research, but it turns out that after a while even scientists can get bored of science. Especially here. Mars, I can tell you, is pretty much rocks, rocks, rocks.

The idea was originally that we would go on to terraform the planet, but we would need more people for that. And at first, *Destination Mars!* did talk about eventually sending more people, but they've been quiet about that for a while.

And now we're possibly making a new person of our own.

"Do you think we should tell them?" I say. Two years ago, when we first got here, the *Destination Mars!* people would already know, because they were filming everything for reality TV back then, but that show got canceled about a year in. Also because of boredom. Now we'd have to actually tell them.

Jenny considers the question. We're sitting in the common room, because that's where we sit. On low, reddish vinyl-ish couches and *chaises longues* next to basically Ikea coffee tables. Orange tables. And here I can see her face now, of course. It's a round face, with extra-round cheeks. Plus those big light brown eyes. It's a nice face. "Well, they'll be angry," she says after a while.

I nod. "But they can't actually do anything about it," I say. "Can they?"

Long exhalation. "I guess not." Then, after a minute, "Well, they could leave something out of the next supply rocket. The freeze-dried cookie dough ice cream, maybe." Outside the common room window I can see the sun going down. Sunsets are the one not-so-red thing about Mars. There's more gray in them here.

"They would totally kibosh the cookie dough ice cream," I say. I wonder if they'd even go farther than that. Every once in a while, I get the idea that the managers of the *Destination Mars!* corporation are getting a little fed up with us in general. And that maybe they have some anger issues.

I can hear Roger in the workroom saying hello to someone back on Earth. Hello and then waiting. "Still, though," I say. "Like, how pregnant are you?"

She raises an eyebrow at me. She calls that her "Say what?" eyebrow.

"I mean, how long?" I say.

"Oh," she says. She picks up her tea from the coffee table. "I think almost two months."

"Oh," I say. Jenny is really, truly pregnant. The psychosomatic buzzing in my blood has become an itching.

After quite a few minutes I hear someone on Earth say hello back to Roger. Hello and a question about what's new.

"Are we really doing this?" she says.

I open my mouth to answer, but Jenny, faster than typical Mars-time, speaks first.

"We'd better tell them what's going on," she says.

We get up and go into the workroom, where Roger is alone in

front of the screen. He's here by default; nobody else has enough patience to have these drawn-out Earth conversations. Sometimes others among us go pop our heads in or say something off-camera, but we don't tend to stick around. Roger, though—he's a botanist and a geologist, so he's used to waiting for things. Also he has trouble saying no. Jenny believes that's because he's Canadian; to me that feels a little speculative. Either way, the end result is he ends up doing the calls. Right now he's starting into a longish update on our rock analysis work, saying it all in one stream for convenience, while the Earth person—a woman called Barbara with rectangular glasses—sits passively, having not yet heard any of what he's saying. In twenty-two minutes her face will show a reaction to the beginning of his update, though by then he'll already be done. It's surreal stuff.

"The deeper samples are still under analysis," Roger is saying. He's really the only one who's still fully invested in research, actively in touch with other geologists and botanists back on Earth. "Though so far they seem pretty similar to the not-as-deep samples. We're also filling out more of the topographical map at a good pace," he adds, "and—"

But then we lean in. "Also," Jenny says, "I'm pregnant."

At which point Roger sort of blushes and lapses into indecision about whether to continue with the map-talk, scratching at his pale, thinning hair with his left hand, which is his hand where the fingers got broken and are still at a slightly uneasy angle from the rest of his hand. I see them and wince. I definitely expected an astronaut with the name Roger to be more dashing and confident than our Roger has turned out to be. I guess that's because of Buck Rogers, which I have never actually seen, but which I have heard about.

"It's true," I add into the screen.

Barbara, of course, shows no reaction. She can't, not for another twenty-two minutes. So, we stand there and we wait. We wait and I try to not think about anything at all.

Well, after about twenty minutes we see her nodding dutifully—

she's taking note of Roger's report—and then abruptly her face registers shock. "Wait—what?" she says. And then, not about to wait twenty-two minutes for our confirmation, which I already gave anyway, she sputters on. "This is why we told you not to have sex," she says.

Jenny rolls her eyes at me, which will probably irritate Barbara in about eleven minutes. In the meantime, we wait for her to continue. But she doesn't. She waits for us to continue. Oh, boy.

"Um," I finally say, "but we already *did* have sex."

Twenty-two minutes later we get Barbara glaring at the eye roll and then leaning forward toward the camera. "You are not allowed to do this," she says.

Jenny and I glance at each other. Because what does that even *mean*?

This time there's only a brief pause before Barbara keeps going. "You sat through the abstinence films. I know you did because I have your signatures." She shakes a sheaf of papers that are almost definitely not the specific ones we signed about the abstinence films, but for the sake of drama. "I mean," she says, slipping into an actual rant, "a baby on Mars? How would that even work? Do people lactate the same in low gravity? Do fetuses in the womb get all their bones in the right places? What about radiation? What if the baby wants to come out feet first or head first or however they're not supposed to come out? And then when they're out, do you do sleep training, or co-sleeping, or whatever all that stuff is? Do they sleep on their backs or fronts? I mean, wow. And how the hell do you raise a child on Mars? You don't even have the right size clothes! I just—I don't even know what to say to you. You two are idiots. Why do we even bother with these idiots?"

I feel myself sweating a little as Barbara turns off-camera to say something to someone nearby. Our communication is probably attracting more than the usual amount of attention.

Barbara turns back and faces us squarely. She says, "You're going to have to terminate the pregnancy."

Jenny and I stand up straight and look at each other. Somehow this idea had not even occurred to me—cognitive overload—though I'm thinking about it now, and I can see that Jenny has already thought about it. The moment stretches on a little bit. Mars seconds. I still don't know exactly what Jenny is thinking, but the feeling I'm feeling, considering this idea—you'd honestly have to call it gratitude. You'd have to call it relief. But I look at Jenny's face and don't say anything. Neither of us says anything. We just look back at the screen and wait.

"Seriously?" Barbara says, after she's had enough time to see that we're not responding. "Nothing?" She leans forward again, almost confidential. "Do you realize who's in charge here? Do you realize," she asks, "that you don't even get to *eat* unless we send you food?"

Whoa. That's a *whoa* comment right there. I look at Jenny again.

"You have to terminate the pregnancy," Barbara says. "It's not like we can come get you so that you can get reasonable medical care."

That's true. It was part of the deal: one way. They had the technology to get us here, but they don't have the technology to bring us back.

"You have to terminate," Barbara says again.

Jenny searches my eyes for a minute. It might be an actual full minute. I almost say something about how ending the pregnancy does sound like the easier thing, especially with food threats flying around. Even without them, though—what about all the risks? To the baby? To *Jenny*? The risks in general? But then Jenny says, not to Barbara but to me, "We should decide this ourselves."

I take that in. I take my time taking that in. There are follow-up questions called for here, but not in front of Barbara. I nod. "Okay."

Jenny turns back to Barbara and leans in. "We're going to decide for ourselves." And then she takes my hand and we walk out of there.

Trixie is in the common room, tapping something on her tablet.

Very likely Sudoku. Also she is listening to everything. Trixie isn't even actually looking at her tablet. She's looking at us.

Trixie and Nicole are the people most likely to get the nickname "Doc," because everyone else is just PhD doctors, whereas these two are MD doctors in addition to Trixie also being a PhD doctor and Nicole being an Air Force captain. But we call them Trixie and Nicole. In any case I guess we might be needing them soon, one way or another.

Jenny and I sit together, both chewing on what Barbara said and on the situation overall, listening to Roger for a while as he somehow manages to restart his cartography monologue, and then he talks about some of the astronomical research we've been doing, just for a few minutes. And then we listen as he falls into silence, and as he waits. I notice that my foot is tapping a little frenetically.

"Well, that was some food for thought," I say.

Jenny doesn't have anything to say to that. She's squinting thoughtfully off into the distance. Looking through the window at Mars, such as it is.

"Are we in way over our heads?" I eventually ask.

She stops the thoughtful distance-squinting and says, "Well, however deep in we are, that's where we are." She turns in Trixie's direction. "Right?"

Trixie nods from across the room, her dyed-red pigtails bobbing, and says in her Australian accent, "I don't think I'd be too keen on trying to terminate a pregnancy here." She gestures around generally at Mars.

"Too dangerous?" I ask.

"Defo," Trixie says. That means definitely.

Jenny turns back. "So here we are."

Here we are.

From the next room, Barbara eventually says, twenty-two minutes after we've walked off the set, "Are you serious? Unbelievable. Completely unbelievable." And then, probably to someone else off-camera, "Can they just do that? Can they?" And a brief pause before,

"Okay. You know what? I'm going to have to check into this," she says. "I'm going to have to check into it."

"Do you want to go outside?" I say to Jenny.

Mars at night is also like you'd expect it. Very dark, with lots of stars, of course, and they're almost the stars that we're used to. The moons Phobos and Deimos are both up. They're both pretty small, though, and actually not much to look at. Deimos is practically just like another star. And Earth isn't up there tonight. You can see it from Mars, just like you can see Mars from Earth, but it's not in our particular night sky right now. If it were there, it would just be a little point of light, of course.

Our helmet lights pointing the way, we bounce-walk in a different direction this time. We go toward a crater that we call the Soup Hole. It was Roger who decided we should name it that—he's really into soup—and he used it so consistently that it stuck. I had wanted to call it the Hot Tub. Even though there's obviously not any water in there, it's just deep enough that you can sit in it and lean back and put your elbows up on the crater wall like in a hot tub. It would be a good place to have a beer, except that there's no beer on Mars—the bubbles wouldn't work right—and you couldn't drink a bottle of anything while you're in your space suit anyway. It would have to come through the helmet's food/beverage tube.

We sit in the crater. Two people relaxing in a night-time soak. Or two lentils in a soup.

I look at Jenny's face, or at the sunglass visor in front of it. Now I wish I hadn't asked her to come out here, because I'd like to see her face. I like Jenny's face. Her eyes are actually sometimes more orange than light brown, somehow. They're unbelievable eyes, and she says nobody else in her family has them.

"I like your face," I say.

I can kind of hear her smiling, but I imagine it's a tense smile.

"Do you want to go to our channel?" she says. "Why bother, right?"

"Right," I say. I mean, I'd actually like a private conversation this time, but that just isn't a thing. I watch Phobos, which moves faster than Deimos. You can pretty much see it move. Go Phobos, go.

"I like your face, too," she says.

I take my elbows off the crater wall. "So," I say, "you're pregnant. That's what we're talking about," I say. "As in, we made a baby, inside of you—" I point, for reference—"and it's some kind of mix of genetic material from you and from me, and we're talking about you growing that baby, and then you would have that baby, and it would come out of you, and, when it came out, it would be on *Mars*. Our baby. That's what we're talking about." I try to keep my voice even.

There's only a brief pause before she answers. "Yeah," she says. "I've been developing an awareness of all that."

"The first Martian baby," I say. From buzzing to itching to, now, a kind of full-on scouring feeling.

"My first baby anywhere," she says.

"Mine, too." I pause. There's a lump in my throat. There's no other way to describe it. Then: "I always assumed Mars was going to be a dead-end planet."

Jenny doesn't respond to that, exactly. Instead she says, in a wondering voice, "It happened," and she tilts her sunglass-face up at the stars. She's an astrophysicist. When she looks up, to some extent she sees data. But I know that's not the only thing she sees.

Then, over the radio, I hear—we hear—Nicole's voice. She says, "The first baby born in America—they named her Virginia Dare. Well, the first white baby. There were the indigenous babies, of course."

And then Stefan's voice, with its half-Danish, half-British accent: "Or you could go with Adam, if you're thinking about firsts. Adam. There's a first for you."

Trixie: "There are older names than that. Gilgamesh, et cetera."

"I'm talking about Biblical time," Stefan says, irritable. It's true that he's irritable. "You can't get older than that."

In non-emergency situations we are able to turn down the volume on people from Home Sweet, and so we turn down the volume on people from Home Sweet.

I say, not knowing what to say, "I wonder what the oldest name in the world is."

"Which world?" Jenny says.

I look up. My PhD is in psychology, strangely enough—the science I'm supposed to be doing here is the science of what people are like when just a few of them are thrown together on Mars—but anyway one upshot of my particular education is that, when I look up, I don't see any data, not even constellations, not even after all this time; I see a dark, dark sky, but just speckled straight through with wild light.

It would be a good moment for a shooting star or a meteor shower. The sky, though, basically stands still. Well, except for Phobos. And except for the fact that everything out there actually *is* moving, whether we can see it or not. Moving at inconceivable speeds, in fact.

I'm about to say, "Jenny, I'm freaking out," when first she says, "Josh, I know you're freaking out."

I turn toward Jenny and it's almost like I can see her face. She takes my hand. Holding hands in spacesuits is not very much like holding actual hands, but it's something.

"I know you're thinking of Lil," Jenny says.

It takes me a very long time to respond, even by Mars standards. "I am," I manage to say. Lil was my fiancée on Earth, before any of this, before I'd ever even thought about Mars at all, really. She was my fiancée. And then one night she was driving home and a very big car in one of the oncoming lanes lost control. It was raining.

We all have our particular reasons why we signed up for a one-way ticket to Mars.

"And I know you thought this would be a dead-end planet," Jenny says. "That you hoped it." She squeezes my hand. It's not like she can see me crying, with my mirror-face, but she knows. "Believe me," she says. "I hoped that, too."

"I know," I say. We all have our reasons, and I know hers as well as she knows mine.

We sit very quietly for a long time.

"Listen," she eventually says.

"Yes."

"I never had my tubes tied," Jenny says.

Everything stops. I look over at her. "What? What do you mean?" She shakes her head. She never had them tied.

"But that was required, wasn't it? I mean, I know vasectomies were required."

"They didn't make me." She's still just looking up. "One of my earlier doctors said that my Fallopian tubes were problematic. And then the Mars people checked them, and they told me my Fallopian tubes were problematic."

"What?" I say. "Are you serious?"

"Yes. I'm not supposed to be able to get pregnant at all."

This is, in fact, staggering. I am staggered by it. Eventually, I say, "So you weren't supposed to be able to get pregnant, and I wasn't supposed to be able to get you pregnant."

"Right," she said.

"And yet, pregnancy. You're pregnant."

"Yes," she says.

I say, "Wow." I think I am feeling all the things that a person can feel. I say, "That's pretty astounding."

There is a moment or two of silence, and then Jenny issues a world-class, a Mars-class, sigh. This sigh might last for a Mars minute and a half.

"Yeah," she says. "Yeah," she says again. "It really is."

My voice cracks a little when I speak next. "Sometimes I don't have any idea what's going on." A lot of me cracks a little. "How it all happens."

"What do you mean?"

"Do you think that," I say, thinking out loud, "in all the cause-and-effect chains of the universe, there's maybe some chain, one thing leading to the next, that goes all the way from the big bang to this exact situation? That we must have been heading for everything—" I stop, and then continue—"that we must have been heading for everything that's happened to us, and heading for this moment, for you and me, for this, exactly this, from the very beginning?"

Jenny thinks for a moment. "A lot of scientists question the theory of any kind of big bang anymore," she says. "It's possible that the universe has always been here. And always will be. Different, but here."

Very abruptly I reach over and hug her, which also is not like regular hugging, and we sort of clonk our sunglass-faces against one another, but still we're able to hold on, and it's worth it.

I hold on to Jenny, who even without the paralanguage I can tell is also crying a little. I think about the fact that what she just said about the universe is obviously true.

What You Can't Bring With You

(Section 9 of the unofficial *Destination Mars!* handbook, as written by the founder of *Destination Mars!*)

Please understand: there is space, which is infinite, and then there is *storage* space, which is anything but.

Not that you will be traveling empty-handed. There is the Communal Resource Stockpile, which will contain the things you'll need in common: tablets containing a significant percentage of the literary, cinematic, and musical output of the human species, along with scenic Earth photos and collections of bird songs and traffic noises from major cities and digitized versions of all the most popular board games (except Monopoly, because Monopoly is of course an interpersonal nightmare); several decks of playing cards; joke collections; freeze-dried food representing your nutritional needs and your diverse tastes as well as holiday favorites; sports equipment that will still be usable on Mars (e.g., basketballs *no*; bocce balls *yes*); yarn for the knitters on board; spices and condiments; first aid kits; and so on. (See Section 11 of this handbook for more detail.) And then there will be your Personal Vestment Allocation (explained in Section 12), which will allow you a modest collection of clothing, including no more than two pairs of shoes, one of which should probably be a pair of sandals, for casual moments. Beyond that, what you have is the Individual Sine Qua Non Ration, which can weigh no more than 6.80 kg (15 lbs.) in total and must fit completely in the personal *Destination Mars!* zippable tote bag that has been provided to you.

This means that you will have to make some difficult choices. You can do this—you've already made the almost incomprehensibly difficult decision to go, to lift your foot off this planet and head to an unknown world and never come back. That's a huge one, which you nailed. Unless, that is, you're reading this section as a potential applicant and haven't yet decided whether or not you're really going to apply, in which case we hope this section will help to clarify some things and help you to choose. But the main idea is that the opportunities—untold knowledge, adventure, a new frontier, fresh hope for a species that really ekes out a living on hope, etc.—the idea is that the opportunities outweigh the costs. After all, just think: *Mars.* You'll be living on freaking *Mars.* (See Section 2 for more thoughts on why it's an unbelievably amazing idea, and why we wish *we* were going.) Of course, only *you* can decide that big main decision, and (after that) only you can decide what you will and won't bring with you, within the stated limitations.

Some guidelines:

- In terms of exercise equipment, small items may fit but most things won't, and weight is an issue here; two barbells worth the effort of lifting will take you right over your limit. Remember that the Communal Resource Stockpile will contain some helpful resources.

- Paper and paper goods are surprisingly heavy. If you decide to bring files and journals, old newspapers and birthday cards, you will rapidly reach your weight limit. And you are welcome to use our scanners here to create digital images of important materials for the tablets.

- No fireworks or other incendiary devices, for obvious reasons.

- You cannot bring very long objects, like non-compact umbrellas. You will not, in any case, need umbrellas.

- You cannot bring your own well-worn comforter, and, if you bring your own pillow, it will probably be the only thing that will fit in your bag. We will, of course, provide bedding especially designed to work with the bunks, both practically and aesthetically. And we ask you to remember that it is never appropriate to associate any particular set of bedding with important emotional states, such as *safety* and *home*.

- You cannot bring your favorite chair, with the body dents already in place.

- No full-length curtains that your mother crocheted.

- No large wall hangings (e.g., oil paintings). No medium-sized wall hangings.

- No bookshelves, regardless of whether you made them yourself. And bear in mind that the library of Mars is obviously going to be digital.

- You are in a room of your home right now, staring at something substantial that you suddenly realize you own and care about but that won't fit in the tote bag. You cannot bring it.

- Have you ever moved before? Even from one apartment to another, in the same building? Then you know it already: some things can't be moved.

- Also, if you've ever moved, you know that you're going to be glad to leave some things behind—the lousy shower in the old apartment, say, with the terrible water pressure, or the neighbor who practices some kind of brass instrument late into the night, or the excessive friendliness of the neighborhood in general when you're just out trying to take a walk. None of that can—or should—come with you.

- In any case, you can certainly bring a teddy bear, though you cannot bring your teddy bear collection, unless it is a very small and unsuccessful collection.

- You cannot bring rugs. Something the size of a doormat may be theoretically possible. That said, note that the Communal Resource Stockpile already contains novelty doormats which can be placed just outside the colony airlock entrances for a bit of light humor:
  Come In: What's Mars is Yours
  Don't Spread the Red (a foot-wiping request)
  Beware of Martian Dog

- Oh—certainly there will be no actual pets, aside from the two goldfish, male and female, that will be included as part of the Communal Resource Stockpile. We will eventually be sending some lab animals for research purposes, probably, but of course you must not become attached to those specimens as pets. (They are also not intended to be used as food.)

- You can bring small toys, if you have toys that you still use as a grownup, like bath toys—but there will be no baths. Mars will be shower-only.

- One way to think about all this is that you can't, in other words, disassemble your home here—not-quite-cheerful yellow walls and race-car beds and tasseled sham pillows, maybe, and leaky pipes and stationary exercise bikes and that giant signed poster of Leonard Nimoy and slipper chairs and inconsistent central heating and stacks of old extreme sports magazines you never read and hardwood floors and that calcification you could never get out of the toilet and whatever figurines you might have amassed in surprising numbers and Barcaloungers and old lamps and breakfast nooks and wallpaper and the fusty basement that kind of scared you a little anyway, not to mention the garden you maybe tended out back—you can't just break all that down here and reassemble it there.

- Nor will you be bringing the neighborhood you grew up in, or the real innocence you had then, the large experience you have whenever you stand at the edge of a large body of water, not that or the rain running behind your ears when you're caught in a storm or the sensation of waking up in sunlight—and of course those things are already in some sense gone anyway.

- Certainly you cannot pack the future that you once had and are now setting aside in order to pursue this other one.

- You cannot bring additional people.

- You cannot bring *any* additional people.

- We have selected the people who are coming, and there are no other people coming. None of the many that you dislike, luckily, but also none of the ones that you like. None of the ones that you love. Please see Section 3 or perhaps one of our counselors if you struggle to comprehend what this means.

- You will not, in fact, be bringing all of your own person. You will not be carrying a gallbladder, an appendix, wisdom teeth. Not anything of the body that is both disposable and dangerous; you will leave all such parts here on Earth. Some of you may request elective, preventative mastectomies, and you will be readily obliged. Tonsillectomy may also be a wise move in some cases. You can have removed whatever might trouble you, can consign it to a jar and walk away. But a note on reproductive systems: although there will certainly be vasectomies and tying of Fallopian tubes, all the associated internal organs will remain in place unless you request otherwise. You won't be using those organs—as mentioned in Section 4, you will not be having sex on Mars—but you'll know that they're there, and that may bring you comfort during the dark hours that may be very similar to, but not the same as, Earth ones.

- You cannot bring the view out of your living room window. You can bring a photo, of course, but you cannot really hope to capture the way the view changes as you move closer to the window or step to one side to lean on one of the jambs, along with

the shift of the trees in the air, unsettling and reset-
tling, and the great variety of cars that come down
your street and cannot hold on to the way that com-
bines with the sound of your difficult neighbor or the
smell—perhaps it's late fall and the city hasn't picked
up the piles of leaves and so they have begun to
decompose—all of this providing somehow a multi-
sensory but nonetheless singular experience which
says to you, *This is mine. This is what has come to me.*

- It's worth noting that you will not be bringing any
windows, in fact, that open and close.

- We might add that there will be no need for window
fans.

- The sunlight on Mars will not be the sunlight that
you know from Earth. You will have sun, of course,
but it will be more remote. This is speculation, but it
may feel like God has turned God's face just a few
degrees away from you, and this will require some
adjustment. Maybe you will feel loss. Maybe you will
feel finally free.

- Also consider your many routines. For example, your
morning routine: In the morning you wake up and
let's say you get right up to walk into your living room
to look at that view, which as we've said you can't
bring with you, not the ugly bits or the nice ones, and
then you get dressed without thinking much about
getting dressed—you showered the night before, to
help you fall asleep—and you eat breakfast standing
up at that same window, even though you do have a
table with chairs, but probably the table is scattered

with mail, a lot of it completely junk. And then out the door briskly to the bus or subway or car. Let's say bus. And on the bus, though these are not people you know, and though largely you are thinking about the concerns of your work, concerns that probably won't come with you, you register each person as she or he walks down the aisle past you or stands nearby, once all the seats are taken. Tall person, you think, or round person, or person who smiles when people are not looking, or person dressed very warmly for this time of year, or marginally scary person, or person who sort of looks like someone else you know. You get off the bus and walk to the building that is the building where you work. The weather is nice or it's not nice. (You cannot bring the weather.) You walk past benches of one kind or another, including the one that nobody sits on because the trashcan is right next to it and always overflowing, and in the summer it's clouded with bees. (There will be no bees.) You get to your building and go inside. Inevitably you encounter someone once you're inside, and she or he greets you by name. He or she asks an innocuous and unanswerable question about your well-being; nonetheless you try to answer it. There are answers available. If it's a certain kind of person who you know a certain kind of way, there are sincere answers available. That person might even walk you to the room where there's tea or coffee or in your case a very cold cup of water, which is all you need to get started. And you talk for a moment more—the lights are fluorescent but they've thoughtfully chosen the light covers and painted the walls and chosen the carpet to warm up the space somewhat, so it's a place where you can pause and talk. And then at some point you both nod your heads and it's time to do the work that you're ready to do. And the point is that you can't bring any of that with you.

- But what if it's not like that at work? What if you go in and nobody seems to care that you're there? What if, when you meet people here or there, they ignore you or they ask you to do things that you don't want to do, or tease you about your shirt, or call you nicknames that you don't like? Or, back before that, what if the crowdedness of the bus makes you itch all over? Or when you step out of your house in the first place—what if you step out into the world full of all its white-collar crime and wars and climate change and people that don't make any sense to you and you think, even though it's the only world any of us have ever lived on, you think, *What the hell am I even doing here?* You can't bring it, that baffling world that you may currently live in right this very second. You get to leave it.

- You can, of course, bring each and every emotion. (For things you will be unable to leave behind—grief, personality issues, etc.—see Section 10.) You can bring your busy mind, that loses and gains.

- But you cannot bring a comprehension of what's to come. You may not understand it when you're there. What do you understand right now, standing perhaps in your garden with a view of everything that you have turned into something that surrounds you? Or standing with a view of yourself?

- You cannot bring your bathroom mirror. Does that matter? We will provide reflective surfaces.

- You can bring yourself.

- You can't bring yourself.

- Can you bring yourself?

- Old printed photographs are allowed, up to the stated limit.

Team Orderly Mars

STEFAN DIDN'T BREAK Roger's fingers because he was cross with Roger; Stefan broke Roger's fingers because Mars was a lawless planet. Well, and also he was cross. But the primary bit was the lawlessness.

This fact—the fact that there was no legal structure, no system of rules or enforcement—had never occurred to him at any point during the months spent on that tight little rocket that he helped to pilot and which, in its all-encompassing technological sophistication and detail, seemed like an extension of Earth and its rules, but the fact struck him the minute he stepped out of the rocket. He realized it as he put his feet down onto the orange sand in his big, puffy suit, surrounded by other big, puffy suits, and under the sun that was not precisely the same sun they had grown up with, the open lifeless landscape spreading off toward all the horizons: he stood there and thought, *Nobody is in charge of this.*

Because there was nobody here. There was nothing here. There was nothing anywhere near here. To the left, orange sand. To the right, orange sand. Above, brown sky. Below, orange sand. Every time you made a footprint, it would be the first footprint. Stefan, just off the rocket, demonstrated this to himself with his own foot. There it was—the tread of a space boot—a first. He could have done it anywhere. Everything was new and ungoverned.

He thought, *I can do whatever the fuck I want.*

Stefan was from Denmark, and Denmark was of course a proper

country of laws. *This is a country of laws*, his father used to say, his finger up in the air. As a matter of fact, they were number one at it; in worldwide "rule of law" surveys conducted by organizations that conducted such surveys, Denmark was tops. A lawful paradise. Stefan had been proud when he read that in the news—he'd actually straightened up at the breakfast table and murmured *Hail King and Fatherland* under his breath.

But then, through many intermediate steps and considerable time and effort, he worked his way from that table to this place. And, he was realizing, this place was a patch of untracked sand that was six months by rocket from the nearest police station. Think about that! Six months from the nearest officer of the law. It changed things. The *Destination Mars!* cameras were rolling for the reality show, of course, but the people running those cameras were on *another planet*.

He turned to the person who happened to be standing next to him—a soft-spoken, pale, balding, Canadian man named Roger in a big, puffy suit of his own—and thought, *I could push you over onto the ground*. He didn't even really *want* to push Roger over, exactly. But he could do.

"I know," Roger said, even though he didn't know, in response to Stefan's silent stare, which in any case he couldn't see past the mirrored front visor. "It's unbelievable, isn't it?"

Stefan didn't do anything then, of course. It was only a thought. A ridiculous one. And there were other thoughts, too, including all the expected things like, *OH MY GOD THIS IS MARS* and *I hope the living quarters are all set up* and *I hope there's breathable air in there* and so on, and there was some joyous low-gravity bouncing about with the five other puffy people, kicking up clouds of dust and sand that were being kicked up by people for the first time ever. But that other thought had definitely found a home in him.

. . . .

Thankfully, the living quarters *were* all ready, thanks to the robots that had landed ahead of them and set up their whole facility, a cluster of interconnected domes where they would live and work and everything else, and there was indeed breathable air and edible food and there was electricity and running water and even some comfortable furniture to relax on—*chaises longues* and so on—and the atmosphere was giddy. Partly because the oxygen mix needed a bit of refining, but mainly because of Mars. And actually there wasn't much relaxation at first, with so much wanting to be done. Jenny started setting up the telescope, Nicole did extensive physicals on everyone, Roger set up procedures to take rock and soil samples and started planting the greenhouse, Trixie pitched in with physicals and the greenhouse, Josh transferred the rocket Experience Logs into the mainframe and arranged his little therapeutic office, and Stefan tooled all the equipment. Each of them turned to his or her tasks with Seven-Dwarfs-level enthusiasm. It must have looked great for the cameras.

Labor, however, was not, in this instance, order. Nobody was doing work because of a requirement; they were all doing it out of excitement. Some organization did emerge along the way—they largely ate meals at the same time, because it was nicer like that, and people generally said *please* and *thank you*, and several of them attended Jenny's open-invitation yoga sessions—but it was the sort of organization that you could opt in to, or opt out of. What they had on Mars were options.

This idea became a strange preoccupation for Stefan, thinking about everything he could do if he wanted to. He looked at the bunks in the bunkroom with their gray mattresses and comforters— they all slept in the same room—and thought, *I could urinate on all these beds.* He realized that he could knock everyone's dinner to the floor and smash their tablets and pitch all their clothes outside into the sand. He watched Trixie, Australian Trixie with the dyed-red hair, playing cards with Jenny one night, and he thought, *I could walk over there and pass gas in her face.* Or he could smack Jenny's head. And then there was Roger, who just for one reason or another rubbed Stefan the wrong way. Slow and steady Roger. Pale, gentle Roger. He was just so *geologist*, maybe. So *Canadian*. Stefan watched him and thought about the fact that he could poison Roger or stab him in the throat.

Stefan was not used to such thoughts by any means. He had not been prone to fighting with other children in primary school, had in fact been praised by his teachers for his obedience and attention to detail. His fourth-form report on Knud Rasmussen, for example, earned him the comment *Very neat work!* from his teacher. He had made it through university and graduate school in the UK by virtue of careful planning and discipline. Certainly he had not spent his dissertation years planning urinating sprees and murder.

Even here in the settlement Stefan was mainly focused on the machinery of the place—the workmanlike, logical devices and systems that gave them air and water and light and everything else they needed. The filters, the condenser, the outgassing machine, the seismography equipment, the portable synchrotron radiation linear accelerator, the fridge. Many, many things called out to be checked. He ran diagnostics meticulously and adjusted settings and tightened bolts, all quite steady and disciplined. There was plenty of order there—even the mini nuclear reactor out back was a plodding, sensible thing—and he appreciated it. Stefan was an engineer, after all. Though he did occasionally whisper to an exposed circuit board something like, *I am unfettered.*

"Did you say something?" Josh asked once from where he was working nearby.

Stefan said, "No," and was keenly aware of his pulse.

To be certain, even without police stations there were fetters, of a kind. There were those cameras, for one thing, and the people watching back on Earth. That was a sort of pressure. And he was not alone here, and the other people could probably stop things from happening if they had the will, and if they were strong enough. But did they? Were they?

At lunch one day Stefan looked around the table whilst people ate their reconstituted freeze-dried dishes, each with his or her own. There was Jenny, the astrophysicist who was somewhat athletic, true, and some mix of African American and Puerto Rican—somehow that made him a little nervous, maybe because of what he'd seen in movies—but the top of her head came up to his chin, and that was when she was in space boots. There was Trixie, spunky and with that dramatic red hair but not very frightening. He gathered, again mainly from movies, that some Asian people knew martial arts, but did not believe she was one of them. In any case, there was also Josh, who was a Jewish psychologist—a naturally pacifist type—and, Stefan observed, a bit distracted by Jenny. Nicole was a question mark—she had been in the military and had a tight buzz cut and usually wore an expression that he would describe as *stern*. Also, she was African American herself. He had really seen quite a lot of movies. Finally, of course there was Roger. The man was soft-spoken—annoyingly so—though he did have access to rocks.

The main thing, in any case, was that they were not a unified force. Nobody was in charge and nobody was teaming up about anything. They were eating, respectively, some curried rice situation, a pot pie, a burrito, a roast beef sandwich, and a bowl of soup. They were all over the place.

If someone had asked him, *Are you planning trouble?* Stefan would have been shocked. He wasn't planning anything. He was just thinking. You could think about something without actually doing something.

One of the things he was thinking was that order, outside the world of machines, was a sort of arbitrary thing, and generally ridiculous. Out by the reactor one day, checking things in his puffy suit, he asked himself: Who had decided which side of the plate had the napkin on it, for example? Or driving—in Denmark they drove on the right side of the road, but in England they drove quite comfortably on the left, and the rate of traffic fatalities was more or less the same. When he'd visited the Space Research Institute in Bulgaria five years earlier, he found out that nodding your head in that country meant *no*. Or NASA in America—he shook his head (which meant *yes* in Bulgaria!) whenever he thought about America—NASA had mostly managed to make the transition to the superior metric system, but had for many years been hamstrung by Americans preferring twelve inches, whatever those were, in an equally unjustifiable foot. Or consider the cinnamon and pepper—in Denmark your friends poured these over you on your birthday if you were still single at twenty-five and thirty, respectively. That was a tradition that an entire country practiced. It had happened to Stefan, cinnamon at twenty-five and pepper at thirty. It was part of the Danish social order.

Ultimately, when the incident occurred, there had been no forethought at all. It arose, almost naturally, out of the Red/Orange Debates; in the early weeks, they discovered disagreement among them as to whether Mars was, as reputation had held, a red planet—red dust, red rocks, et cetera—or whether it was actually orange. To Stefan it was obvious. They had already tracked orange dust all over their white floors, so the evidence was all about. But some of the people, looking straight at it, insisted that the color was red. They debated about it over meals, and while at first the argument had been friendly enough, eventually people became incredulous at one another, and voices were raised.

"Have you been tested for color blindness, you mug?" Trixie said, wagging an olive loaf sandwich at Josh. It was lunchtime.

"Have *you*?" Nicole said.

"This is bizarre," Jenny threw in. "You don't have an argument. Check the spectrophotometer again."

Roger shrugged. "The songs will work better if we go with red. Songs about Mars. You can't even rhyme anything with orange."

And that's when Stefan reached over. He wasn't even that cross. Well, he was a bit cross. But it was more that he had thought to himself, *Right in this moment I could reach over there and grab one of his fingers.* And so he did, grabbing hold of the middle finger of Roger's left hand and twisting it sharply—there was a feeling of snapping and a yowl from Roger, and a surge of pleasure in Stefan's chest—and then, before Roger could even recoil, Stefan grabbed the ring finger on that hand, with the same results, and then he sat back again in his chair. He was actually rather stunned. His body buzzed. The entire event had taken less than three seconds.

Subsequently there was a certain amount of chaos. Roger's yowl went on well past the three seconds, and people started leaping up from their chairs uselessly. Their eyes bounced like ping pong balls between the injured and the injurer, trying to make sense out of things. Trixie was the most on task, rounding the table to test Roger's fingers and provoke more yowling.

"They're . . . broken," she said, her voice broad with Australian vowels and wonder.

"I know," Stefan said. His voice was full of wonder, too.

Of course they had to convene a group meeting in the common room once the fingers were splinted and Roger had been given some pain meds. He sat on the opposite side of the circle from Stefan—well, approximately a circle—staring at him warily.

"So," Josh said to Stefan. In role as the team psychologist now, he was sitting on the edge of his *chaise*, leaning forward, his hands clasped between his knees, his blue eyes attempting to be soothing. There was something quite odd about the somber tone of this gathering in counterpoint with most people sitting on *chaises longues.* "What happened there?"

Stefan considered that for a moment. He wasn't sure what he was feeling in the aftermath. That hadn't become clear yet. "Well, I wasn't keen on what Roger was saying," he started, "and it occurred to me that I could do *that* instead of listening to him say more things."

"It occurred to you," Josh said.

"Yes."

"And then you did it."

"Yes," Stefan said. "That's what happened."

There was a pause. Then Trixie half-whispered to Nicole, "Has he gone crackers?"

"Crackers," Roger said quietly, almost to himself.

Josh spoke again, his eyes steady on Stefan. "So, you know you can't do that," he said.

The rest of the room nodded. "Too right," Trixie said.

But, "What exactly does that mean?" Stefan said. "I don't know if I *want* to do that again, but I *could* do it again."

"Stefan—" Josh began.

"Here—give me one of your fingers," Stefan said, holding his hand out. "I'll show you."

Nicole stood up abruptly, and Stefan retracted his hand.

"He *has* gone crackers," Trixie said.

"Crackers," Roger stage-whispered.

"I'm not going to give you one of my fingers," Josh said.

"Still on your hand, I meant."

"Right. Still no." Josh cleared his throat. "What I think I'm trying to say is that you're not *allowed* to do that kind of thing."

"Not allowed by whom?" Stefan said, glancing uneasily at Nicole, who was settling back down on her *chaise longue*, her eyes locked on to him.

At this, Josh looked around at the group. They nodded at him. *Go on*, their nods seemed to say. "By us," he finally said. "By this group."

Stefan sat back in his *chaise*, as though about to start suntanning. This was the first law ever, on the planet of Mars: *You cannot break the fingers of other people.*

Josh looked back around at everyone again. "I think," he said, almost as though he could hear Stefan's inner workings, "that maybe we need to establish some ground rules, here."

"I think that's an excellent idea," Nicole said with some intensity.

"What rules, exactly?" Jenny said.

Trixie tapped away on her tablet and then held it up for the group to see. "We could look at some of the classics," she said. "For inspiration. I've pulled up the Ten Commandments."

"I'm not sure if religion's going to help things," Jenny said.

"Thou shalt not," Roger said quietly.

Only Stefan seemed to be aware of the humor in these commandments being displayed on a tablet.

"Hammurabi's Code," Trixie suggested, tapping away some more.

"Ruuuuuuules," Roger said at length. The pain meds were really settling in.

"I'd like to make an observation," Nicole said. She sat like a military person. She always sat like that, no matter how relaxing the chair. The tight buzz cut added to the effect. "We haven't talked about enforcement."

"Enforcement?" Josh said.

Nicole nodded crisply. "It's one thing to say that people can't do certain things, and it's another to make *sure* that they don't."

Stefan felt his heart going.

"Because that's what Stefan was saying earlier," she said, indicating him. "It doesn't mean anything to say something's illegal unless you also have an enforcement plan."

"What does that mean, practically?" Jenny said.

"It means two things," Nicole said, and then she counted them off on her fingers—unbroken, of course. "It means figuring out what happens when people violate the rules, and it means figuring out who makes those consequences happen."

"I think we have to all be in charge," Jenny said. General agreement ensued.

"Okay," Nicole said. "We all enforce the rules. That means we have to come together to do that. But what happens when the rules get broken?"

"Well," Trixie said, shrugging, "punishment, I reckon."

Stefan was definitely feeling alert at this point. But it wasn't precisely fear. "Wait," he said, just as Nicole was opening her mouth, clearly about to ask for specific punishment ideas. "There's an alternative to this."

"An alternative?" Trixie asked.

"Sure," Stefan said. "We could just do what we want."

"We could do what we want?" Jenny said.

"Right. We could *not* make rules. We could all be allowed to do what we want."

Trixie blinked. "But I'm pretty confident I don't want you to do what you want, mate."

Stefan shrugged. "Then you could stop me, on an ad hoc basis. That would be you doing what *you* want in response to me trying to do what *I* want. And if you're able to stop it, then it doesn't happen. If you're not able, it *does* happen."

"So, chaos," Josh said. Over his shoulder there was a camera in the wall, passively filming this whole thing.

"No," Stefan said. "Anarchy. It's a political philosophy," he added, speculatively.

"I don't think that what you're describing meets the definition of true anarchy," Jenny said, raising one eyebrow.

"I don't think so, either," Josh said.

"Sure it does," Stefan said. "In any case, listen to me: the point is that we're on our own out here. We could be perfectly free."

Stefan spent the next twenty-four hours locked in the rocket that had brought them to Mars. He hadn't known that the door could lock from the outside, but apparently it could. It was an odd feature.

He was in a spacesuit—there wasn't any power to the rocket any-more. So that was awkward, though there was air and there were food and water tubes in the helmet which mostly worked and the others had been thoughtful enough to put a diaper on him as well. They gave him a tablet so that he could read or watch movies if he liked. It wouldn't be a terrible place to be if it had light and heat and oxygen. But it didn't.

"You're essentially making me sit in the corner," Stefan said. "So I can think about what I've done."

People shrugged and nodded. *Pretty much.*

"We can talk about it more, after," Josh said. "We probably should talk about it, after."

So at present he was in the rocket, in his puffy suit, sitting in the mostly dark in one of the navigation chairs. He buckled the seatbelt for no particular reason, and then he unbuckled it for no reason. Doing that a lot more times allowed a minute to pass by. Then he got up and looked out of one of the portholes.

"That," he said, looking at the obvious landscape, "is fucking or-ange."

Presumably the *Destination Mars!* camera and microphone in his helmet had picked that right up.

It was actually sobering to be in the rocket, almost right away. Especially with the view of the landscape, which was, among other things, completely inhospitable to human life. It served as an effec-tive reminder that a person couldn't do all that much on his own here.

Perhaps there was something to this time-out business after all.

Stefan didn't know what had been going on with him. Certainly he was not thinking or acting the way he had thought and acted on Earth, where he had had a very organized sock drawer and was scrupulous about traffic laws and taxes and had never broken any-one's fingers. Not even his own. He had voted consistently for the Conservative People's Party, had always preferred a leader who kept a grip on things. And now here he was, an anarchist on Mars. He had to admit that it was not necessarily a good sign about his character or, in fact, his mental well-being.

There had been a lot of exposure to cosmic rays between Earth and Mars. Hard to say what that did to a person over nine months.

On the other hand, he did have a bit of a point. After all, When in Rome; he had been born into a place, so he'd acted as the Romans had. But now the situation was When in Mars. And there was no such thing as Doing as the Martians Do. The Marsonauts would have to invent that. And was there such a thing as an ethical imperative when you were no longer under the umbrella of society, so to speak?

Of course, he could see where people wouldn't want to have their fingers broken.

Stefan gave himself a little squirt of applesauce from his food tube. Then he sat back in the chair with his tablet. He could basically read even with his helmet on, so he pulled up Søren Kierkegaard's book *Enten-Eller*, which he had always meant to check out. After a short while, he fell asleep.

When he woke up, though—he thought he heard somebody's voice but nobody was there—it was still daytime. He checked his watch. It wasn't even quite dinnertime yet.

He turned on the radio in his helmet. He said, "Did you call me?"

A minute went by and then Josh came on. "Nope," he said.

Stefan felt a strange pang of sadness. After a moment, he asked, "I genuinely have to stay here for twenty-four hours?"

"We think it's for the best, yeah," Josh said.

"It's an arbitrary amount of time." An hour wasn't even the same thing here as it had been on Earth. They had just taken the Mars day and divided it into twenty-four pieces. Which were, he acknowledged to himself, actually fairly similar in size to Earth hours.

"We can talk more tomorrow."

"You have to admit it's arbitrary," Stefan said.

There was no response.

He played solitaire for a bit on his tablet. And then he went back to the Kierkegaard, but didn't get very far, and then he pulled up Hammurabi's Code himself. *If a woman who owns a tavern won't take corn as payment for a drink, and she gets less money than the worth of the corn, she has to be thrown into the river.* You see? That ridiculousness was civilization! Though some of the other ones about renting and marriage and inheritance did seem reasonable. Then back to Kierkegaard; the man was a Danish giant and you had to read him. Still Stefan didn't get very far. He did a crossword puzzle in English, and there was a clue that went *Two wrongs*, for which the answer was obviously and irritatingly *notright*. He had more applesauce.

Eventually the sun went down, and Stefan could see it through one of the portholes. It wasn't much on Mars, the sunset. It had to do with the kinds of particles that were in the air: the sun got a bit blue-gray and then it went down.

After that, it was quite dark in the rocket.

Sitting awake in the dark—he could have turned on his helmet light but didn't, for some reason—he tried to think his way through the situation. One question: if the idea was that he could now, for the first time ever, do whatever he wanted . . . what did he actually want?

After a while, he fell asleep again.

The next day, by the time the early afternoon rolled around—Stefan's release time—he was not sure that he was much wiser than he had been. He had spent the morning on calisthenics, some episodes of the old TV show *Broen*, and a few attempts at reading. He had yogurt and a sort of pancake paste from his feeding tube when it was breakfast time and he had a pureed rye bread fish sandwich for lunch. The spacesuit had a nice selection, honestly. You could get by on helmet food.

What he knew for sure was that soon they were going to come to let him out, and he was going to have to make a statement of some kind. *I have seen the error of my ways*, is what he was meant to say. *I'm ready to play nice for Team Orderly Mars*. And of course he could just say it.

God fucking damn it.

Stefan paced around in the small space available to him. The situation, he'd decided, was clear enough. On the practical side, anarchy wasn't going to be possible if you were the only person doing it. Mars was not friendly enough for rugged individualists to make their own way. You couldn't, for example, just wander off on your own and live off the fat of the land. The land had no fat. It didn't even have breathable air. And so perhaps you did need some co-operation, for survival purposes, he considered. And, besides, he could empathize with Roger's likely point of view on the situation. On the other hand, he was still right that he *should* be allowed to do what he wanted. Also, he didn't like Roger. Honestly, he wasn't sure who he did like, among these people. And so there was the ideal, and there was the real. And apparently you had to choose. They were making him choose.

At some point Stefan used his tablet to look up the word "anarchy." The dictionary did its usual mealy-mouthed work, offering several definitions—everything from chaos to ungoverned utopia—and he found a few conflicting articles about what it might actually look like in practice. The things everybody agreed on seemed to be a lack of a central authority or hierarchies, which fit what he was thinking about. Though also a lack of coercion. Which, he wasn't sure how that exactly fit what he was thinking about.

He put the tablet away again.

The others showed up at 2:30 pm, Mars time. He was given five minutes' notice—"We're heading over there," came Josh's voice in his helmet speaker—and while he waited for everyone he asked himself that same question again: *What, Stefan, do you really want?* And then he asked it aloud, perhaps for the cameras. There was no answer, of course. In any case, it wasn't, he realized in the pressure of the moment, precisely a philosophical question for him. You could get philosophical about it, but for Stefan it was ultimately something more practical. Not that he specifically wanted to break fingers or wee on beds; there was nothing particularly great about those things. It was that, regardless of exactly what it was he wanted to do, which perhaps he didn't even know himself, he bloody well wanted to be free to do it.

Why should *they* be allowed to coerce *him*? That was how it fit.

Through the porthole he saw all five of them bouncing toward the rocket in their spacesuits, a matching little troop of puffies. It was clear: they weren't going to let him have that thing that he wanted. And in that realization was another realization, which was the realization that this whole thing left him quite angry. Anger that it was not safe to show.

A minute or so later, the door opened. With the helmet masks on, they all looked exactly the same. And of course he looked just like them, too.

"Are you ready to come out?" Josh asked via helmet radio. It wasn't clear which one of the puffies was Josh.

"I'm ready," Stefan said, in a sudden burst of decision. "I was wrong and you were right." That was what he decided to say, and that was what he said.

After a moment of helmets checking in with other helmets, the group came to its own decision. As one, the group waved him forward out of the dark rocket, out into all the breathless orange landscape a person could ever handle.

How to Organize Yourselves
(Section 19 of the unofficial *Destination Mars!* handbook, as written by the founder of *Destination Mars!*)

The truth is that we wish we were you. Not so much that we would trade places—as we said in Section 2 of this handbook, the thought of trading places is both thrilling and also frankly terrifying—but enough that we have significant doubts at night while brushing our teeth and we wonder if we've turned out to be who we hoped we'd be.

And why do we envy you? We envy you not only because you get to go somewhere that people have never gone, but also because you get to be in charge of a world. Think about it: you will be the entire population of your new planet. You will be *everybody*. As in, when people say "Martians," it'll just be you. And so you get to start over—you won't have the United Nations looking over your shoulder, won't find the taxman at your door, won't ever get called for jury duty again in your lives.

The question is: what will you do with this fresh start?

We want to be clear that we have no intention of telling Martians how to run Mars on a day-to-day basis. Aside from one crucial rule—no sex (see Section 4)—we're really going to leave everything in your capable hands. This is your chance to build the ideal society for *you*, the vision that you imagined loosely when you were young and that you're now old enough and wise enough and lucky enough to create. You're free—out of reach of anything more powerful than yourselves. What will you do with that freedom?

All that said, we encourage you to consider a few principles:

- You may want to choose a leader, or a leader may emerge naturally; some people are just built for it. Studies show that monkeys with enlarged amygdalas and hypothalamuses tend to become the alpha monkeys. Serotonin is involved, too. In other words, some brains are leader brains, and people with those kinds of brains are the ones you might turn to. Just bear in mind that sometimes people have too much of that kind of brain, as studies also show, and they become serial killers.

- In fact, you might decide that you don't want leaders. The Quakers, for example, sit around quietly in a circle until they get a good inner signal, and then they come to consensus. It's kind of amazing to watch. Or there's always direct democracy, where you vote on everything. It gets old fast, but even an ideal society is going to involve a little tedium. And you're less likely to nod off mid-decision than in the Quaker model. Or you may have a more fluid system, with different kinds of things happening in different ways at different times—organically, you might say. This idea makes us nervous, but it's not our planet.

- But, we wouldn't want you to panic about *Lord of the Flies* scenarios. If you read that book as an adult instead of as a high school student, you'll see that it's actually pretty manipulative; Golding obviously knew where he was going from the start. To us, that suggests a lack of open-minded artistic exploration, and it leaves his conclusions very much in question. Certainly he tapped a nerve, but just because we're afraid of something happening doesn't mean it's bound to happen. It's also worth noting that Golding wrote a dozen other novels and you haven't heard of any of them. Not even *The Scorpion God*, which has quite a title on it.

• In any case, a chore wheel is probably a good idea.

• One of the ways to look at this is that there's a question of how much societal structure you're going to import to Mars, and how much you're going to completely reinvent. We suspect that it's a difficult balance to strike. On the one hand, it's true that there's opportunity in front of you—you could do virtually anything, even something that no philosopher on Earth has ever imagined—but on the other hand there's comfort in things that you already know. An old sweater, special desserts from your childhood, even the feeling of being a small element in a larger sociopolitical system that you could never hope to individually influence and whose presence in your life was generally unpredictable. With this in mind, you might consider incorporating into your lives at least some of the trappings of your former world: a flag, perhaps; a kind of Mars anniversary celebration with, if not actual fireworks (not allowed per Section 9), at least sparklers (included in the Communal Resource Stockpile outlined in Section 11); staged political campaign ads; formalized mail delivery by a designated person in a makeshift uniform, whenever one of the unmanned supply rockets arrives. (See Section 13 for information on the supply rockets.) In other words, sometimes new wine tastes better if it's presented in old bottles. *Destination Mars!* will be happy, if it helps bring you comfort, to play the role of the impenetrable, inaccessible bureaucracy.

- Indeed, please don't forget that, as remote as we will be from your daily lives, we will make many significant decisions that affect you, not least of which will be the contents and timing of those supply rockets. (Do take a look at Section 13 when you get a chance.) While you are free to construct your own society, you will continue, of course, to intersect with forces larger than yourselves, as you always have.

- It probably wouldn't be helpful to create Martian currency.

- What about the moments when a decision has to be made quickly, military style? We, for sure, won't be able to respond to your communications at a moment's notice. This concern is an argument in favor of a leader, definitely, and again this may just arise naturally, even right there in the moment. In our experience, emergencies tend to bring people out in ways that you'd never anticipate. Some people turn out to be cowards howling at the back of the group; others—sometimes the ones you wouldn't expect—become startlingly bold. They're the ones who say things like, *Okay—I have an idea that's a real long shot, but I think it gives us a chance.* In situations like these, you don't need to have a leader already in place because they just stand up when you need them—and, interestingly, sometimes the leader already in place isn't the one who steps up when things get scary. Sometimes they're the first to the exit.

- Usually, though, the situation won't be an emergency. How do you build a society that can handle emergencies but usually doesn't have to? You could say, *Hope for peace, but prepare for war.* Or you could say, *Only prepare what you're willing to eat.* They're both good sayings, and they both hold some truth.

- Whatever you do, remember that all groups are divisible. All groups are divisible. *All* groups are divisible. For this reason, working in even-numbered groups is best, so that the resulting groups have a shot at coming out equal. Working in threes is of course just foolish.

- What a lot of this boils down to is social dynamics, which play out in many different ways, and in many different forums. Take, for example, the dining room table. You'll note that the table, which will be set up by the rover bots by the time you get there, is mold-able. You can make it any shape you like. It will, as a starting point, be set up in the form of a circle because the circle is a perfect shape. There are no bad seats at a circular table; there are no invidious distinctions in the round. Nobody is automatically the metaphorical turkey carver, nobody holding down the precarious end. But it's your table and you can do what you want with it.

- It's a good idea to try to uncover common interests in order to facilitate group bonding. Mars will offer ample opportunities for hiking, for example. The larger point is that group bonding is essential, whether through shared values, shared customs, shared recreational activities, or the emergence of a singular Martian identity. You all do different work, are different bright stars in this universe, but you are on a common path and there's much to connect to in one another. There's a reason why we made all your spacesuits and jumpsuits the same color.

- Mars is unlikely to be a very formal place, but there's always time for *please* and *thank you*.

- In terms of humor, bear in mind that some people just don't understand sarcasm. And not just people from the American Midwest, either—you'd be surprised how many people you can stump with a piece of sarcasm. Keep things straightforward, is our advice.

- We will have no objections if the *Destination Mars!* logo becomes inspirational for you—if it ends up on a flag, say—or if in any way *Destination Mars!* becomes symbolically significant as you construct your new society.

- We're not sure what to say about religion.

- Well, okay—we'll say this much: if you're going to do religion, it might be time for a new one, something you build from scratch yourselves, so that everyone can sign on. It shouldn't be that difficult to come up with something; if you are even the tiniest bit openhearted, you will experience some awe, at least in your first days on Mars. You will be on *Mars*. Put another way: you're the first humans to set up lives away from Earth. You're like the proverbial first humans outside the proverbial Garden of Eden! So awe should happen automatically. All you have to do is call that awe God, come up with a couple of occasions and rituals, and you're off and running.

- We emphatically do not recommend the development of multiple religions.

- Will you even use anything like the calendar system we use? Mars has years whether you want them or not, and days, of course, but what about months? Mars' moons are different from our moon. Will there be weeks? Will there be weekends?

- Wouldn't it be funny if this handbook, unofficial as it is, became something like a Bible for your new religion?

- As you know, sex is not allowed on Mars, not only because it could lead to deformed babies (see Section 4) but also because it splits a group right up (seriously see Section 4). (It seems implausible, doesn't it, that those legendary utopian free love communes of the sixties and seventies actually existed? More likely our older relatives told us those stories so that we would think our older relatives were cool. Which of course we still did not.) So the question becomes: how do you spend your life among a group of other humans and not end up having sex with any of them? Even if you don't find the others attractive at first, surely over time your desires will shift, won't they? And then what do you do? What the priests tell us is that you have to get married to something bigger than yourself and get your satisfaction from that. Maybe you will put that new religion together, and you will find that your awe of the manifest breadth and beauty of the solar system, of the universe, of reality itself, will lift you above bodily preoccupations. We also strongly suggest that your new religion allow for masturbation.

- Oh—and we wouldn't mix religion and government. It would be terrible to see Mars become a totalitarian theocracy. Really a shame. Remember that Earth is counting on you to model a viable future for the species, because we're having trouble doing it here. So go forward boldly. Make a new world. Maybe an *Egalitarian Paradise of the Flies*.

- Above all, be kind to one another and have fun with this! What you are doing is truly amazing, so different from anything the rest of us will ever experience. As we make our way through the many norms, expectations, legalities, and civic responsibilities of our daily lives here on Earth—every day a gauntlet of sorts—we will have you in our thoughts. We'll have you in our thoughts as we temporarily shuck our social world each night to cozy into our beds. Sometimes we will be overcome with envy and we'll curse our timorous dispositions that kept us here in our complicated, systematized life instead of letting us go off with you. It really is every day; I mean, who wants to go through all kinds of paperwork to renew a driver's license or stand in some long line to register to vote? Laws and regulations and laws. They keep a lot of us safe, but you can remember the feeling: sometimes the blanket is pretty heavy. In those moments before we fall asleep we might curse ourselves.

- Please get this right.

The Interaction of Weight and Light, or: Birds' Holiday
(an excursion report)

Purposes of Excursion:

- Non-routine inspection of, and maintenance on, our Mt. Nearby telescope during a period of minimal atmospheric dust and while still at an early enough stage of my pregnancy to be able to do it easily. (While still able to get into a spacesuit!)

- Given the opportunity provided by the maintenance run, to also collect a subsurface water sample from Trixie's latest drill site. In Trixie's words: "It's like giving Mars another pregnancy test. Maybe one of these days she'll turn up preggers, hey?"

NOTE: Trixie has not had any luck in our time on the planet, after many samples. Sometimes in the first year I heard her crying in her lab, and for a while it seemed she had given up altogether. But lately she seems to have found some renewed energy—quite vibrant energy—for the research.

Personnel:

- Me (Jenny)

- Trixie
- Nicole, who is not an engineer but is nonetheless a handy one as a result of Air Force training, stepped in in place of Stefan. (See below.) Which provoked Trixie to yell "Birds' holiday!" Australian slang, I understand, for a trip involving only women. (Question: is the derivation for this rooted in the manner in which birds, according to the saying, flock together?)

- Scratched:
  - Stefan, because he is supposed to be our engineer, was asked to come help with the telescope, but did not want to come. Perhaps because he is uneasy around me and/or all people of color, and perhaps because he just didn't want to go somewhere/do something.
  - Trixie's gendered declaration meant that Josh was not allowed to come. For that matter, neither was Roger. But Josh, I had been thinking, would come.

Necessity of Report, Given That *Destination Mars!* Has Recommenced Filming for the Reality TV Show, Including Via Cameras and Microphones in the Rovers and Spacesuits:
Unclear.

Summary of Excursion:
Leg 1: Habitation Unit to Telescope
As I've mentioned in other reports, Mt. Nearby, despite its name, is not especially near to the habitation unit, especially given the way the rover travels over rough terrain—indirectly and slowly. And of course the mountain is also tall. Not by Martian standards (against

that standard, it's more correctly called a hill) but compared to the surrounding area. The trip to the top of it took 5 Martian hours, during which we discussed the excursion and other matters. Nicole, having very seriously hung her lucky Mardi Gras beads off the dashboard—I have learned that people in the Air Force tend to be superstitious—drove the entire way.

Trixie noted that it was good to have 2 medical doctors present in order to keep an eye on the pregnancy. While en route, she "stethoed" me regularly (her term), took blood pressure and temperature readings (all apparently normal), and asked me repeatedly about my physical comfort level. Nicole was mainly quiet, until late in the trip when she unexpectedly suggested we shift from medical questions to some car games. (I welcomed this, and Trixie, all happiness, repeated her reference to a birds' holiday.)

License plates being in short supply on the planet, we did "first letter last letter," where one person says a word in a category and another person says a word whose first letter is the last letter of the previous word. Despite the category—Mars—Trixie somewhat fixated on reproductive terms. E.g., part of the transcript recorded by the rover's internal microphone, starting with Nicole:

"Banh." (a crater on Mars named after a city in the African country of Burkina Faso)

"That ends with an H, correct? Hm. Hartwig." (crater named after German astronomer Ernst Hartwig)

"Well, gestation. What? That's happening on Mars, too. It's not *all* craters, you know."

"Okay. Huh. Nereidum Montes." (Martian mountain range)

"Great. Syrtis Major Planum." (a surface feature on the planet)

"Motherhood. *What?*"

Et cetera.

Eventually Trixie fell asleep. Josh believes that she's working very hard at her life-of-the-party personality, that it's in fact exhausting to be her. In any case, with her asleep, conversation slowed and, when in motion, restricted itself mainly to expedition goals and concerns. Though at one point we passed a particularly empty stretch of landscape and Nicole said, "Some kind of a world for a baby." Face characteristically hard to read; I didn't pursue further.

The last portion of the trip, when the slope became impossible for the rover, was done on foot. Was uncertain as to whether I found the climb more difficult than usual. Certainly our muscles had already atrophied in the low-gravity conditions of the planet. Trixie, back in the rover, in constant contact with me via radio all the while.

Telescope Maintenance:

- Upon arrival at telescope (which has been, as far as one can tell from the readings back at the habitation unit, functioning within normal specifications, though turning up few findings of any significance), Nicole and I inspected and cleaned exterior of telescope housing and then opened the housing and connected tablet to test all important parameters and components. Dusted mirrors and, upon closing the housing again, checked all seals. Though knowing that dust always finds a way in, no matter what you do. Summary: all functioning well within normal, even ideal, specifications. No repairs, part replacements, or adjustments necessary.
  - See attached chart for complete listing of components, tests, readings, and observations.

- Nicole, afterward, said, "We drove all this way out here for an all-clear report, huh?" Has been irritable. Trixie responded, "Oh, you wet blanket. We're *bonding*." Bonding being in the nature, I gather, of a birds' holiday.

Leg 2: Telescope to Drill Site

The drill site is not far from Mt. Nearby, in relative terms; we drove the 1.5 hours on the same day we inspected the telescope. "Samples won't take a minute," Trixie said. Bouncing in her seat. Talking about the depth of the sample area—"Feeling lucky"—she said, fingers crossed on both hands. "Mama needs a new pair of microorganisms." Also "stethoed" me repeatedly. "Bummer it's too soon to hear the baby's heartbeat, eh?"

Note that I am not yet feeling significantly different from how I've always felt before. Breasts slightly tender, increased need to urinate (unpleasant device available in rover), some nausea. Considerable disbelief. Concerns. Questions, including one about whether I'm doing the right thing, bringing this baby to term, though both Trixie and Nicole believe it's safer than the alternative. In any case, many questions.

What's happening? What am I doing? What *will* happen?

Presumably normal thoughts for a woman who is pregnant. On Mars.

Nicole, during this leg of the trip, mostly silent.

Drill Site Sampling:

Am leaving this summary to Trixie, who will presumably be writing a report of her own. From all appearances, sample easily obtained. Trixie extremely careful with it. Cradled it, you could say.

Overnight:

Because of the length of the trip back, we elected to stay overnight at the drill site, sleeping in the rover. Awkward, cramped. Also, Trixie is a very loud snorer; it took some time for Nicole and me to fall asleep, which led eventually to conversation there in the dark, lots of stars visible through the window. Transcript, starting with me:

"It's really something, isn't it?"

"What, the snoring? I'm pretty sure I snore, too."

"Yours is more like . . . like a cat purring."

"Are you listening to me at night, now?"

(long pause, even for Mars, and then me again) "What's going on with you?"

(long pause and then sigh from Nicole, audible over Trixie snoring) "I'm sorry."

"What is it?"

"I don't know. This whole situation just has me thinking."

(long pause)

(Me feeling like Josh, who is much more likely to ask questions than I am) "About what?"

(long pause)

"I see you and Josh, getting ready to have a family. It's nice. It's a good thing. But I . . . I have a range of feelings about that." (Quiet but still audible) "I had a real shitshow of a family back Earthside."

(long pause while I try to think of what Josh would say in this situation, until I finally give up, and just say the only thing I can think of) "Of course. That's hard."

"You got that right."

(End of transcript)

Eventually—it took a fairly long time—Nicole was purring from her seat in the rover. There was a lot of sound in there. I considered that it may be exhausting to be Nicole, too. Perhaps most people. Remembered my father coming home from work, or after dealing with some trouble from my sister, saying, "Just so damn tired." Moaning it, more precisely. I looked at both women in the rover and considered what both must be carrying around.

Then in the midst of the sounds of sleeping I thought about how birds—actual birds from the taxonomic class Aves—are supposed to fall asleep automatically when placed in a darkened atmosphere. And how the rover was in that sense like a birdcage with a blanket over it. (Mars is, as I have mentioned in numerous other reports, very dark at night.) Except that I was awake. Unbirdlike. Perhaps it was the light of the stars; I continued to stare out the window at them. Are some birds more light-sensitive than others? Some less able to sleep? Obviously there are owls, who are presumably on reverse settings. And of course not all birds flock together. All that said, as much as I stared at the stars, I was not precisely seeing them. Of course I'm not in the habit of studying astronomical objects with the naked eye, and simultaneously my education has demystified and deromanticized them. Still clearly the light reaches you.

I sat awake in the rover and thought about all the things that people want and don't have. This is not an easy subject to contemplate. I know from personal experience: terrible things can happen when people want things that they don't have. Which is something I try not to think about.

But sometimes that's a challenge.

What will the baby need and not have?

That night, after my own exhaustion won out, I dreamed that someone was calling my name.

Comment on Report:

Uncharacteristically unfocused; will almost certainly need to be rewritten.

Leg 3: Drill Site Back to Habitation Unit
A lot of talking. A lot of silence.

The Patterns

WE KNOW YOU'RE HERE. It's not like you're sneaking about, with all the giant things that weren't here but are now here and that put you out and which you go into and which you come out of again all the time. You make noise. You're extremely visible. You might say there's a smell.

We think you would use the word smell.

It feels like the temperature is rising. Do you feel the temperature rising? You might not notice; you don't seem to be big noticers. Anyway, it's small, so far. Of course, that may be how it starts.

The impression we have is that you're looking for things that you're not finding. There's been a whole lot of cutting into rocks and pushing down below the surface and moving things from one place to another. A lot of those things go back into the big objects with you. Like we say, noisy. And a whole lot of it. We thought you'd just do this stuff once or twice, but you keep doing it. So we think you're not finding whatever it is. This is just an observation; in any case, probably we couldn't help you even if you noticed us. We're not big lookers-for-things.

That said, sometimes we're right there with you, inside, watching you as you look at the pieces of rocks and the amounts of liquid and as you don't find what you're looking for. At least we think that's what's going on. To be honest, there's a lot of guesswork involved. And we don't stay with you inside that much because of all of the walking right through us. Well, actually, we're always inside with you—how could we not be?—but there's a question of how *there* we *really* are. Because it certainly varies.

For sure the air is moving differently now. It's navigating around you. Do you feel that at all? That affects us, believe it or not, messing—trifling?—with the air currents. How north and south we are, from the air currents. And besides they don't taste the same as before.

It's almost as though we can't tell what's happening or what's going to happen.

Here's how it was before you got here. Before even the every-once-in-a-while objects that crashed onto the surface and roamed about making scoops of this and scoops of that, roaming right through us, which is always an awkward experience. Before objects circled around at the top of the air, also circling right through us, at the edge between where there's something and where there's basically nothing. Awkward no matter where it happens. And it affects how in and out we are. Anyway, before all that, there were the Patterns. Temperature and air and where liquid was and where solid was, and the way things turned and moved. Moons and sun. Magnetism. Arranged in comprehensive ways but also in subsystems of ways. We knew all of that very intimately. You could actually say that we *were* the Patterns—*are* the Patterns. You probably would say that, if you were good noticers. You'd say, "Oh—they're the Patterns."

But of course those things change. They always change, so that what we were before you got here isn't the same as what we were a very long time before you got here. Naturally. It used to be a lot warmer, in fact. And that affects how big and small we are, among other things. So we've seen change, always. And change is part of the Patterns, so we consist of the changes, partly, or we *have* consisted of them. Well, it's hard to explain, even to ourselves. We just sort of *get it*. But so change isn't new or remarkable, and we're never the same, but it turns out that there are different kinds of change. There's a difference. Natural versus unnatural kinds, we were thinking? After all, your objects don't seem natural. But then we realized that we don't know what unnatural means, because it's all made of the same stuff, really. Everything is. We're not even sure how the word unnatural got into the conversation. But so we're having trouble bolting down the difference between how things used to change and how they're changing now.

We think you would say bolting. Possibly nailing?

Maybe there's no difference at all. One of the most important things is that Patterns have many orders of magnitude, and that across time we discover new, larger orders of magnitude around the other ones that we already knew about. I think when we started out it was just mass and less mass, mass all here and mass in different places, but then there was light, which affected how massive and not-massive we were. It happens over and over again, if you take the long view. We might be thinking, right, we've got this all sorted out, and then it turns out there's something else and it's part of things and of us, too. It keeps things interesting, believe me. So we're wondering if maybe you're part of the next order of magnitude.

At the same time, some of us are wondering if you're something else. The idea is that you might not be part of a larger Pattern, but that, with your new objects and your going this way in objects and that way without them and scooping and different things, that maybe you're some kind of Unpattern, or that you *do* Unpatterning, or however you'd want to think about it. And the reason some of us are wondering that is because we haven't ever before had a *some of us*. It's always just been *us*. It's a pretty big deal around here, having some of us this and others of us that. And it may be part of something and it may be unpart of everything.

We think you would use the word chaos.

And so there are different points of view. Some of us actually want to spend more time with you, be really *there* when we're there, because for sure the whole deal is pretty interesting. (That word—interesting—is interesting. Because it could be good or bad, but it's still interesting.) Those ones of us want to really be with you as you move through your big objects and go from one smaller object to another, and as you sort through the pieces of things. And maybe, given that we're starting to understand what you're thinking about or at least *how* you think—certainly we've picked up a lot of vocabulary just by listening—the interest is understandable.

What does the word preggers mean, by the way?

Those same some of us have suggested that communication is possible—not just listening but also speaking to you—and that there have been one or two semi-successful tries. This whole deal is new to us, so who's to say? Anyway, those ones of us want to know more of what you're thinking about. Because there could be a Pattern there.

Others of us, though, want you gone. You weren't here before you were here, so the thinking is that you must have been in another place. We know there are other places, although we aren't there. And those others of us think everything would be better off if everything was where it originally was. But then still others object and say that, technically, nothing is where it originally was. And the first others say, You know what we mean.

This is how it's gotten with us.

But how has it gotten with you? That's what some of us want to know. Because when you move it doesn't seem to have that much to do with magnetism or mass. Light and dark, maybe—some of us say, See? Patterns?—but that's only the sunlight and not the position of the tiny lights way beyond in the place where there's basically nothing. Mostly, despite our progress listening in, we really don't know why you do what you do or even exactly *what* you do.

Maybe there will be another change, a change we can all handle, a change for the good, if you do find what you're looking for. Is that a possibility, you finding what you're looking for? Are you maybe getting any closer? Some of us say faces, and claim to see wrongness on those faces. Or rightness? Others say that that's just part of a larger Pattern, and that soon the faces will change. Things looked for will be found, and Patterns will be Repatterned, and you will be you rather nicely and maybe not quite as loudly and that will be part of us and nothing more will be confusing. That's where some of our hope is these days.

Although, honestly, that's only some of it. Because then you go around some more and Unpattern this and that, and *what* are you even looking for? You've broken all those rocks, and taken pieces of things and you're below the surface all over and farther and farther than ever. And we don't know why. *Are* you even looking? We don't understand. Even if you weren't so loud and with the smell, it would still be on our minds. The things you do—they go on *in* us, basically, and they affect how right and wrong we are. It's a lot. It's possibly too much.

And so the rest of the hope is still on you being gone somehow. We think that there are a lot of ways you could be gone. So that's a thing that we think about.

And, even better, about how maybe we can make that happen.

We think you would use the word hope.

What You Can't Do (Part One)

(Section 4 of the unofficial *Destination Mars!* handbook, as written by the founder of *Destination Mars!*)

We are not big on rules here at *Destination Mars!* We have procedures that we follow on Earth, and obviously we've thought about what you're heading for, and have advice for you on a range of issues and circumstances that you're likely to encounter—but we are also aware that we don't *really* know what you're going to encounter at all, and that of course we can't prepare you for things that are ultimately unknown. (Though see Section 27 for some thoughts on how *you* might want to deal with the many unknowns that are going to be coming at you.) On top of that, we also don't want to get in your way, and would be limited in our ability to do so even if we wanted to; we're sending you to Mars, but we won't be there with you. And so, in the realest possible sense, Mars is going to be yours. Yours to put your hard work and sweat into, to inhabit and to till, hopefully, eventually, and to shape. To fill with whatever culture and customs and social structures you like. (Though see Section 19.) That's as it should be. All this to say that we don't want to hamper your creativity with a variety of rules around how to behave on a new planet. But we do have one rule, in part because you've got to have *something* to start with, and in larger part because this rule is a very important one. So let's be clear:

You are not allowed to have sex on Mars.

You will hear this from us quite a few times and in a variety of formats, but it bears repeating because we're not sure how easy it will be for you to follow:

YOU ARE NOT ALLOWED TO HAVE SEX ON MARS.

Let us explain, in the following three subsections:

Subsection 4:1: Social Impacts

There will only be a handful of you on Mars.

If you want an analogy, think of your situation as similar to a big off-campus house that you might rent with a bunch of friends in your senior year of college. You start off with lots of enthusiasm, naturally—you're going to have chore wheels! everybody will cook together! house parties! thoughtful house meetings every week where you discuss every conceivable issue in an enlightened and sensitive way! it'll be the way society *should* be!

And maybe for a while it is like that. Everybody's happily exhausted after moving all the boxes in. The chore wheel that one of you made is colorful and spins perfectly. While the good weather lasts you have beers on the porch in the evenings. Then the first party is amazing—full of the joy of living, and of living together. Everybody's happy to be eating the same thing. Even when the toilet breaks you all rally around and get it fixed somehow, and you don't even get too aggressive about figuring out who flushed what crazy object to break the toilet in the first place, because you're all in it together.

But then something ruins everything. And you know what that thing is. We all know what that thing is: one of you has sex with another one of you. Which is, frankly, the end of every utopia. (We consider the apple in the Biblical story to be a kind of metaphor.) Here's what happens:

- You start spending more time with each other and less with everyone else, which creates a kind of gravitational shift in the house, which goes from being one big *us* to something more fractured.

- The two of you start echoing each other's points at the weekly house meetings, becoming a voting bloc of sorts, a fact that is not lost on your increasingly resentful housemates.

- This escalates. When one of you uses up all the hot water the other pretends not to know who did it. When one of you breaks the chair in the living room the other one gets rid of the evidence. When one of you leaves a thousand dirty dishes in the sink the other one makes excuses, or even lies about who left them there.
    - This can create issues within the couple that's having sex, of course, which is a danger in its own right. More on this below.

- Meanwhile, inspired by your thoughtless example, other people in the house begin thinking about having sex.
    - They think, for example, about having sex with other people in the house.
        - Maybe they think about having sex with one of the two people who are now having sex with each other, which naturally causes a lot of tension.
        - Maybe they think about having sex with one of the people in the house who is not in the couple.

- If the other person is amenable, the house continues to further balkanize.
- If the other person is not amenable, discomfort spreads and people start to dislike each other actively.
  - Or people might start leaving the house for sex, which fractures things even more.

- And then there's always the possibility that the couple having sex *stops* having sex. People are very unpredictable, after all; you can't really count on them. So whether the two are fighting about all the tension in the house or something else, the relationship falls apart. Probably unpleasantly. And now there are two sides in something very explosive, and everyone has to take sides, and the whole thing gets very ugly. And what was once a potential utopia where each person kept their feelings and impulses safely to themselves is now a bunch of disgruntled people who talk behind each other's backs and yell at each other and maybe even throw things. Everybody finally hates everyone else and you're all just wishing for graduation to hurry up and get there so that you never have to see each other again.

- And the thing is that on Mars it's going to be worse than that, because:
  - You are not friends to begin with.
  - There is no graduation, and nowhere to go outside of the metaphorical house. You will be stuck with each other, forever, in the *only place on the entire planet where there is food*

and breathable air. Outside of the metaphorical house is only death.

- Sex, in other words, is a selfish pursuit that can probably only happen at the expense of the community. The community that is your only chance of survival.

Game Night with the O'Marses

THINGS HAVE BEEN so boring on Mars for so long that I more or less forgot that I'm a psychologist. But now Jenny's pregnancy is making everyone weird, so all of a sudden—I realize it one morning when I wake up and see Trixie hovering over sleeping Jenny, quietly applying a stethoscope to Jenny's pooched-out torso—I'm a psychologist again.

When we first got here, I had this little office—well, it was more like a booth, just big enough for two chairs—off the common room, and I would sit down with everybody regularly and ask how they were doing. That was why I was there: to keep an eye on how everybody was doing. And primarily how everybody was doing was *excited*. I mean, we were on *Mars*. We had traveled through space for six months and landed in our rocket, and that was pretty exciting, obviously—we didn't crash or die, for starters—and then we were the first six people to ever set foot on Mars. Which, all by itself, wow. That thought stays with you for a while. And there was the buzz of the early weeks, setting things up and getting our feet under us. Absorbing the red landscape. We were on *Mars*! Lots of excitement to be experienced. Everything was new; everything was unknown. So Trixie was bopping all over the place singing her favorite pop songs and digging up subsurface water samples, and Roger was gathering up rocks upon rocks and going on about tholeiitic basalt, and Nicole was walking around with her hands on her hips with an open-mouthed expression that was basically *Well, would you look at this*, and even sometimes sort of giggling when she couldn't help it—she would clap her hand over her mouth each time and then right away get super-serious again—and Jenny had these big big eyes (beautiful, light brown) and she would go out to look at the sky every night and go totally silent for an hour at a time, and Stefan—well, Stefan was decompensating, apparently, which basically means losing it, and that turned into some alarming but luckily minor early violence, but I'm telling you there's more to Stefan than that.

As for me, I knew my mission was to watch over everyone else, and so I did. I was there because nobody knew what to expect from throwing a few not-totally-random-but-still-kind-of-random people together into a completely crazy situation for the rest of their lives. And as it turned out, at first, the main thing—aside from the early violence—was that good old-fashioned excitement. Fast heartbeat, fast breath, busy brain, wide eyes. Each person would sit down in my booth and would tell me, in one way or another, *I AM SO EXCITED.*

Which I was, too. How could anybody not be?

We had all signed up for this, of course. We had our reasons. And I guess the reasons were good enough for someone. Supposedly the way this not-totally-random group happened was that we were chosen from among all the other applicants by TV viewers—the reality show started back on Earth—but I've never believed that. I mean, I would be surprised if *Destination Mars!* paid attention to any of that voting. I think they just thought we'd make for good drama.

But things are only new until they're old, and they're only unknown until you know them. And drama can run out.

In the beginning of our time here, when the *Destination Mars!* cameras were still rolling for the reality show and when everybody here was sampling and drilling and scanning and analyzing and mapping and communicating with fellow scientists back on Earth and doing all the kinds of things people of a scientific mindset like to do, at first we produced and shared one finding after the next—*Look at this rock! Look at that rock!* And I had a lot to say into the cameras about all the dynamic and in fact layered personalities and so on. But after a while the findings started to find the same things over and over. There were no signs of life anywhere. The much-reduced gravity and increased radiation weren't doing anything especially surprising to our physiology. The stars were pretty similar to stars as seen from Earth, and anyway dust made it hard to see them a lot of the time. Things slowed down, and slowed down some more, and then they slowed down even more. Two-plus years in, most folks have stopped sciencing at the same rate, have stopped reading the professional journals and sending findings back home. Two-plus years in, it's more like, *Would you look at all these damn rocks?*

So: the *Destination Mars!* cameras stopped rolling, the reality show canceled for lack of interest, and Trixie got more interested in Sudoku than water samples (or, in my opinion, got to the point where she could handle a Sudoku puzzle a lot better than another sterile sample) and Stefan was always off muttering to his machines and Nicole mainly focused on the chore wheel and Jenny and I started falling for each other, which turns out to be a lot more interesting, at least to us, than being on a planet millions of miles from Earth, and Roger—well, Roger continued to gather his rocks, but that's Roger.

My booth has mainly become a place where we keep extra towels. *Destination Mars!* sends us more towels than we need, and they've got to go somewhere.

Also sometimes Jenny and I go in there and canoodle.

And so somewhere along the line I forgot that I'm a psychologist. When you're watching excitement and even alarming early violence, it kind of keeps you on task. But when it becomes the psychology of boredom, you might forget that you're supposed to be doing it. Anyway I did. And what I was letting myself ignore was the fact that there was a lot more going on than boredom, actually.

Now, though—Jenny's pregnant now, and it's so obviously affecting everybody that I can't be in denial about it. There's a lot to keep an eye on. The cameras are, in fact, back up and running. And on the morning when I wake up to see Trixie hovering over Jenny—and I sleep in the same tiny bunk as Jenny, so the hovering is kind of hard to miss—the way Trixie has been doing throughout the day lately, I know I've got to pick my mission up again.

I tell Jenny about it when she's awake—Trixie and the stethoscope. "Oh, boy," Jenny says.

"Everyone's behaving kind of strangely," I say.

"It's true." She scratches at her messy hair. Jenny is still next to me in the bunk, but now it's me hovering over her, up on one elbow. We are, as usual, the last ones out of bed.

"I'm going to look into it," I say.

"You sound like a television detective," she says, blinking at me.

I consider that. "There are some TV shows where the detective is a psychologist."

"How are *you* doing with everything, Josh?" she asks me.

"How are *you* doing?" I say.

"Wow," she says. "You really are on the job, huh?"

I give Jenny a kind of salute. Which is awkward in a very tight bunk.

Since I can't really use my office and also I want to be a little more nonchalant about it, I do my eye-keeping out in the common spaces, where there are not so many towels.

I start with some of the people who are having what look like sweet reactions. First of all, Roger. It's almost like he's nesting. Recently he sewed the baby three onesies, all by himself, using a couple of those extra *Destination Mars!* towels—and we didn't even know he could sew! And then he made a rattle using a little plastic sampling bottle and some Mars pebbles. It seems like every day he's working on something new for the baby.

I go into the greenhouse, where he spends most of his time, because he's our botanist in addition to being our geologist. I don't really like to be in the greenhouse, to be honest, because it brings up old memories—Lil, my fiancée on Earth until that night of the car accident, gardened. But I'm back in the mode of keeping my eye on people, and Roger is in the greenhouse, so that's where I go.

It's warm in here, and humid, the air thick with oxygen. Roger is at a workstation tucked away behind the crops. He works on his things there—plants, rocks, et cetera.

"Hey," I say.

Roger startles. He startles pretty easily. "Oh—Josh. Hi, Josh." There are vegetables in front of him, looking like they've been cooked, and some kitchen implements, and little jars.

"Whatcha working on?" I say. Though honestly I can sort of already tell, and my insides are going *Awwwwwwwww.*

Roger smiles a little, and scratches at his thinning hair. "I'm figuring out"—he says "out" in that Canadian accent that makes it sound like "oot"—"how to strain peas and spinach and then can them."

"For . . . baby food?" I say. This is what I mean by sweet. Though I know there's more to it than sweetness. People always have their deeper reasons. But it's also sweet.

"Yeah," he says, blushing a little. "I'm doing peas and spinach, and also radishes and tomatoes."

Those last two sound like question marks as far as baby taste buds are concerned, but I don't want to quash his excitement, for sure. I pat him lightly on the shoulder. "You're really getting into this," I say. Which I mean partly as a question.

"Well," he says, in his soft-spoken way. "We all are, I think."

I smile and nod and study him a little. "Hey—why do they call it canning when you use jars?" I say.

But Roger doesn't know. I pat him lightly on the shoulder again—clapping him on the back might knock Roger over, is one thing you have to know about Roger—and leave him to his vegetables.

When I tell Jenny about Roger and his baby food, she says, "Awwwwwwwww."

"I know," I say. We're getting our lunches ready. I put one last spread of peanut butter on the peanut butter half of my sandwich.

Jenny, whose stomach is easily upset these days, is just toasting toast. Maybe she'll do some margarine. After a few moments, she says, frowning a little, "I hope he's careful about it. Is there botulism on Mars?"

It's hard to know. Mars is sort of a restart as far as diseases are concerned. If we didn't bring it with us, it's probably not here. But maybe we did bring it with us, or one of the supply rockets did, without meaning to.

Trixie, who has come in to grab a bowl of cereal, says, "You never know. You should be very, very, very careful about home-canned foods. In fact, you probably shouldn't eat them at all."

"I'll keep an eye on it," I say.

"Detective mode," Jenny says. "Psychologist-detective mode."

"I'll keep an eye out, too," Trixie says. I can see she's about to reach for her stethoscope, so I unite the jelly half with the peanut butter half and lead Jenny out of there.

Nicole's gotten very family-oriented, too, in her way. Unlike the rest of us, she actually has a lot of relatives back on Earth—living parents, siblings, aunts, uncles, cousins (first, second, etc., once removed, twice removed, unremoved, etc.), nieces, nephews, and so on. Which makes it sound nice. But Nicole describes her family as a "shitshow." What stories I've gleaned from her back that description up. Which means that she came here in part in search of something better even among the six of us. And then she got bored of Mars like the rest of us, and we didn't fill the void for her, which made her struggle with it more for a while, and then eventually she just settled into boredom like the rest of us. But it seems now the pregnancy's brought the longing back again; the whole thing seems to have fired her up to make us more of a family here.

For example, there's that chore wheel, where she's getting very intense—*We all have to do our share, because I'm not here to clean up after you flumps*—and, in the more-fun category, she's been organizing game nights. She started when Jenny announced she was pregnant—charades and Apples to Apples and Taboo and, one time only, Twister. Stefan is usually too grumbly to play, but the rest of us get into it, at least up to a point. There was talk of potato-sack races outside, where we would use pillow cases, but people were concerned that we could trip and rip our spacesuits open on rocks, which would be very, very bad, and Trixie pointed out that the risks were especially big for pregnant Jenny. But the point is that Nicole's been trying to instill that family feeling in us. At one point she even suggested the possibility of us all adopting the same last name. *O'Mars* is what she's suggested. Currently that suggestion is tabled, but you never know.

I ask Nicole about all of it after lunch as we clean up. The chore wheel has the two of us in the kitchen, loading the dishwasher. Could the kitchen be my new office? It could be good for people who do anxious eating.

"You've been doing a lot of team-building lately," I say.

Nicole looks up from a little plate that she was rinsing, eyebrows up. Her buzz cut seems almost to tighten.

"I mean, the way you're pulling us all together," I say. When we were all out there for lunch—she's really been encouraging everyone to try to eat at the same time—she proposed Trivial Pursuit for tonight.

She keeps staring at me with those up eyebrows. In addition to being a medical doctor, Nicole is in the Air Force—or she was when she was on Earth—and she can be intimidating.

Roger comes into the kitchen, gingerly places another few dishes in the sink, and tiptoes out again. It's probably too busy in here to be my new office.

"It's nice," I say to Nicole, "what you're doing. You know, Trivial Pursuit, et cetera." I don't say anything about her need for a family of her own; it's not the moment.

Nicole seems to decide that there's nothing to be suspicious about. She sighs a long, slow sigh, and nods. "It's true," she says. She hands me the plate, which I put in the dishwasher. "Is it disturbing folks?"

"I don't think so," I say. And then, with a little chuckle: "I mean, maybe Stefan."

She rolls her eyes.

I say, "It's nice, really." And then I take a small step toward her. Emotionally, I mean. "Do you think it's because of the pregnancy?"

Nicole gives me up eyebrows again.

I say, "I guess it's a big deal, the baby coming."

"You *guess*? You ought to know—you *are* the father, aren't you?"

I laugh. "But I mean it seems like it's making you think we ought to be closer than we are. More like a family." There—I said it. I rack a water glass.

"Well, it seems to me we have two choices," she says, her voice losing some of its military polish: "We can be a family, or we can be strangers thrown together for no apparent reason or purpose."

I see Roger pause at the kitchen entrance he's entering, and then, sensing that something is happening, he turns around again, taking the dirty dishes back into the dining room with him.

"Mm," I say.

Anyway, right now she says, very decisively, "And I don't need strangers in my life." She hands me another plate with such intensity that it's like she's giving me a hand grenade that I'm supposed to throw before it explodes. But it won't explode. I just put it in the dishwasher.

That afternoon Jenny and I are sitting wrapped up together on a *chaise longue* in the common room, the two of us working on a crossword puzzle on my tablet. Trixie is a couple of *chaises longues* away, eyeing Jenny a bit. I whisper about Nicole into Jenny's ear, which is right there next to my mouth. "She says we can either be family or strangers, and she wants us to be family."

"Hm," Jenny says quietly. Then, after a while: "So those are the choices?"

"That's what she says," I whisper, eyeing Trixie eyeing Jenny.

Trixie's the one who I'm really watching, because she's assigned herself the role of primary doctor to Jenny and the baby-to-be, and she's taking on the job with a lot of zeal. Like, she's always checking Jenny. She carries her stethoscope around with her everywhere she goes so that whenever she wants she can "just get a quickie stetho," which is how she puts it. And then she leans in to hear that heartbeat. And she takes Jenny's temperature. And checks Jenny's weight, multiple times a day. And watches the food Jenny eats, and checks on her sleeping, even sometimes while she's actually sleeping, apparently. It's a lot.

But here's the thing: Trixie is a biologist and a medical doctor, and she was hoping that Mars was going to be swimming in new life. After all, she grew up in Australia, where some animals have *pockets* in them, and there's an animal called a devil, and there are giant birds that don't fly, and mammals the size of foxes that do, and poisonous octopi, and also they have mammals that lay eggs, one of which is the platypus, which has a duck's bill. So she had become accustomed to the idea that life was plentiful and strange and full of surprises. If there are pythons that can eat crocodiles in Australia, she figured, who *knows* what must be on Mars. And she was *so* excited about that possibility, *so* looking forward to seeing what she might find, that she gave up everything to come looking.

But no.

Trixie's lab has been, since the very beginning, a total blank. All of Trixie's underground water samples—*all* of them—have turned up sterile. One after the next, dragged up from ten meters, a hundred meters, a thousand meters below the surface, totally devoid. Her notes read *Negative, Negative, Negative.* She's taken to ending her conclusions with frowny emojis—I know because she told me—which apparently makes her feel less professional but also a little bit better.

What you have here is a woman who's traveled more than a hundred million miles in order to become, I guess, a biologist with no *bio* to *ology.*

Trixie was probably the most frequent visitor to my office back when I had one. She was very cheerful out in the common spaces—flashing her smile and her dyed-red hair everywhere, and singing those pop songs—but in my office she was another person. In my office she would at first chatter about music or television or the way people were talking about us on social media and on blogs back on Earth—she used to follow that kind of thing more than a person should—but after a few minutes of me waiting for it she'd slow down. Slow down and start *really* talking. And a lot of times she'd cry quietly and say things like, "If this planet was a pregnancy test, it would be a great big blue minus sign."

The Trixie who bops around and sings is not the whole Trixie, is what I'm saying.

And then—this is where the pregnancy comes in—right in front of her, one bunk over on a planet that has yet to cough up a bacterium, suddenly Jenny is cooking up brand new life. And you can actually hear it, that life—we don't have ultrasound, but a stethoscope brings the heartbeat right up. It's *detectable*. And so Trixie keeps that stethoscope on like a necklace and she stethoes Jenny whenever she gets half a chance.

I get it.

Still—that doesn't mean it's a good thing for Jenny, and I have already been spending a lot of my time lately heading Trixie off at the pass. Like, I hear her coming and I warn Jenny, who zips off to the bathroom. Or I'm with Trixie and I hear Jenny coming and I pull Trixie away to ask her something random, like how she liked her stew at dinner or what she thinks about the soap we've been using. I usually don't have much time to think. Maybe I should plan some things in advance.

Today I actively go looking for Trixie, but I keep finding her preoccupied—lab stuff—or she's with someone else. Then at one point at dinner when everybody's chatting, she mouths to me, "Talk later?" And I nod.

Which leaves me, in the meantime, with Stefan. And anyway there's obviously an extra level of urgency to keeping an eye on Stefan. I probably should have started with him.

Early on in our time here, Stefan decided that he wanted us to do anarchy, and, in a sign that he probably didn't understand what political philosophers meant by the word "anarchy," he marked the occasion by breaking two of Roger's fingers. Very unsettling. So we gave him a kind of time out and he said he'd give up anarchy. Ever since then he's just mainly been sticking to his engineer duties, which involves a lot of poking at machines and getting under them and behind them and using tools on them and apparently also talking to them a little. What it looks like is that Stefan has gone from being Mars' Most Wanted to our quirky sourpants roommate who keeps to himself.

What it looks like is not entirely what it actually is, of course.

With Stefan there is the quirky, cranky layer and then, deeper, the very angry layer. Under *that*—this is what I'm counting on, but Jenny's not sure I'm right about it—under that is, I believe, something better.

Lately his pants seem to be sourer than usual. He's generally the first person awake and the last person asleep, so we don't really see him in the bunk dome, and he skips game nights, of course, and usually does his meals at odd hours so that he doesn't sit with us. And his conversations with the machines are more muttery and grumbly than they used to be; you'll suddenly realize he's nearby when he starts cursing at whatever mechanical thing he's working on. And people—he snaps at people. So for the most part we leave him alone. Including me—I came to the conclusion a while back, and I know maybe I've been rationalizing, that he's better with a little space around him.

But with Jenny's pregnancy the stakes are bigger. So I go looking for him, because that's my job.

This evening, Stefan's out working on the reactor, so to find him I have to suit up and step away from Home Sweet. Because I'm being nonchalant, I saunter over his way. Or I try to, in the big, bouncy steps that you naturally do on Mars, because of the very low gravity.

"Hey, Stefan," I say through the radio, when I'm still a few bounce-saunter-steps away from him.

He straightens up from the reactor, which has a panel open, dials and meters showing. As is usual, I can't see his face, which is hidden in a mirror-fronted helmet. Plus his helmet light is now pointing in my own face.

After a minute, I realize that his straightening up is as close as I'm going to get to a *hello*, so I shade my eyes and say, "I'm just out for a walk. You feel like going for a walk?"

"Not especially," Stefan says. His accent is British, though he is Danish. The accent makes him sound very dry sometimes. Like now.

"Beautiful night," I say, looking up and seeing that in fact there's a lot of dust in the air and that you can't see many stars.

Stefan bends back down over the reactor, taking his helmet-light beam with him. This means *goodbye*. But I'm not quite ready for that yet.

"How are you doing, Stefan?" I say.

He straightens up again. Light back in my face.

I continue. "I just mean that there's a lot going on lately. The baby coming, et cetera."

"You've got that right," he says.

"Right. So how are you doing with it all?"

Stefan takes a minute to answer. This is not unusual for us; things are slow on Mars. But it feels more tense when it's Stefan. Especially because I can't see his face. Eventually, he says, "I'm not doing anything with it all."

"Well, right," I say. "Not that you have to *do* anything. What I mean is: how are you *feeling* about it?"

This is the wrong approach with Stefan. I'm off because of not seeing his expression.

There is another long pause. I can hear him breathing over the radio channel. I stare past the light into his mirror-face. The dust swirls around. Finally, he says, "I'm feeling that I'd like to be alone with my machines."

"Right now?" I say. "Or in general?"

After a pause, he says, very drily, "Yes."

Well, there isn't much I can say to that, so I just say "Okay," and then, "Have a good night, Stefan."

In response, he bends back to his reactor, which makes things darker again and which means the same thing it meant the first time he did it.

I will need to continue to keep an eye on Stefan.

. . . .

Before I can go back to Home Sweet I have to take a walk for appearances' sake, because my whole pretext for talking to Stefan was that I was taking a walk. So I roam around for a little while, worrying about him, before returning.

Trixie's waiting for me, right there in the airlock area.

"Josh," she says, startling me.

"Oh, Trixie," I say, helmet still in hand. "Oh, hey."

"I heard you talking to Stefan," she says in a conspiratorial whisper.

"You did?" This should not really be surprising; people are always listening to each other's radio conversations. It's easy to tune in from Home Sweet and, like I say, people are bored.

"I did," she says. "Now I really get it."

"You get it?"

"What Jenny said earlier, about psychologist mode. Detective-psychologist mode. You're back in business. The doctor is in."

It's taking me a minute to catch up, but now I see what's in front of me; Trixie is making my segue for me. "Do you want to talk?" I say. I'm still in my spacesuit, and we're standing awkwardly among a bunch of other spacesuits, but I'm not going to pass up the opportunity.

"Yes," she says. "Yeah."

I nod a *Go ahead* nod.

"Okay," she says. "I've been dreaming. Heaps."

"Dreaming?" I say. I lean back against the wall of hanging spacesuits.

She nods vigorously, which makes her bright hair bounce—it's been pink instead of red lately—but her face is all seriousness. This isn't the party Trixie. "Heaps."

"What about?"

Her eyes go fuzzy. "It's like I'm floating through these worlds, these teeming worlds. Worlds just chockers with possibilities—I can't even really describe it. I can't even totally remember it." She screws up her face, thinking. "Well, I remember *pieces* of it: some fluorescent light, maybe, or like the edge of a form. A form with inter-locking parts. But not exactly a *form*. Do you know what I mean?"

Without setting out to do it, I do a thing that's half a nod, and half shaking my head no. Meanwhile there's a wall hook that's sort of in my upper back.

"But mostly it's ideas that are so bonkers that my brain doesn't even know how to think about them. Just bonkers as," she says. "Mostly I've just got this feeling, after, of having felt a feeling. Like there's something in my peripheral vision, and it goes away when-ever I look right at it."

"Wow," I say. Usually I don't remember my dreams.

"But also sometimes I think I hear someone calling my name."

"Huh. In the dream?"

"Well, yes. But once—" she looks around before continuing, as though checking for spies— "one time it happened when I was awake."

"Oh," I say.

"What do you think it means?" she says in a low, conspiratorial voice.

"What do *you* think it means?" I say. It's an old psychologist move, that one.

"You know what I think?" She says this last bit in an even lower voice, leaning toward me.

"What?"

She looks around again. "That there's life on this planet after all."

"Life?" I say.

"Yeah. Life—but life that I can't find with my lab tools. Life that I can only find in my dreams. Or in my mind." She taps her head.

"Interesting," I say. It's actually less worrisome than it sounds; dreams are dreams, and it's pretty normal for people to hear their name being called when it's not. We're all kind of egocentric. But Trixie does probably need to be calmed down some.

"I know." Her eyes are burning.

"That's some theory."

"I know."

"So . . . ." I'm just going to begin. "Do you think it's all related?"

"What? What's related?"

I say, "Let me ask you this: do you ever think that maybe you're even more excited than other people are? About the pregnancy?"

After a moment, Trixie says, "Really?" Another moment. "Wait," she says. "Hold on. Really?" She taps her lower lip with a fat space-suit finger. "I mean, Roger's been making the onesies, hasn't he? I mean, Stefan isn't, but. . . ." She's pretty much talking to herself now. And then she returns to the conversation. "I *am* a biologist," she says. "It's my thing."

"Exactly," I say, leaning in. "I mean, here you are on Mars, and you haven't found any life here—*yet*—or not definitively—" I emphasize, because she's getting ready to protest—"but I wonder if that's why you're sort of latching on to Jenny." I'm thinking the word "displacement" though I don't say it.

"Wait," Trixie says. Her eyes aren't burning anymore. "Wait— you wouldn't say *latching on*, would you? Because of course you have to keep an eye on the pregnancy, and of course it's professionally relevant. But—but is it too much?"

I don't say *yes*, but I make a face that says *yes* for me.

"Is it bothering her? Is that what's going on?" Trixie asks.

I keep my face the same.

"Really?"

Same face.

Trixie stares at me for quite a while. "Oh," she says. "Oh."

She looks shaken enough that I put my hands on her shoulders and look her in the eyes. Hers are a little trembly, a little wet. From there I give her a hug, and it's the right thing to do; she hugs back.

When we're done, Trixie leaves the airlock area, silently, and I get unsuited, feeling bad and proud of myself at the same time. And I know I'm still going to need to keep an eye on her going forward.

. . . .

When I walk into the empty common room, I hear a "Psst!" and I look around. There's my old office, the door partly open, Jenny poking her head out from inside.

Canoodling? Canoodling is always nice, though I feel a little distracted right now. Or maybe she's hiding from Trixie and Trixie's attentions.

Jenny beckons me over silently.

Inside, she's got the light on, and has carved out a little space by stacking some towels very high and leaving a couple smaller stacks to sit on. Everywhere you look, white towels with big blue *Destination Mars!* logos on them. She's already sitting, and she gestures for me to sit down, too. I do, right on a logo. My stack isn't next to hers—it's across from hers.

"How's it going, detective?" she says.

I chew on that for a minute. There's a lot going on, I think. Plus the towels that are stacked very high look like they could topple over. I also feel aware that the cameras in here are probably rolling. Of course, they were probably rolling when I was outside with Stefan, and when I was in the kitchen, and the greenhouse, and the airlock, and even when Jenny and I were in the bathroom. What do the people on Earth think about all of this? As I say, there's a lot going on. "I was just talking to Trixie," I say.

"You're concerned about her," she says.

"Well, yeah," I say. "I am. But I think maybe we made some progress."

"Okay."

"Yeah—we were just talking about—"

"And you're concerned about Stefan," she says, looking at me closely with those eyes, those light brown eyes. She's leaning forward, her forearms on her thighs, her hands clasped together. Almost like *she's* in detective mode.

"Well, Stefan's the kind of person you worry about," I say.

Jenny tilts her head as if to say, *True enough.* But then: "And you're concerned about Roger and Nicole."

"Concerned? I don't know about *concerned*," I say. "They seem like they're doing okay."

"But you're keeping an eye on them."

I nod decisively. "Yeah."

Jenny waits a minute—probably a full minute—before she says the next thing: "And you know who you're *not* keeping an eye on?"

My mouth falls right open.

Jenny.

Oh, Jenny.

This pregnancy is, obviously, a very big deal for Jenny. First of all, growing a baby inside you—a person inside a person—is just a crazy thing to be doing no matter who or where you are. Could there be a bigger deal? It happens on Earth all the time, so it's common, but common and ordinary are not at all the same thing. And this pregnancy is crazier than it would be for other people under the same circumstances, and crazier than it would be for her under other circumstances. For one thing, on Earth the doctors told her she was never going to be able to get pregnant, so she never saw this coming. Plus I'd had a vasectomy that apparently didn't take. Plus the *Destination Mars!* people told us not to have sex here because it wasn't going to be a good idea to have a baby on Mars, so we didn't ever consider the possibility of babies on Mars, even though Jenny and I were ignoring the don't-have-sex rule. Again, we weren't even supposed to be able to get pregnant.

And then—I lean forward and reach out to take Jenny's hand—there's the question of what will happen when the baby is born. The *Destination Mars!* people told us not to have sex on Mars because they didn't know if it was safe to have a baby here—safe for the baby or safe for the mother.

And even if the birth goes okay and the baby isn't affected by being conceived and carried and getting born on Mars, who will that baby be?

That has to be the hardest thing for Jenny. Her sister—her sister was not a well person. Jenny is on Mars partly because she just couldn't stay on the planet where her sister used to be, which is understandable. But the genetics have come with Jenny, and she knows it.

We've talked about all of this before, but not recently. I do ask her how she's doing sometimes. Usually she deflects. But still—I should deflect the deflections.

"I'm sorry, Jenny," I say. "I'm sorry. I should be paying more attention to you." I want to smack myself in the head.

"It's challenging," she admits. "It's a heady time, certainly."

I take her other hand with my other hand, so both of my hands are holding both of her hands. They are, I notice again, almost the exact same color as her eyes. "I'm sorry," I say. "Let's talk about it."

"It's a whirlwind for me, emotionally, definitely," she says.

"Totally."

"But that's not what I'm talking about."

"Huh?" I say.

She takes a long moment—not too long by Mars standards, but certainly by Earth standards. "I'm talking about *you*," she said.

I straighten up, which pulls my hands away. It also makes me knock against a tall stack of towels, and the stack wavers a little. "Me?"

Jenny nods. "Do you know what I think?" she says.

I breathe in and out. Now that she asks, I do know what she thinks, but I don't feel like saying it out loud. I don't think I even want to hear it. "You don't have to worry about me," I say.

"I'm not *worried*," she says. "But I think you've got stuff going on."

"Who doesn't?" I say, gesturing around like everybody else is there in the towel closet with us.

"Josh," Jenny says. "I'm trying to talk about *you*."

I look up at the wavering stack of towels. Why does *Destination Mars!* keep sending us all these towels, anyway? They're not even very good ones, because the *Destination Mars!* logo is so big and embroidered on so thickly that they don't dry a person well.

Jenny tries again. "I think you're in this detective mode so that you don't have to think about how *you're* doing."

I look back at Jenny. "I'm doing fine," I say. "I'm crazy about you. You're having a baby. It's great."

"I know it's got to be difficult."

"Can we stop?" I say.

She sighs. "I know you're crazy about me. But there's still Lil."

I want to knock a stack of towels over just to stop the conversation. "Lil isn't here," I say.

"Yes she is," Jenny says. "It's okay. My sister is here, too. Everybody who was there is also here."

"I mean, I know that," I say. "I understand that."

"I just know it must be difficult," she says. "It was okay when this was casual. You could be crazy about me and it was okay. But now—"

She doesn't finish her sentence. She waits.

I wait, too.

So eventually she starts a new sentence: "You were going to make a family with Lil," she says. "And you left Earth because, when she was taken away from you, you were sure you never wanted to do that with anyone else, ever. Never even try. Which is why it was okay when we were just casual. But now—"

She leaves the same unfinished sentence sitting there. Neither one of us touches it.

After a very long wait, I say, "Thank you, Jenny. I'm hearing you. I'm okay. We're okay. Everything is okay. You're right that it's hard. But it's okay."

She looks at me with a face of not believing me.

I reach over to give her a hug, and also so I don't have to see her looking at me that way. Looking over her shoulder at all the towels, I think about how she's completely right. And we've talked about Lil before; it's not like I won't talk about her. It's just that it's one thing to be sad about Lil, and it's another thing to go forward anyway.

The truth is not that I'm crazy about Jenny; the truth is actually that I love her. And sometimes, when I think about this baby, I'm as happy as I can possibly be. But it's still another thing to go forward anyway.

It's a Jewish tradition to be worried about the future. A superstition, really. But in my life it's been the accurate way to be.

"Josh," Jenny says quietly in my ear.

"Yeah," I say.

"Nicole is right about that choice we have to make," she says.

Over Jenny's shoulder, I press my face into a stack of the towels, white with too-big blue logos. It feels nice, having Jenny in my arms. But the room is very close around us. It's so different from when we first got here.

When I speak, my voice goes right into the towels. "I know," I say.

Pregnancy as a Location in Space-Time

Observation: Nosebleeds

- Are the occasion for beginning these notes. The notes are, I suppose, for posterity.
  - Documentation for future generations?
  - Possible article(s)?
  - ?

- In any case: after dinner tonight I had the first nosebleed of my life (the technical term is epistaxis, I learned from Nicole and Trixie—our doctors here), and it's an alarming experience. You feel it—not pain, but the tangible sense that something has come loose—and then, before you have a grip on that first sensation, it's running down your face. Blood. Blood is running down your face. Josh (sweet) knocked his chair over when he leaped up to help me. But it turns out that epistaxis is not uncommon during pregnancy, or at least on Earth. And apparently it happens here, too.

- At least in my case.

- Which is the only case there is.

Observation: Singularity

On Earth:	On Mars:
Pregnancy is common; there are more than two billion mothers on the planet. These mothers get together to discuss their experiences, to ready new mothers for their experiences. There is a sharing of accumulated wisdom.	I am the one person who has ever been pregnant here.

Observation: Back

On Earth:	On Mars:
Aches in this region of the body are common during pregnancy, because of weight gain, hormones, and a shift in a woman's center of gravity.	Nothing yet. Is this because of the dramatically lower gravity here? Though presumably muscular atrophy would mean that my back is equally unready for the extra weight as it would be under normal conditions. Question: What are "normal conditions"?

Observation: Midsection

On Earth:	On Mars:
Would be distending (Josh calls it "pooching out") noticeably. I would be shifting into maternity clothes. Elastic waistbands; big tent-shirts.	Am, per expectation, pooching out. I already look different than I ever thought I would look. It's hard to pass a mirror without checking myself in it.

	Checking myself for? Also, there is no such thing as pregnancy jumpsuits, no such thing as pregnancy spacesuits. All we have is the clothing we've been wearing all along—and the upper part of my jumpsuit is starting to get tight. How tight is too tight for a developing fetus? Soon I'll be in my bathrobe all the time.

Observation: The need, in case of an emergency that would force us to evacuate Home Sweet, to have a spacesuit that fits

As my father would put it, it's best not to think about some things.

Observation: Things that can go wrong with a pregnancy on Mars

In every life, there are many things about which it's best not to think.

Observation: How you can stop yourself from thinking about things you shouldn't think about

Still unknown.

Observation: Months

On Earth:	On Mars:
There are months.	There are no months.

A woman could be four months pregnant on Earth, and there would be general agreement: she is four months pregnant.	That is to say, there is the Darian calendar, but between the fact that (1) there are twenty-four months in the Darian calendar and (2) the calendar requires a person to drop days sometimes to keep the calendar working correctly, which is as annoying as it sounds like it is, we stopped using the Darian calendar a long time ago, and never came up with a replacement. Which means there are no months on Mars. What this means is that I have been pregnant for a period of time that can best be described as: since I got pregnant.

Observation: Darian calendar

Thomas Gangale invented this calendar in the late twentieth century, but he did not name it after himself. He named it after his son, Darius.

Observation: Family support system

On Earth:	On Mars:
Would be the same messy thing it was when I was living there and not expecting a baby. When, some years ago, my	Is Josh. Who came here, like me, expecting (hoping for) a barren planet. He lost someone, too.

OB/GYN told me that I would never be able to get pregnant (!), I shared the news with my mother and she said, "Well, *nena*, that's one thing you won't have to worry about." She was thinking about my sister. My sister was still alive then. But my sister's life was not much easier than her death.

My parents and I communicate via email now. But it took me several weeks ("weeks" are also not actually real here) beyond the positive pregnancy test before I sent my parents a video message to tell them the news. In their response video, they held one another very tightly as they congratulated me. They did smile. Though Josh tells me that it's only called a Duchenne smile—a true smile—if it reaches the person's eyes.

Sometimes he looks at me the way a person might look at an unexploded bomb, or like someone falling, away.

Other times he smiles in a way that reaches his eyes, his whole face, his whole body, beyond.

Observation: What you might think when a doctor tells you you're infertile

I am not like other women. Am I a space alien?

Observation: Heartburn

On Earth:	On Mars:
Over fifty percent of women experience heartburn during pregnancy, particularly during the second and third trimesters.	One hundred percent of pregnant mothers on Mars experience heartburn.

Observation: Months II

Question: If there are no months, are there trimesters? Also, could the length of a pregnancy increase in proportion to the longer Martian year?

If p (length of pregnancy) = 280 Earth days (approx.) = 0.7671 Earth years (approx.), and if t (length of Martian year/length of Earth year) = 1.88 (approx.), then:

$$p * t = 0.7671*1.88 = 1.44 \text{ Earth years} = \text{approximately } 526 \text{ Earth days!}$$

I suspect that some of my questions are not quite scientific questions.

Observation: "Morning" sickness

On Earth:	On Mars:
Common during the first trimester—common all day long—and, though unpleasant, possibly an important sign of a healthy fetus. Associated with lower rates of miscarriage. Though of course there are other things, aside	Has begun to fade, now in what would be the second trimester, if there were months here of the traditional kind. (It is September on Earth.) The decline in nausea does not mean a danger to the fetus on Mars any more than it would

from miscarriages, that can go wrong. Generally fades in the second trimester.	on Earth. It is normal, and does not indicate any problems. Though of course there are other things, aside from miscarriages, that can go wrong.

Observation: Foundation for claims about pregnancy

On Earth:	On Mars:
Two hundred thousand years of experience and stories and scientific investigation.	Analogies. Maybe what happened there will happen here, a kind of unwavering pattern. Optimism. Me. Me looking at me. Nobody has done this before me.

Observation: Time

Classical Physics:	Relativistic Physics:
Time passes. "The arrow of time," in the words of twentieth century astronomer Arthur Eddington, moves in one direction. Time is asymmetrical. As in, getting pregnant is behind; the rest of this pregnancy, however it turns out, is ahead. My old family is behind; my new family is ahead.	Time is. Any sense of unidirectionality is a human illusion. If the universe can be described as four-dimensional space-time, then the past and the future are just locations in that matrix. The night when Josh and I had sex and (unlike the other nights we had sex) fertilization occurred; the night decades before that when an egg and sperm combined to produce proto-me; the day

when there will be a baby on Mars for the first time; the time when my sister was alive and so young that everything seemed entirely promising; the end of the universe; the night when I was awakened by a text from my sister—it came as a text—and I called her and couldn't reach her and had to call the police instead—all of these, locations in a space-time continuum.

If you had the right kind of vehicle, theoretically you could go to any of these locations whenever you wanted.

The mind might be that kind of vehicle.

If you had the wrong kind of vehicle, you might find it difficult to leave some of these locations.

The mind might also be this kind of vehicle.

Observation: Mental habits

Josh once observed—we were in his bed, whispering together—that sometimes I reach for theoretical physics as though for a teddy bear.

Observation: Fetal development

On Earth:	On Mars:
Assuming all was progressing normally, fetus would be approximately six or seven inches long—maybe the size of a small banana. Though it's been a long time since I last saw a banana.	No way of knowing. We don't have ultrasound equipment. We don't have anything that allows us to see inside. We have stethoscopes, so what we have is a heartbeat. Nicole and Trixie say it's a fine heartbeat. 140 beats per minute, right in the normal range.
Assuming all was progressing normally, the fetus would be starting to grow hair and teeth, might be sucking a thumb. For comfort?	Of course you can never see all the way inside. Not on any planet. Some things will always be hidden.

Observation: Possibility that the child will be born with a brain like my sister's brain

On Earth:	On Mars:
Low but not insignificant. Bipolar disorder is one of the most heritable disorders; estimates suggest that c. 80-85% of variability among people on this dimension is attributable to genetic factors. Still—even with a bipolar parent, odds appear to be below 10% that the child will also be bipolar. Odds surely lower if the relation is an	Radiation can affect genes and genetic transmission. Because the atmosphere is thinner, we are routinely exposed to more radiation here. And the rocket trip, through unshielded space for six Earth months—radiation radiation radiation. Does this increase the odds or lower them?

| aunt rather than a parent. And Josh does not have this history in his family at all.
Note: Depression is also like-lier among relatives of people with BPD. | |

Observation: Distribution of anxiety

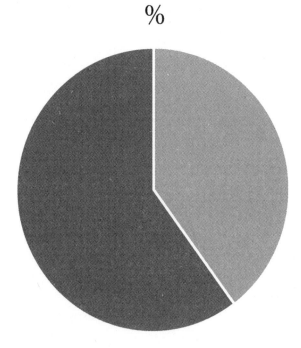

%

■ Time spent worrying about dangers from outside me on Mars

■ Time spent worrying about dangers from inside me

Observation: Gravity

On Earth:

The rate of acceleration while falling is 9.8 m/s².

The rate is the same whether you fall, or whether you jump.

There are many tall buildings on Earth.

Nobody can state with certainty how far one has to fall to produce a necessarily fatal result.

On the one hand, a flight attendant named Vesna Vulovic once fell 10,000 meters and survived it. She broke many bones, and there was a brief coma, but eventually she made a full recovery. Though it's worth noting that her fall was not a case of a human falling free in space; a food cart kept her pinned in the tail section after the plane broke up. And she landed, in that tail section, in snow. Still—that's a long fall, and she lived.

On the other hand, it's possible to slip on a puddle and hit your head and die that way. Falling hardly at all.

My sister's apartment building was a brownstone. It was

On Mars:

The rate of acceleration while falling is 3.75 m/s².

There are very tall mountains, but no tall buildings, on Mars.

When we approached the planet after those six months in space, we were traveling at nearly 24,000 kilometers per hour. At that speed you could fly from Boston to San Francisco in less than 11 minutes. And as the planet was looming, I had the strangest thought; it occurred to me, just for a second, that we could change our minds and decide to *not* brake. We could maintain our speed, be slowed hardly at all by the atmosphere, and become Mars' next great crater. The first that would be human-made.

And then, while I was thinking of that, almost paralyzed by thoughts of that, of course Stefan and Nicole were turning on the braking jets, and we slowed down, and there was a parachute, and we slowed down more, and we fell all the way to the ground, but more and

only four stories high. Vesna Vulovic died in her own apartment at age 66, of unknown causes.	more slowly, and then we land-ed—completely unharmed.

Observation: Boston and San Francisco; Uncrossable distances

Boston:	San Francisco:
Where I lived for most of my adult life.	Where my sister lived, for the year up until her suicide. She texted me—*texted* me—right before. Even eleven minutes would have been too long to get to her in time. The police, who I called, only took six, which is fast, compared to the national average for police responses. And that was too late. Eleven minutes would have been an eternity.

Observation: Time II

Fertilization:	Getting to the roof and jumping:
Can take place as soon as a half hour, or as long as five days, after sex.	In one sense, it only takes five minutes. In another sense, a more accurate sense, it takes your whole life up to that point. My sister was climbing, in this understanding, for thirty-four

	years. Which means that we had plenty of time to reach her, even on foot. Even from across the world.

Observation: God

On Earth:	On Mars:
At best: Absent.	Josh asked me once how I would feel about raising the child Jewish. It's like asking me what I would prefer in an imaginary friend.

Observation: Paradoxical feelings

- If r = relief (e.g., like what I felt when my sister first moved to San Francisco, which meant that I could no longer be called on to rush to her side again and again and again when her life was falling apart in one of a thousand ways);

- and if g = guilt (e.g., how I felt afterward because I had been at a distance where I couldn't be called on to rush to her side); then

$$g = rm$$

- where m = the magnitude of the consequences brought about by the distance.

Observation: Uncrossable distances II

Mars is so far from where things have gone wrong in the past that the relationship between r and g are no longer certain. Which produces more r.	The distance between Mars and present and future potential disasters = 0.

Question: Siblings

Is it possible that this child inside me will ever have a sibling?

Observation: There were good times with her

There were!

Question: Age

If—I looked it up—the average lifespan of a human being on Earth is now 76.1 years (Earth years), and 80.2 years in the United States specifically (interestingly, at 80.6 years it's actually slightly higher in, even more specifically, my mother's home territory of Puerto Rico), what is the life expectancy on Mars? The people here are healthy, but we're also less equipped to handle medical emergencies, and then there's the increased radiation. And if a person takes her own—the point is that it's hard to predict.

But say we each live exactly to the unknown average Martian lifespan that I will assign the variable x. Let's say that. And also say the baby lives a full life. Let's say that. And that I will be 34 years old (Earth years) at the time of the birth.

- That means that I will have $(x - 34)$ years left to live, $(x - 34)$ years to spend with the child.

- The child, on the other hand, would have x more years to live, including $(x - (x - 34)) = 34$ years without me. 34 years without me.
  - By that same formula, 36 years without Josh.
  - By that same formula, 29 years without Trixie, who is our youngest.

In other words, if *Destination Mars!* doesn't send any more people to Mars and if this baby lives—please—a full lifespan, that person, our child, will be alone on this planet, this place that nobody's currently working on terraforming, where you can't even breathe, for probably decades. Alone.

Unscientific question
Is death always an abandonment?

Unscientific question II
Can making *life* be an abandonment?

Observation: Gravity II
As we already know, F (gravitational force) = $G(m_1 m_2 / r^2)$, where G is a constant equal to 6.67×10^{-11} Nm^2/kg^2, m_1 is the mass of the first object, m_2 is the mass of the second one, and r is the distance between the objects. With this formula you can calculate the pull between any two objects, whether they are two planets or two people in the same or different rooms.

I would calculate the pull between Earth and Mars as it currently stands at the current distance between the planets, but it's getting pretty late.

I would calculate other pulls, but some of them are incalculable.

Question: Notes

Who, again, are these notes for?

Unscientific question III

Is it possible that, if I had stayed on Earth, I would have stayed infertile? That I *couldn't* have produced life there? That I had to be this far away for it to happen?

Observation: Linea Negra

On Earth:	On Mars:
In some cases, a darker line develops between the navel and the pubic bone. Caused by increases in hormones.	The line is not a metaphor, but it seems like a metaphor. The line between the navel (the place where my umbilicus once was) and the pubis (the place where the baby will, if all goes well up to that point, enter the world): the line between generations, maybe. The symbol of continuation. Is this a beautiful thing or an awful thing?

Observation: Genes vs. environment vs. . . .

Genes:	Environment:	. . .
Studies routinely suggest that around 50% of a baby's personality can be explained by genetic background.	If 50% is genetics, that leaves a lot of room for something else. Environment is the prime candidate. And what is	It is possible that we are the product of more than genes and environment. That there's something else shaping

(Though see above re: bipolar disorder.)	the environment, the one around me and this developing fetus right now? It's a planet, an orange planet, where a person can't breathe, where there are no trees. Also, where there is none of my past. Not my parents, not my sister, not anything they ever did or knew. None of that is in this particular location in space-time. But there *is* Josh. And there is me. Is this, taken all together, a beautiful thing or an awful thing?	us, mapping out directions and constraints and possibilities. What that something else would be, I'm not sure science can say. But is it real anyway?

Observation: Quickening (first movements)

They say it doesn't feel like *movement* right away, like an actual baby moving inside of you, where you might think *Oh, that's the elbow nudging, that's the leg kicking.* They say it typically feels like gas. Like the aftereffects of a burrito. Like bubbles. I am experiencing something like bubbles, something like gas. Like so many other things—all things?—it's impossible to be certain about a cause. And impossible to be certain about an effect.

Maybe someday Josh will observe that I retreat into indeterminacy as though under a blanket.

Note: The term quickening apparently comes from the fact that the word "quick" used to mean *alive*. As in, "the quick and the dead." Before ultrasound, before even stethoscopes, the quickening was the first compelling sign that the baby was alive.

Tonight I felt the quickening for the first time. Which is the actual occasion for beginning these notes—not, honestly, the nosebleed. It was that sensation of gurgling or tickling or bubbles. That sign of whatever it signifies. I have been writing this ever since, re-researching all the things I've researched before, for several hours now. Josh has twice come out from the bunk dome to ask me if I'm going to come to bed soon. I should.

My nose is no longer bleeding.

This is not a sign of anything.

Observation: Probability

On Earth:	On Mars:
Unknown.	Unknowable.

How to Deal with the Unknown
(Section 27 of the unofficial *Destination Mars!* handbook, as written by the founder of *Destination Mars!*)

You are not new to the unknown. Every day, whether you think about it or not, you wake up into mystery. You have plans, very likely, and maybe even a routine that you're ready to settle into even as you rub the sleep out of your eyes, the slumber from your face—but that doesn't mean you know what's going to happen, because you very obviously cannot. You don't even know what you'll be *thinking* later, let alone what you'll be doing or what will be happening to you.

And it's bigger than that, bigger than the unpredictable future. You also confront the unknown on a daily basis in the sense that what you understand about the world around you is infinitesimal in comparison to what you don't understand. What you really *get* is basically nothing. This is just as true when you're looking at the world of the self.

Not one person has a decent grasp on the future, the past, or the present. Not the world, nor themselves.

That said, you are already accustomed to this much mystery, and it probably doesn't even register anymore. It's an everyday thing; you don't think about it. It's only when you're facing something dramatically new—something vivid and unprecedented—that you are struck by the limits of your knowledge.

Going to Mars is likely to be one of those occasions.

With that in mind, we've written this chapter to support you as you confront these new realities, and, even more, as you sit in uncertain anticipation. As you, in other words, wake up once again to the profound inscrutability of everything that is. We of course don't know exactly when those situations will come up, or what they'll be about—that's sort of our main point here—but some general thoughts may help.

- First of all, the best approach varies by personality. For example:
  - There are people whose preference is for control, and who see knowledge as control. These are the people who will read up exhaustively on Mars before going. Of course, you will all have to absorb an enormous amount of information before getting on the rocket, but some people will go well beyond the requirements. Not content to study the behavior of dust storms on the planet's surface, or even the chemical structure of Martian dust (this varies, but there will often be iron and magnesium involved), these folks will need to study the seventeenth century physicist Evangelista Torricelli's groundbreaking theories about the origins of wind and dig up the etymology of the word dust (which, as we understand it, derives from the pre-Germanic word *dunstaz*, a word that meant the ultimate minute and scattered product of human decomposition). They will need to *taste* the dust (which we do not advise). For these people, a piece of knowledge is a fingerhold. Never mind that still their ignorance is to their understanding as the universe is to a grain of rice; the fingerhold is their salvation.

o   Then there are the head-down types. They set aside the unknown and get back to work, doing the things they already know how to do. These are not, admittedly, always the most exciting people in the world. But they do tend to show up on time and meet deadlines. No group of people is likely to survive without a few of this kind sprinkled among them.

o   People with a more philosophical bent, or people who are religious in a certain kind of way, often like to do something they call *sitting with the unknown*. They face it and take it in and continue to face it some more. Without moving. We find this attractive but itself fairly mysterious. There are times when we don't believe this is even possible.

o   There are also individuals who, when faced with the unknown, want to destroy it. This is probably not a good tendency to indulge.

o   Artists and other creative types, meanwhile, generally dive—without even thinking about it—right into the center of whatever it is they don't know, just to kind of *poke around* in there. Results vary.

• Speaking of religion, different religions have different understandings of the nature of the unknown. In the Qur'an, for example, only Allah is described as *knowing the unknown, seeing the unseen*, which means that the rest of us have to do without. In the Bhagavad Gita, one reads, *Knowledge is superior to mechanical practice. Meditation is superior to knowledge. But best of all is the surrender of attachment to results, because this leads immediately to peace.* So you may be able to do something with that. And St. Ignatius has a great quote on the subject: *Less knowledge, more virtue!* he said. There's even part of the Passover Seder where you break a piece of matzah in two, and you hide the bigger part, because what's hidden is larger than what's revealed—which is just what we were saying above—and then the kid who finds the hidden piece at the end of dinner gets a prize. Real life may or may not work in this way.

- The point is that these traditions may have some answers for you, even if most of the answers are, in one way or another, *Deal with it.*

- Relatedly, you will find that your tablets and computers are stocked with a healthy set of aphorisms on just about any topic you could imagine. A search for "anxiety" should bring up thousands of possibly helpful quotes.

- In terms of these various styles and strategies, consider doing some mixing and matching. Like, maybe you can try to dive into some unknowns, and sit with other ones, and pursue virtue here and there, and learn your way into others, and do some surrendering, and ignore the rest of what you don't know. You can't deal with everything at once, is one thing we've observed.

- We have included in your Communal Stockpile (see Section 11) some helpful psychopharmaceutical medications. We will be happy to replenish as necessary.

- Side note. This is not the main point of this chapter,

but here are a few very specific unknown things we would like you to look into on your new planet:

- o What are the effects of all the extra radiation on human physiology, health, and life span? Not that you are an experiment, the first humans ever to live on Mars, but you're sort of an experiment.
- o What is a Martian sunset like? Emotionally?
- o Did the planet ever have a fertile Earth-like period? Was it once teeming with life?
- o Is Mars our future?
  - ▪ Like, is Earth going to end up the way Mars is now?
  - ▪ And also, is the future of the human species on Mars?
- o Is there life there now? Oh, please please please. And please let it not just be something like bacteria. It seems like bacteria's the most likely thing, and it would be cool in a way if there were bacteria there, we guess. Biologists would be electrified. But here at *Destination Mars!* we have to admit we're rooting for charismatic megafauna. Come on, charismatic megafauna!
- o (As long as it's friendly.)

- Anyway, back to the focus of the chapter: dealing. And we've left a big unknown for last. Specifically: at some point on Mars you will be forced to confront the enormous question mark that is yourself. The self is, as we said above, an enigma on any planet, obviously, but you will be in a new and challenging landscape, one that will test and provoke you in many ways, and so—especially in a context where you will be one of only a very few people anywhere around—you will probably be brought face-to-face with yourself more than once. Who are you? Who will you turn out to be? Even we, who have run you through an exhaustive battery of physical and psychological examinations, cannot answer these questions. Probably you are not able to answer them, either, and perhaps you never will be, or perhaps the answers will come to you too late, *after* a watershed moment when you really needed to know. But maybe you'll come to a few timely conclusions. Maybe even wisdom. We hope so. We're rooting for you, too.

- It's interesting, isn't it? People have been wrestling with this probably since the beginning of the species, and yet, even now, nobody really has the answer.

- Though there's one thing we *can* tell you:
  - When it comes to life's most frightening questions—
    - What's going to happen to me?
    - Will I be equal to the biggest challenges of my life?
    - Is it safe to hope?
  - —the one thing you can count on is this: you're damn sure going to find out.

We Are All in Tents
(on Earth, back before we ever left it)

FIRST IT'S DIAL-TURNING. They tell me, tell all of us, to turn dials, one notch every forty-five seconds. Each time, once every forty-five seconds, there's this soft *thunk* in our hands as the dials settle into their new notches. We do this for four hours straight. The dials don't control anything or measure anything. They don't make anything light up or start or stop. They just move through notches.

This is the part of the weeding process, I know. The test is boredom.

There's not much going on up there, the people in charge have told us. *Or, what's going on is a whole lot of maintaining equipment and checking readings and cataloguing them and keeping things clean and then doing it all again.* They say that they don't mean to be buzz-kills, but that we need to know what we're getting into. *It's not boisterous up there.*

There have been other kinds of tests—wearing backpacks full of old encyclopedias all day, for example, to see about our endurance levels; timed simultaneous crossword puzzles and Sudoku for a kind of intelligence check; color chip sorting and balloon-filling and even some juggling performance tests for various other purposes, some of which never became clear to any of us. But now it's about boredom.

And so the people in charge start this unit with dial-turning. After that, they tell us to sit at our metal desks which are bolted down in rows and move sand, grain by grain, from one Tupperware container to another. If we accidentally move more than one grain at a time, we have to start over. And then we write the alphabet repeatedly until we've filled a five-section, college-ruled, spiral notebook. We have to clasp and unclasp and clasp and unclasp all the clasps on our standard-issue white jumpsuits until our hands feel like lobster claws. At night, we are literally asked to count the stars. The candidates stand in the bare cement courtyard that's at the center of the whole giant complex we're in, and we turn our faces upward, and we count.

We are trying to demystify the stars, the people in charge have said, *so that you can live productively among them.*

Some of the candidates are starting to decompensate a bit. Elena has taken up muttering in streams of mysterious Bulgarian; Marcelo has developed a twitchy eyelid. Julia, who looks a little bit like Lil—maybe the curly dark hair that's long enough to get to the middle of her back, or her smile, or more likely just me wanting someone to look like Lil—Julia whistles to keep herself cheerful. One person, a man from Bali named Pramana, took himself completely out of the running by sweeping his Tupperware containers to the floor during the sand exercise. We haven't seen him in the *Destination Mars!* complex since.

Honestly, though, I don't mind any of it. If you've ever been through a PhD program, you're pretty much habituated to this kind of thing.

The workroom could be nicer. The cement floor is painted gray-green and the walls are just green, a dull shade of it—I once heard that they paint the inside of submarines green so that people forget they're a half a mile or however deep underwater and instead feel like they're in a meadow, which is supposed to keep them calm—and there isn't anything on the walls in here at all. Especially not windows. That's like a submarine, too. But you sort of forget about the surroundings after a while—maybe that's the calming effect of the green, or maybe just another example of habituation—and you get into the work. Like, here I am bent over a copy of the King James Bible, using two different-color highlighters to highlight the words "and" and "but" wherever they appear, one color for "and" and another color for "but," and the main thing it is, is peaceful. *And*, I highlight. *And. And. But. And.* Peaceful for me, anyway. Kirsten, at the desk in front of me, is drumming her long fingers and her yellow highlighter is trembling just a little in her other hand, which is maybe or maybe not visible to the several cameras positioned above us.

They are filming us for a reality show. Supposedly audience votes will decide who gets to go to Mars and who won't. We'll see.

There are, naturally, breaks for meals and sleep. The eating breaks are nice, not because the food is good—the food is not good—but because you get to find out more about the other candidates. Like Marcelo is from Argentina and is a sculptor, or Molly is from Ireland and drives a cab there. Or Bruce chews with his mouth open.

Sometimes we talk about why we're here, why we want to go to Mars. Tom, who has advanced degrees in several different sciences, wants to study the effects of reduced gravity on human physiology. Dalit, who refuses to tell us what he does for a living, says he wants to help spread humanity throughout the galaxy so that it can go on forever. Yiran is a musician—she plays the guzheng, which she says is a kind of zither, which I guess is a kind of instrument—and she wants to compose "truly Martian music."

When they asked me about it, when they asked me why I want to go, I told them the answer I tell everyone, my best answer. "Why not?" I said.

And then everybody blinked at me.

"Seriously, Josh," a red-faced guy named Eddie said, pointing his sandwich at me and losing a slice of tomato as a result. "Why do you want to go?"

"Seriously," I said. "Why not?"

"Well, if you're really asking: because you'll never see Earth again, or feel a breeze on your face, or be in the same room as anybody you've ever known, ever again."

"But all of that *on Mars*," I said, using my hands to show how that balanced out.

"I think that rhetorical move is just Josh keeping his cards close to the vest," Nadine said. She's an English professor, which makes her something like a psychologist herself but with her own vocabulary set.

"Or he's kidding," Julia said. A peacemaker, like Lil often was.

"Or crazy," Kirsten said, and everybody laughed. But not in a mean way. In a let's-move-on kind of way. And so we did.

But I wasn't kidding, or not totally. Because that's what got me to sign up in the first place, those *Destination Mars!* ads that asked that exact question. I saw one in a newspaper. There was a picture of a planet—very red, kind of like you'd expect it to be—and, underneath it, only those two words: *Why Not?* And it was a Tuesday, and I was at the tail end of a deeply strange five-day weekend, and maybe wasn't very recently showered. So there was all that. Above all, though, when I saw that ad, I remembered being a kid and, like most kids, thinking from time to time, *Hey, wouldn't it be amazing to set foot on another planet*—which was a pretty invigorating memory. I remember my mother encouraging those fantasies. *What do you think it would look like, Josh? On Mars?* When I went to the website, all they wanted right then was an email address. It was very easy and surprisingly exciting.

Things kind of escalated from there.

"This is really something," says Eddie now, in the wake of the highlighting. He's sneering—he's a sneerer—a few seats down at the cafeteria table where half of the candidates are sitting, the others being at the next table. Eddie says, "They're turning the screws on us, aren't they?"

"I wonder what they'll hand us next," Marcelo says, giving his stubbled face a good scratching.

"Fill a bathtub with an eyedropper," Yiran says.

"Put ten thousand phone numbers in numerical order," Eddie says.

"You know what I always hated?" says Molly in her Irish voice. "Poetry. Maybe they'll make us read poetry."

Everybody laughs. I like poetry fine, actually, and I think Nadine might be a little offended, but the thing we're doing right now is laughing at Molly's joke. It's understandable that the people are bored. The work is supposed to be boring.

I'm not sure that this makes for the best TV, but I'm not the one rolling the cameras.

The next task involves a ream of paper each. We're supposed to take each sheet and cut it into eight pieces that are exactly equal in size, and then we have to fold each smaller piece in half so that it can stand up like a tent. We number our tents sequentially with a pencil and stack them, nested, on the upper-left corner of our desks. It isn't a long time before somebody makes a pun of a joke involving the conflation of *intense* and *in tents*. Still folding, again I laugh along with everyone else.

This time, though, there's a hitch, about a half hour after we get started. Kirsten, who's wearing sandals with her jumpsuit as maybe a kind of fashion statement, notices it first—there is a sheet of water on the floor. She stands up. "There's a leak," she says.

Everyone looks around and sees the water. *Huh*, I think.

"Uh-oh," Yiran says.

A crackle over the PA system, and then: "*There is no leak. You can keep working.*"

"There's water on the floor," Kirsten says to the cameras, which they also use to monitor us in real-time. She points at the water for evidence, up on her tip toes.

As a matter of fact, the level is rising. Like everybody but Kirsten, I've got canvas shoes on, supplied by the people running this, and the water's seeping in at this point. The water is cold.

"*The point is that you don't need to worry about it,*" the somebody-in-charge says over the PA. "*You can keep working.*"

"Oh," says Bruce. "Ohhhhhh."

William snaps his fingers once. "Do you remember when the microwave broke, a couple of days ago?" he says, eyes wide with comprehension. "Or when they woke us up early '*by accident*' yesterday?" Air quotes and all.

It's true. I'm still sleepy from the wake-up call thing. When they made the *oops* announcement yesterday about the early start, I got the idea: the people in charge are testing our ability to do boring tasks while under stress. It's a wrinkle, but fair enough. Space is probably going to be wrinkly. So to speak.

"*Remember that you have a deadline,*" advises someone-else-in-charge through the PA.

"God damn it," Eddie says.

But everybody gets back to work. There aren't a lot of other good options. Even Kirsten, who seems for a minute to have forgotten how to sit down, eventually does, and, with a shake of the head and a splash of the feet, picks up her scissors. The water is now up to our ankles, and it's definitely cold.

I don't like to be cold, but I've been cold before—winter is an annual thing in many places, after all—and it doesn't kill you. Well, it can, actually, but I doubt that the people in charge want to kill the candidates. I mostly doubt that. The water works its way up into the legs of my jumpsuit, and meanwhile I refocus myself with a little effort and fold a new tent, extra precisely. Then I fold another one.

Things did build up slowly. First there was the email address, and then they asked for some basic information, which I sent, and then they sent me some basic information in return, and they asked for more involved information, which I sent, and they sent back some of their own, and so on. It was a fairly slippery slope, is what I'm saying.

But the other thing is that the *Why Not?* question never stopped being a good one. *Destination Mars!* would send me an email asking for an essay or an application video or a couple of recommendations and each time I'd ask myself why, in fact, not? For one thing, what was keeping me on this planet? I don't have siblings, and my parents are gone—my father died years ago, and my mother more recently, both pretty young. And then there was Lil, of course. Lil—it was her very, very unexpected funeral that had started the surreal five-day weekend when I first saw the *Destination Mars!* ad.

Of course, I do still have friends here on Earth—all of them pretty concerned about me, in fact—and I like the breeze on my face as much as anyone. It's a nice planet, Earth. Those are answers, reasons not to go. But studies show that you can replicate the feeling of being in nature by stimulating the right part of the brain. So: as long as you have your brain and some equipment with you, you're good. And these days you can always do space-age video calls with the people in your life, which means you can hear their voices and see their faces and take in their words. And that's not as good as in-person stuff but it's still pretty good. The big difference in terms of relationships isn't Earth versus Mars; it's alive versus dead.

Or maybe it *would* make a difference. As in, if I could get that much farther—millions of miles farther—from the place where the one car smashed into Lil's car on a rainy night, you have to admit that it's a good question: *Why not? Why wouldn't I?*

The tent-folding task goes on for a while, and the water keeps rising and rising, until it's to a level just below the seats of our chairs, at which point it holds steady. That's nice, anyway; at least we're not sitting on water directly.

"Is anyone else starting to feel a little numb in the foot area?" Eddie says.

I'm pretty sure that Eddie, who is usually the first to complain, is not a real candidate but has instead been planted here by the people in charge in order to draw complainers out into the open. In any case, everyone in the room nods a *yes* or says one aloud, me included. The water is cold.

"Is this supposed to be a simulation? Because there's not a lot of water on Mars," Eddie says up to the cameras. "I mean, as a liquid."

"Not yet," chirps Julia from across the room. She's a trier, like Lil was, and I smile over at her. It comes out as a sad smile, though.

For a while, everyone reminded me of Lil, and I mean everyone. Height didn't matter, or eye color, or the sound of the person's voice, or their ethnicity, or personality, or gender. I would be walking slowly down the street or picking my way through a grocery store or staring out of the window of my office and seeing Lils everywhere. Especially in my peripheral vision, but even when I looked directly at people, too. People in dresses, in suits and chef's outfits and police uniforms, in hardhats. Even the person in front of the seafood restaurant dressed as a lobster. It felt like any one of them could secretly turn out to be Lil, and then there would be Lil again. That lasted for at least a full two months. These days, though, there has to be an actual resemblance for me to see a resemblance.

Maybe if Julia and I both get picked, it'll be like—I don't know. I don't know what it could be like.

"WHOA," Bruce says suddenly, jumping to his feet. "What was that?"

"What?" Elena says, and this is the first non-Bulgarian word we've heard out of her in a long time.

"Something brushed my leg," Bruce says.

Several of us are pooh-poohing this when Yiran yelps and jumps to her feet, too. "There is something there," she says.

Out of the corner of my eye, I see a shadow zip through the water, and I stand slowly. Looking around, I can see several shadows, each maybe the size of my hand, zipping around. "Fish," I say.

There is general incredulity at this.

"*Fish?*" someone says.

The PA comes back on again. We, as usual, don't know who's speaking. We've met some people in charge, but the PA voices are always different from those people-in-charge's voices. This time, it says, "*The fish are not important.*"

"I think fish are inherently important," Molly says upward, "in a workroom."

This strikes me as pretty reasonable. "Does anyone know what kind of fish they are?" I say. As far as I can tell, from the moments when the shadows slow down, they're bristly, ugly things, though not very big. Everyone in the room is standing now. They all shrug, collectively.

The PA makes a sound like a sigh and then speaks: "*They are two-horned sculpin. The fish are safe, as long as you don't touch their spines.*"

We all exchange glances.

"*The fish are not important.*"

I look up at the cameras. "Are there going to be more kinds of fish?"

The PA voice says, "*There will not be any important fish.*"

I stand there thinking. And for some reason I think about Lil's garden, which I guess is not surprising, because actually I think about it a lot.

When she was a child, Lil moved over and over again. Philadelphia, Maine, the suburbs around Baltimore, Wisconsin, Florida, New Jersey. Once they even lived in Mexico for six months. It was job stuff that moved them around—sometimes her mother, sometimes her father. And according to Lil all the places were nice. There would be an interesting house or apartment. Kids at school who needed new friends. But still it was always upsetting to move, and even with the same family and same furniture it was hard for her to see the new place as home. And so her mother would make a flower garden each time, or try to. Even though this was Lil's childhood, not mine, I met her mother, and I can picture her kneeling there, getting the knees of her jeans dirty. She probably had special dirty-kneed jeans for that. Lil told me that when the flowers came up, they'd go out and admire them, and something would shift, and they would arrive the rest of the way.

That was a story I almost told on my *Destination Mars!* application video—*I want to make a garden on Mars!*—but then I didn't. I didn't know what I wanted to do on Mars. And in any case I wanted to keep the story for me.

Lil grew up to be a gardener herself. She even made a tiny garden in the tiny lawn in front of the house we shared together—flowers of all colors whose names I could never keep straight. The plot has gone wild since her death. It's like the opposite of what happened in Lil's story; when her mother made a garden, it allowed the family to arrive. As the one in front of our house became wilderness, I knew I had to leave. I knew I had already become homeless.

I look across the room and catch Julia's eye. She doesn't look too optimistic at the moment. It occurs to me: it's possible that she won't make the final cut, won't be sent to Mars. That's definitely possible.

And Julia is of course not Lil. Nobody is.

I look at my desk, which is where things are right now.

Nearby, Eddie asks the cameras, "Are there going to be any more surprises?"

The PA voice offers the exact words that occur to me in response: "*Yes and no*," it says.

I think for just one more moment. It's possible that I won't make the cut, either. I've thought about that before, and I think about it now. And I get the same jolt that I always get: a jolt of anxiety, of loss in advance. Not because I think Mars could become home, but because of that distance, those millions of miles—away from the place that used to be our home, from the garden Lil once made, from the neatly trimmed plot where she is now—and at least that's something. In fact, it's the only thing.

Even though the seat is now wet, I sit, and I reach for another small rectangle of paper. My hands are already in the shape of a tent.

There Are Owls in the Moss
(on Earth, before anyone departed for Mars)

By the time his toothpaste had disappeared for the second time, and in the context of his showers having temperature variations unexperienced by the other candidates, and waking up with sand in his sleepsack all this week despite having always been in a spacesuit with built-in boots whenever he was outside—a spacesuit that they made all of them wear even though outside it was only Mungo National Park, Australia—a spacesuit that seemed to make him sweatier than it made anyone else and which he removed meticulously in the airlock every time, eliminating any chance of him having tracked any sand into the simulated colony units, and yet his sleepsack, and only *his* sleepsack, was suddenly all grit—given all that, Stefan was pretty sure that they were messing with him.

For another example, that morning. Just that morning, he had gotten an email sent from the producers to his special account that was only meant to receive simulated *Destination Mars!* Mission Control emails, written as though Stefan and the others were actually on Mars. But this message read, in its entirety, *We need you to sound more Danish.* He had written back, somewhat incredulous, *What do you mean? Accent? Expressions? Do you want me to mention King Frederik?* but he had yet to get a response.

He had the suspicion that none of the other candidates were getting odd emails.

Stefan, formally educated as an engineer in England, had in fact very little in the way of a Danish accent, little enthusiasm for the Danish monarchy, and, when it came to idioms, he was more likely to say, for example, that someone *cocked it up* than that he *trådte i spinat*—which is to say, *stepped in the spinach.*

Still—the man wanted to go to Mars. Quite a lot, in fact. And if that meant putting up with some bother, then *Hil drot og fæderland.*

Stefan tried it out over lunch. Despite the fact that they were all, after three months, fairly tired of one another, and despite the fact that there wasn't a common meal served but instead a scatter of individually heated up freeze-dried food portions, they still largely ate meals together. And so they were in the mess dome, along the long table, eating their various revivified items. Stefan had heated up some sausage and red cabbage, with a slice of bread and some mustard, which he now realized was all available because of its Danishness. In any case, he said, into the settled silence of people who have nothing left to say to one another, "Is it the horse's birthday?"

Four other pairs of eyes looked up from food at him. (Eric was, as ever, napping in the bunkroom, just biding his time until this was all over and he could go home.) Stefan was also aware of the several cameras and microphones hidden away throughout the room. That was his real audience: Television Land.

"Is it what?" Orna said, down the table.

"The horse's birthday," Stefan said, and he tried to swallow his r's in the Danish way instead of in the British way. In England it was more a matter of ignoring the r's altogether. "It's a Danish expression," he said. "You use it when you get a thick slice of rye bread."

Everybody looked at his bread, which was not thick.

"I think that's whole wheat," Jackson said.

Stefan glared at him. Or somewhat glared at him. Jackson was a little bit intimidating.

"Are we going out for samples after lunch?" Mary asked. And there was her Nigerian accent—*Ah we going out fa sahmples ahfta lanch?*—and, for the first time, Stefan wondered if it might be intentionally laid on a little thick. Had she gotten an email asking her to be more Nigerian? Or Orna—was Orna's Israeli sound a put-on? Or was it only him? Did everyone else naturally sound more the way they ought to? He looked around the table a little feverishly. *The lunchdome*, he thought, narrating the scene, *was a den of deceivers.*

"I think we're supposed to," Tiago said.

"What?" Stefan snapped.

Tiago's eyes widened, big, wide, and brown. "Go out for rock samples."

Stefan nodded slowly, his eyes sharp on the Brazilian. "Okay," Stefan said. "Okay."

Orna leaned in. When she leaned in you knew it; she had a *lot* of wild, dark hair. It was like a lion leaning in. She said, "Are you okay, Stefan?" She was also a medical doctor.

He shook his head. "There's no cow on the ice," he said.

Orna frowned at him speculatively.

"There's no problem," he translated, his accent somewhere in between.

A half hour later he was outside, in his spacesuit, surrounded by what might as well be Mars—everything vast and orange, or brown, depending on the light, and the landscape all crags and ridges with sand, of course, underfoot—and accompanied by Mary and Tiago this time. Three people in white spacesuits and helmets, looking exactly the same as one another and not quite human. You couldn't see Mary's increasingly ragged Cowrie-beaded braids or her Super Eagles T-shirt or Tiago's black beard, his pug nose. You could only see the suits, the sun-gleam off the helmet's visors.

Rock samples. Given that this was well-explored Mungo, there was little doubt that they would just find more calcareous soil, but they had to be good sports and collect it anyway.

Tiago asked, "Which direction, do you think?"—Tiago was too annoying to make the final cut, Stefan thought—and Stefan pointed toward an outcropping they hadn't visited yet and said, "Over there," but he buried his r's again; he was going to play this thing out a while. Mary turned her opaque, helmeted face in his direction. Though she couldn't make eye contact that way, Stefan felt his face blush. Which would in any case show up on the cameras positioned inside his own helmet.

The fact: this was not proper science, not yet. This was really money. The reality show was funding the rocket. The reality show was funding the colony. The reality show would fund all the rockets and all the colonies. The reality show would fund everything, until everything was funded.

It was also how they were going to decide who would go on: audience votes.

Under a heavy sun—Stefan felt itchy with the first sweat—they walked off with big, slow steps, the way they supposed they'd have to on Mars. They communicated via radio. Or they would have, if they had anything to say. Mostly they walked and looked at the crags and ridges. They walked and looked while Stefan did what he'd been doing quite a bit lately: he silently narrated, in his head, his own experience in third person. *They walked across what used to be the bottom of a gigantic lake and was now a semiarid desert biome,* he thought. It was not the first time that he had narrated that exact line. Though sometimes he would add some poetry—*With broad strides hard into the wind, they crossed the emptied bowl that had once been a vast and teeming lake,* etc.—and other times he added more science—*claypan, magnesite, Pleistocene*—or, on some days, he might just say, *He was really starting to loathe Australia.* Sometimes Stefan did it as though they were already on Mars. *The small team of scientists crossed what appeared to be a large impact basin, the result of a meteor strike that had happened literally billions of years before.* That sort of thing.

Anyway they crossed the dry lake.

Stefan was keenly aware of the pointlessness of this practice experience. He didn't usually narrate that truth, even to himself, but he knew.

When they got close to their destination, the outcropping looming in front of them, he said aloud, laying on the Danish, "Do you want to go to the other side of the structure?" It sounded, even to him, like *Do you want to go to de udda site off de stwuctcha?*

Mary stopped and turned her helmet toward him again. "What *are* you doing?" she asked, in her perhaps-real and perhaps-fake Nigerian accent.

"What are you talking about?" he said, sweating. He thought it was very possible that the producers had put some sand inside his suit somehow, and added an extra layer of suit to it, just to make it hotter.

Mars is meant to be cold, is something he would have liked to say to the producers.

Maybe they weren't just messing with him; maybe they were trying to drive him insane. And certainly he'd been increasingly irritable.

"Your voice," she said. "You're not talking in your usual voice."

"I am," Stefan insisted, sticking to words that sounded about the same either way.

They stood there for a moment, with her studying his helmet, presumably.

"I would go to the other side," Tiago said, and he managed a visible shrug in his spacesuit.

And so they agreed, Stefan thought. This involved going up a dune, a basically slapstick affair that none of them had mastered, but luckily it was not an enormous dune, and they got up there readily enough. *They crested the lunette, and found themselves with a breathtaking view of the landscape, the countless aeolian features. This was land sculpted only by the hands of wind.*

"Pain in my ass," Mary said. It was her inability to fake enthusiasm that was going to keep her off the rocket, in Stefan's estimation.

Though it had, it's true, been a bit of a pain in the arse. And the hands of wind were in fact rather pushy today. In Denmark you might say it *was blowing half a pelican.*

"Well," he started, aiming for an accent somewhere in the middle, "the next part is easier." He pointed downhill.

And indeed the next part was largely a spectacle of sliding that resisted dignified narration. But then they were on the other side of the structure, and they opened up the sampling kit to get to the process of unearthing. UnMarsing. That was going to be a new word, Stefan reflected. Unmarsing. Plus a grounded person was going to be described as *down-to-Mars*, might even be the *salt of the Mars*, and people were going to have to *move heaven and Mars* to get things done, and nobody would have *any Marsly idea* what anybody was talking about.

Stefan let out an unprofessional giggle.

Mary looked at him again.

"I'm just a bit uncomfortable in my suit," he said, scratching himself ineffectually with his enormous spacesuit fingers.

"Where should we dig?" Tiago asked.

Stefan looked around. Orange everywhere. Basically barren. Occasionally on these forays they would see an emu, but, since there were obviously no emus on Mars, the team was under orders to ignore them here on simulated Mars. And today there weren't even emus. Stefan pointed to the base of an outcropping thirty meters away, basically at random. "That one," he said.

And so they tromped over there and started digging. The process was to bag a few surface-level rocks and some surface-level sand, and also to dig down a meter or so into the clay to see if anything interesting was there. Nothing interesting would be there, obviously; it was just an exercise. But Stefan supposed it prepared them for what they'd be doing on Mars, and apparently the TV viewers found the digging entertaining. Stefan supposed heavy editing was involved.

While they dug—steadily but also carefully, in case they miraculously came across something precious and fragile—the conversation died away. Probably the producers would have preferred some snappy dialogue, but there wasn't very much to say. In any case it gave Stefan time to think. And not just narrator-style thinking— *With hearts full of resolve, they dug deeper, in hopes of unmarsing something human eyes had never seen*—but also bigger-picture stuff. Such as the old recurring question of why he was so keen to do this. Why on Earth, so to speak, did he want—need—to go to Mars?

Hvorfor ikke gå? said the *Destination Mars!* ads in Denmark. *Why not go?*

But the opportunity had been more urgent to him than "why not?" It had felt almost like a duty, sending his application in, clicking "submit" on his computer with a buzz in his chest. A duty, yes. He had engineering skills that could help take humanity to other planets, to help spread civilization to other worlds. He had the strength of character to help carry the species' footprints beyond the confines of its millennia-old home and out into the vast reaches of space and the known and unknown universe.

Stefan pictured himself standing on a landscape much like this one, but millions of kilometers off into the darkness and the unknown. Orange mountains, swirling clouds overhead. A sandy wind rippling the air. And Stefan there, standing with his hands on his hips, the orange glow of a new land on all sides, nothing but the yet-to-be-discovered. *The lone adventurer took a bold step forward, his whole soul—*

"How much deeper should we go?" Tiago said.

Stefan blinked. "What?"

"How much deeper?" Tiago said, pointing into the hole.

Stefan felt a surge of unexpected anger. "The normal amount," he said. "Why would it be different this time?"

"You don't have to bark at me," Tiago said.

Oh, God, Stefan thought. *I'm stroppy lately. And now I'm going to have to talk about this for the video journal later.* The TV people loved interpersonal drama. Stefan, in fact, wondered whether the most dramatic types were the ones who would get voted onto the rocket in the end. So maybe he needed to lean into it. Stefan tried to come up with a relevant Danish expression for the moment. The closest that occurred to him was *Jeg er kold i røven*—*I'm cold in the ass*—but that meant *I don't care*, and it wasn't such a good fit. And the Danish for *wanker* would probably get him in trouble. There were limits to even this stupid game.

"I'm just trying to be a team member," Tiago said.

"Well, I'm cold in the ass," Stefan said after all.

"Boys," Mary said.

Stefan plunged his shovel into the hole with considerable force, and there was a cracking sound, and Mary yelped.

In the hole they were digging, which was now perhaps a meter deep, Stefan's shovel had hit something. Something hard and yellowish whitish brownish. In fact, more than that—his shovel had cleaved that yellowish whitish brownish hard something in two. A small thing, a small ridge of a thing, in two. Tiago and Stefan leaned closer, blocking out the sun until Mary shoved them back again. It almost looked like—

"What the bother?" Stefan said under his breath.

They all wordlessly switched from shovels to brushes, the kind of brushes that archaeologists used. But it felt like they all already knew what they were about to find. Stefan didn't articulate it in his mind, but he knew all the same.

And so it was. After a while of brushing away at the dirt, there it was.

A skull. A human skull.

With a shovel in it.

"Oh, bollocks," Stefan said.

Mary sent Stefan and Tiago back to the base, standing watch over the skull herself, as though it was going to be snatched up the minute their backs were turned, or perhaps, Stefan reflected, as though she worried that Stefan would break it further if he was the one who was left to keep an eye on things.

Over the lunette, back across the dry lakebed, panting in the heat—they moved as fast as they could while still using the simulated big, slow Mars steps. The cameras were always watching.

Or would the producers want them to drop all that pretense, because of the drama of finding a body? Maybe the producers would have preferred them to abandon the façade in the face of something surprising. Or maybe they preferred the absurdity of them maintaining the façade.

Stefan was getting very tired of wondering what the cameras wanted.

Back at the base, everybody already knew the news because the three diggers had radioed ahead with that news. Stefan and Tiago had only come back because it seemed like the thing to do. In a situation like this, you had to come back and, with hand gestures and facial expressions, convey the significance of the moment.

"Oh, wow, my friends," Tiago said, holding his helmet out in front of him like he was the prince of Denmark or something. "We've really found something."

Everybody was already getting their spacesuits on. Well, Orna and Jackson were getting their spacesuits on. Eric was still in his bunk, still waiting for it all to be over.

"Have we heard from Mission Control?" Stefan said. "Do we know what they want us to do?" If the team was meant to ignore emus as unmarsly, perhaps the same logic was meant to apply to human skeletons.

"We haven't heard a damn thing," Jackson said. "We're on our own with this one."

"I hear you broke the skull," Orna said, winking at Stefan as she wrestled her hair up into a massive and chaotic bun so that she could get her helmet on.

"Well—"

Tiago freed up one hand so that he could lay it on Stefan's shoulder. "It was an accident," he said.

For a very brief and unexpected moment, Stefan pictured himself grabbing that hand and giving it a good, hard twist.

"I guess it's the cow's birthday after all," Jackson said.

. . . .

On the way back to the skull, still walking Mars-style—there was apparently implicit agreement that the façade should be maintained—Stefan thought about the sound-more-Danish email he'd gotten that morning, which had been just one more thing piled onto the big pile, under which he was struggling to keep it together. A terrible thought had occurred to him: What if they had asked him to be more Danish because they believed that the TV audience *hated* Danish people? There was a difference between messing with him and actual *sabotage*. Stefan's breath felt hot in his throat.

After another undignified tumble down the far side of the lunette, they all assembled around the hole. Mary had done a bit more excavating, had brushed away the rest of the dirt surrounding the fractured skull, which was now essentially out in the open under the enormous sky. Both empty eyes looked up at them. And what looked like another bone—collarbone, maybe?—was starting to show through the dirt alongside.

"I think we've found something truly remarkable," Mary said, shaking her head. *Re-mah-kah-ble.*

They all shook their heads, including Stefan. It *was* remarkable. The sun stared down all over everything.

"Do you think it's recent?" Tiago said.

Orna squatted down by the hole and carefully picked up half of the skull. "It's heavy," she said after a moment. "And you see how dark it is?"

Everybody nodded.

"This is fossilized bone," Orna said.

"Now, hold on," Jackson said. "You're saying we've found a *fossil*?"

"*Homo shovelensis*," Orna said, probably winking from inside her helmet.

"Now, see here—" Stefan started.

Jackson held a hand up to shush him. "Really, Orna? A fossil?"

A sandy wind swept over them all, and Orna set the skull-piece back down in the hole, very carefully, where she'd picked it up. "I'm not a paleontologist," she said. "But I don't think it's bone. I think it's fossil."

"Remarkable," Mary said.

"This is the park where they found Mungo Man, after all," Orna said. "And Mungo Lady." ·

"Mungo Lady?" Tiago said.

"More fossils. The oldest humans discovered in Australia, I think."

"Wow," Tiago said.

Jackson stepped back from the hole, clapped his hands against each other as though wiping dust off. "We really shouldn't be messing with this. We've already broken one piece—" Stefan started to protest, and Jackson cut him off again. "It's probably not your fault, okay, but this could be a major discovery. I know we're not supposed to knock down the fourth wall—" he meant the TV show, and in fact he started talking to the people watching, which is something the candidates never did—"but hey, somebody out there, it seems like this is a major find, and it'd be good to send some experts in here, wouldn't it, which we are definitely not."

"Maybe we should go back to the base," Tiago said. "Wait and see."

"But *we* found this," Mary said, almost mournfully.

Suddenly Stefan felt possessive, too. "It's *ours*," he said.

"None of this is ours," Jackson said.

Back at the base again, Stefan took a long shower to get at least most of the sand off. The water was an unpredictable mess of very hot and very cold, as usual. Still he stayed in there. There wasn't anything else to do for the moment, with the digging mission cut short and Jackson off in the video journal dome, trying to communicate with Mission Control. So Stefan tried to get the sand off, and tried to calm himself, too. He was starting to feel a bit paranoid about the TV people and their control over things, and he wasn't keen on the feeling. Unfortunately, the wild temperature swings didn't help him calm down.

After, Stefan went back to the bunkroom to grab his sleepsack; he was going to shake it out once and for all. Eric was there, on the bunk above his own, staring straight up at the ceiling.

"Hey," Eric said, or maybe he just sighed loudly. He was an unshaven, unshowered, and underfed man with very pale skin. He hadn't started out that way, but, three months in, he was that way now.

"Did you hear?" Stefan said. "We found a fossil."

Eric didn't take his eyes off the ceiling. "That's bullshit."

"No, truly," Stefan said. "We were digging, and we turned up this skull. And Orna says it's a proper fossil."

"That's bullshit," Eric said, his voice completely flat.

Stefan felt another surge of anger. "What are you going on about? I'm telling you what happened."

Eric turned his head in Stefan's direction. The turning was geologically slow, but eventually he met Stefan's eyes with his own gray ones. "They probably just *put* it there, you dipshit," he said.

"Who?"

Eric just stared at him.

Stefan's jaw fell open. "The TV people?"

Eric turned slowly back up to the ceiling.

They—they—could they have *planted* a fossil?

Our hero was beginning to wonder what was even real.

Stefan, gobsmacked, left the bunkroom.

Orna, Tiago, and Mary were all out in the sitting dome, their arms crossed, feet tapping, watching the door to the airlock.

"What's going on?" Stefan said.

Orna nodded at the door. "They told Jackson to go by himself back to the hole. I guess they're going to meet him there."

"They argued for a long time first," Tiago said. "They wanted him to forget about it, but he insisted."

"He did," Orna said.

"Are we going to tune in to his radio channel?" Stefan asked. "To hear what happens?"

"They told him to turn it off," Mary said.

"Oh. Really?"

"Yeah."

Still gobsmacked, Stefan sat down, too.

Maybe fifteen quiet minutes went by. And then there was a ping from a variety of sources—the main control panel, the PA system, and the individual tablets scattered around—which was the ping of an important official communication from Mission Control. They all picked up tablets, and there was the message.

Our condolences. We understand that, while on a solo mission for the good of the colony, Jackson Thomas' spacesuit developed a catastrophic rupture, and he rapidly depressurized and suffocated in the Martian atmosphere.

There was a fresh, stunned silence.

"Wait," Tiago said. "They don't mean—did they *kill* him?"

Orna shook her head. "Um, no," she said. "Couldn't be. They probably just took him out of the running. That's all."

"Right, right," Tiago said.

"Nonetheless," Mary said. "That is really, really something." She sounded even more Nigerian than usual.

Stefan thought the thing they were probably all thinking: *It was not a good idea to break the fourth wall.*

"*Baruch dayan ha-emet,*" Orna said in quiet Hebrew. It sounded like a very small prayer.

. . . .

Dinner that night was quiet. Eric was in back, and otherwise it was just the four of them. Orna was eating a falafel sandwich, Tiago a black bean and beef stew, Mary pepper soup with a side of yams, and Stefan a smoked herring, and they ate it all in near silence.

At one point Tiago piped up. "Should we have some kind of funeral ceremony?"

"We don't have a—" Mary said, stopping short of the word *body*.

"We could say a few words," Orna said. "But I don't know much about Christian funerals."

"May he rest in peace with God," Tiago said.

Orna put down her sandwich. "Sure," she said. "Be well on your journey, Jackson."

"God bless," Mary said.

For his part, Stefan sat there fuming. Jackson wasn't dead—he was only expelled. But of course you couldn't acknowledge that. There were many things you couldn't do, and many things you were meant to do. The pile was bigger and bigger all the time. How was a person meant to carry a pile like this one?

"God bless," he said, fork and knife in hand.

That night, while everyone else slept, Stefan lay awake in his sleep-sack, which—God damn it—still had sand in it, or had sand in it again, or whatever it was. His whole world was itchy.

Eventually he got up and went out into the common domes, and to the airlock, where he put on his spacesuit, mainly just so he would have the boots on; they were his only boot options. But he put the helmet on, too. Probably the cameras were running. He had to assume they were running.

It was quite dark outside, once Stefan was outside the range of the dome lights. This was the Outback, after all. So he turned on his helmet flashlight, which opened up a beam of visible landscape in front of him, all familiar barren landscape without the color, and off he went. *The stupid man was on the move again*, he narrated.

He found the lunette. He went over it.

And there on the other side was the hole. It was the same hole, of course, though it was now quite a lot larger than it had been. And—Stefan stepped up to it and shone his helmet light down into the opening—it was perfectly empty. There was no skull, no edge of collarbone, nothing at all. Just a big emptiness.

He wondered where Jackson was at that moment. Most likely headed back to America, or possibly in some long or even endless debrief with the TV people at *Destination Mars!* It was conceivable that the TV part never ended. Maybe they followed the ejected candidates for the rest of their lives, making them do things and say things.

It was an increasingly unbearable thought.

He now did something he was definitely not meant to do: he took off his helmet—cool air for a moment, the first fresh air he'd felt on his face in months, like a miracle. Should he keep it off forever? Should he walk off the set, so to speak?

Stefan looked up. Somewhere up there, or out there, was Mars. Where they could watch you if they wanted, but they couldn't do anything to you.

He bent down to the hole. The sandy soil was loose, and it was easy to scoop up a handful. It was easy to pour it down the neck of his suit. He felt the sand go all the way down his overheated body, into his clothes; he put another scoop into his helmet. And then he put that helmet back on, sealing all the heat and itchiness inside. From the roots of his hair to his sweating feet.

"*Jeg er her stadig,*" he said, directly into the helmet-cam, before turning to head back to the lunette, the dry lake bed, the base, his uncomfortable sleepsack.

I'm still here.

Ghost Martians at the Baby Shower

THE FIRST-EVER Martian baby shower seemed like it was doomed from the start.

At least, that was how it looked on television. What the viewers on Planet Earth saw was an edited version of the events, a couple of weeks pared down to fit into two hour-long episodes of the *Destination Mars!* reality TV show. Certainly there would be some manipulation on the part of the producers in order to get the maximum drama out of the situation, particularly given that the show, which had started off with such a huge audience—people living on Mars!—had actually gotten so dull after a while (it turns out there's not much to do on that planet) that it had been canceled, and was only back on now that one of the Marsonauts was pregnant. So the producers had to be feeling pressure to make sure it was good TV.

But in fact it may not have required much effort. Even before things started going wrong in the planning and execution of the baby shower, consider that:

1. The Marsonauts were not supposed to be having sex at all, but two of them—Jenny and Josh—had apparently left that rule behind after the series' first run. Some viewers had picked up on romantic tension between them, but nothing actually *happened*,

which was part of the reason the show was canceled; it seemed like another will-they-won't-they scenario, a well-worn television cliché that lost its appeal pretty fast. And then it turned out that they got together once the cameras were off. A lot of people were annoyed about missing that. But the news did make folks want to start watching again. (Some people on Earth got themselves T-shirts featuring a picture of a red planet on which was superimposed an even redder heart, and underneath were the words *I want a Mars love.*) Anyway, the reason they weren't supposed to be having sex was because it could lead to pregnancy, which wasn't thought to be safe on Mars— and now here Jenny was, dangerously pregnant. The commercials for the show all had voiceovers that said things like, *Have these men and women traveled farther than anyone else ever before . . . only to reach tragedy???* (You could hear the extra question marks in the way that they asked it.)

2. Another thing was the fact that, as viewers learned when the show started up again, Jenny had been told her whole life that she was biologically incapable of becoming pregnant. When she managed it anyway, totally by accident, a whole new set of T-shirts (and bumper stickers, and so on) cropped up, this time with a religious message: *God is Great—on Every Planet.* But those were met, as most religious messages are, with religious counter-messages, in this case from people who felt that other people were turning Jenny into some kind of immaculate conceiver, even though she was in fact a completely secular scientist who had gotten pregnant having—they were careful to point out—premarital sex.

3. And meanwhile there was the way that the impending birth was affecting all the Marsonauts. Jenny and
Josh, who had both experienced tragedies back on
Earth, were going through psychological turbulence
throughout the pregnancy, the kind of turbulence
that made for good close-up shots of conflicted faces and additional ominous voiceovers at the end of
the show. For example, after the first of the two baby
shower episodes: *Next time on* Destination Mars!*:
Can the two lovebirds survive what's to come?* And
meanwhile one of the doctors—Trixie—had gotten
kind of obsessive in her prenatal attentions, developing something of a manic vibe, or maybe even slightly
mad-scientist-esque—at least until Josh talked her
down a little. Everybody wondered if that talk-down
would stick. Meanwhile the engineer who had in
the first season demonstrated a tendency toward
violence was getting more antisocial by the minute.
There were a lot of closeups of him muttering unset-
tlingly.

4. Though actually he did have legitimate things to mut-
ter about. Because, on top of all of the other things,
strange things were starting to happen in the habitation dome. Lights were flickering sporadically; water
pressure was fluctuating now and then. More alarm-
ingly, appliances were sometimes turning on and
off without anyone touching them. Stefan was busy
trying to figure all of that out. But meanwhile—and
this didn't seem like an engineering problem—a few
of the Marsonauts said they were occasionally hearing something like voices—distant, muffled, sounding like questions—when nobody was talking. It was

unsettling. And enough of that kind of thing was going on that some people back on Earth were talking about gremlins.

Suffice it to say that quite a few nails were getting bitten among the television audience.

Despite all this, the Marsonaut who was an Air Force captain and a doctor and who had a big following among the African American demographic—Nicole—suggested one night during dinner that they plan a baby shower. She said that it was "a beautiful family tradition." She had in the new run of the show become very interested in family activities.

Reactions among the Marsonauts varied. Trixie, for one, actually jumped out of her seat and pumped her fist. "Paaaar-TY!" she said. She was on the whole well-liked in her home country of Australia, and certainly much-discussed there. Australia had in fact been one of the last countries to stop watching the original series. One of the big questions about her was how she managed to keep her hair dyed up on Mars. Usually red; sometimes pink; very occasionally orange. And her roots never showed! It had to be a regular part of her grooming regimen, but somehow and for some reason the show kept the process secret.

But Jenny, the presumptive focus of the event, waved Nicole's idea off and said, "Oh—come on—you don't have to do anything like that."

Josh, who had lately been frustrating viewers with his hot-and-cold attitude about becoming a family man, put his burrito down, leaned over, and put his arm around Jenny. "I think it sounds nice," he said. (You could feel the public Josh-o-meter shifting more positive.)

Roger, the Canadian geologist and botanist who had a following mainly among other geologists and botanists, said, quietly, "Sure."

But Jenny pushed her dish away and asked, "But what's a baby shower *for*? Isn't it for giving gifts? Everything we have is already here. Wouldn't you just be forced to give us things we already have?"

Some of Earth's audience found her difficult. And some of that reaction may have been racism.

"I'm learning how to knit," Roger said, dipping back into his bowl of soup. It's true that there were a few non-scientist viewers who had fallen for him as this new side—crafty and paternal—had started to come out. And he was somehow looking more buff in the new series. Lighting? Camera angles? Every once in a great while you'd see someone wearing a T-shirt that said *i prefer roger*.

"An event of this nature is also about marking the transition to parenthood," Nicole said crisply. "And it's an occasion for us to come together."

"Plus it's a *party!*" Trixie said. She was still standing. "It'll be *fun!*"

Stefan was not at the table—he had given up on group meals—but, as Trixie said "It'll be *fun!*" the editors cut to an image of him, working alone under the Mars rover outside, muttering in his unsettling way.

Overall, there was enough support for the idea that it went forward. Nicole and Trixie took charge of the planning, and started having meetings to talk about food and party activities. There were disagreements. Nicole wanted something more sit-down, and Trixie wanted something involving more dancing. Not so much Jenny, obviously, at this stage of the pregnancy—she would probably dance in her chair—but everybody else. Also, Trixie was thinking pub munchies—fried, savory things—and Nicole was thinking petit-four-type things. Small sweets. So these disagreements were problem number one. Not insurmountable, but needing to be surmounted.

It did also take a while to figure out what to do about gifts. It was true, what Jenny had said—it wasn't like there was a store to go to, and all the new stuff they would need for the baby was on a supply rocket that was expected pretty close to the due date. Nicole didn't want to wait for it. "Consider this: what if the baby comes early?" she said. "You can't have the shower when the baby's *here*."

"You can't?" Trixie asked.

"You can't," Nicole said.

The viewers had not realized that Nicole was so traditional—she never talked about family in the first run of the show—but there it was.

"Plus, those supplies are issued from HQ," she said. "They're not from us."

Which decided that. In the end they took their cue from Roger, who was starting to knit a pair of booties, and decided that everyone had to make something for the baby.

"Gender neutral colors," Trixie said when she told Stefan by the oxygen distributor he was working on, wagging her stethoscope at him. She had definitely gotten better, wasn't examining Jenny seven times a day now, but she still kept her doctor's tools with her at all times, just in case.

"I'm not going to come," Stefan said, with a slight frown, like he was explaining something very obvious.

"You're . . . not . . ." Trixie started.

"Coming," he said, before returning to the distributor.

This, then, was the next problem: Stefan wasn't coming, and on the one hand it didn't seem like a great idea for him to be there if he didn't want to be, but on the other hand losing him would reduce the number of non-parental party guests by twenty-five percent. In the end they resolved it by having Nicole go tell him that he had to show up and had to play nice. It was a longstanding dynamic that he was scared of Nicole.

Stefan, who was Danish, was nonetheless not wildly popular among the Danish audience. And some engineers were not sure that he represented them well, either. It was his presence on the mission—and, to a lesser extent, Roger's—that made some people wonder if the *Destination Mars!* corporation had really listened to audience votes when putting the group together.

Anyway, Nicole found him in the bathroom, brushing his teeth. "Attendance is mandatory," she said. She didn't even say *baby shower* explicitly (or, if she did, the editors cut it out); she just said "Attendance is mandatory," and waited for him to nod his understanding, and then she left.

As you can imagine, the T-shirt people got busy right away on *Attendance is Mandatory*.

Another problem was the argument Jenny and Josh had about whether the shower was just for her or whether it was for both of them. He thought it'd be nice to make Jenny the focus—she was carrying the baby, after all—and she thought he was resisting fatherhood. "Do you want us to be a family or not?" she said.

Meanwhile, Stefan found himself getting busier, because things were going a little more haywire throughout Home Sweet in the lead-up to the party. The lights got flickerier and also started glaring at other times, and the HVAC became newly unpredictable—too hot and then too cold, randomly. The same thing was happening with the water heater, and the water pressure was up and down more wildly and frequently. The oven went fully on the fritz, putting party snack prep in doubt. Some faint but odd smells came and went throughout the dome. And though viewers were beginning to wonder if Stefan was behind all the mechanical problems—trying to get the party canceled, maybe—he actually looked pretty bewildered by the whole thing, even when the other Marsonauts weren't watching him.

It was not lost on anyone—Marsonaut or Earthling TV watcher—that these minor glitches, if they became major, could cancel the party by, well, killing everyone on the planet.

So Stefan rushed around looking into everything that had an electrical pulse, as the others (and the viewing audience) looked on with some anxiety. The thing about Mars is that it may be dull, but only until your oxygenator stops working.

There was also some speculation online about whether the *Destination Mars!* corporation itself was messing with the six inhabitants, either as revenge for the pregnancy or in order to drum up drama for the show. But nobody could come up with a good explanation for how they could wreak so much havoc from so far away, and it was pointed out that they had a lot to lose if something went *too* wrong and everybody on Mars died—not only the profits from the TV show, but also their whole reputation as a company that had started the first civilization on Mars. And that was a good point.

There were those people who felt something more astounding was responsible. People on Earth who had been saying "gremlins" started to use the word *aliens*.

Of course, there were also people who used the words *ghost Martians*—mainly because the flickering lights had a kind of supernatural quality—which, aside from inspiring a name for a one-hit-wonder band that same year, served mainly to remind the public that a lot of people were prone to questionable thinking.

And then the virus hit, or the bacteria, or parasite, or whatever it was. Trixie and Nicole couldn't figure out what it was—it seemed like proof of Martian life until they failed to find any sign of anything in anyone's blood or anywhere else—but it hit each Marsonaut in turn, or almost each. There was a fair amount of vomiting. The show handled it tastefully enough; the stricken person would dash off to the bathroom and the editors would stick to a shot of the rest of the people, glancing uneasily at one another while sounds of disgorgement—muted sounds—could be heard in the background.

It was not lost on anyone that some viruses killed you.

Luckily, the "Mars flu" didn't last long—just a few days—but it was nasty while it was there, and it left everyone wiped out after. They spent days on the *chaises longues* in the common room just rehydrating.

Again, none of the analyses—checkups, throat swabs, blood tests, examination of the foods people had eaten, et cetera—revealed anything. They couldn't even tell how it was being spread. There were only two clues: (1) the disease progressed in age order, beginning with the youngest person (Trixie, who was still in her twenties in Earth years) and ending with the oldest person (Stefan, who was fifty-three), and (2) the disease skipped right over Jenny. But no-body could figure out what the clues meant. The Marsonauts didn't actually call it the Mars flu—that was an Earth thing. They called it the *WTFlu* and hoped it wouldn't come back.

Trixie pulled Josh aside and said, in a voice right out of a sci-fi thriller, "You see? There's *something* here on this planet. Something we can't detect with human tools."

The band Ghost Martians dropped their first (and only) hit soon after. The song was also called "Ghost Martians."

Party planning went on anyway—Nicole insisted on it, even when she was the sick one. "We can rally," she said to Trixie in one rousing between-vomits scene by the toilet.

"But what if it hits Jenny next?" Trixie asked, biting her nail.

That's where the first of the two-episode sequence ended—*Is Jenny next?* over a shot of Jenny looking worried; then, *Can the two lovebirds survive what's to come?* over a shot of Josh and Jenny look-ing worriedly at each other; and, finally, *Will there even be a party?* over a shot of everyone worrying out in the common room, aside from Stefan, who was off in the bathroom making muted regurgita-tion sounds, the lights flickering.

They started the next episode by picking up a few seconds before where they had left off.

"We can rally," Nicole said to Trixie by the toilet.

"But what if it hits Jenny next?" Trixie asked, biting her own nail.

"It won't," Nicole said, closing the scene.

And of course she couldn't be sure, but it turned out she was right; Jenny never did get sick. Trixie checked her relentlessly, as she had before Josh talked her down, but the mother-to-be never showed any symptoms, and eventually Trixie relaxed again. On Earth there was speculation that the pregnancy protected Jenny because the disease was focused on age, and the fetus didn't tech-nically have an age yet. But then certain religious people got up in arms about that and there was a brief but passionate move-ment for all true believers to petition the government to add nine months to their official age, to signify that they had begun living at conception.

In any case, the party went forward. The disease was winding down and the mechanical problems weren't getting worse, at least. People, once their hydration levels had recovered, were busy making their gifts. Nicole and Trixie settled on a menu that didn't involve using the ongoingly-fritzy oven—little sandwiches, mainly. Things came together. Not neatly, not tidily—honestly there was a lot of obvious anxiety all around—but of course neat and tidy would have made for bad television.

Then, on the day of the baby shower the bathroom showers stopped working altogether, and the heads started making very loud noises when on. It was an intriguing coincidence, shower/ showers. ("You *see*?" Trixie said to Josh.) Or it would have been intriguing if it hadn't been another entry in the *worrying* column. These people had lived together for more than two years already, so they were not particularly put off by the prospect of a little extra body odor—it was hardly the first time that any of them had gone unwashed for a day—and Stefan got to spend the morning working in the bathroom, muttering almost cheerfully. (As astute viewers had observed, he was most content when his machines needed him.) But most everybody would have felt a lot better if things stopped going wrong.

In the early afternoon, Nicole and Trixie determinedly made the sandwiches—little ones, made little by cutting regular-sized ones into quarters, and of various kinds: turkey, peanut butter and honey, cream cheese frosting (as a concession to Nicole), pepper jack and potato chips (as a concession to Trixie), and so on, all presented on plastic plates that were used in the place of silver trays they didn't have. Mars had not been set up for classy entertaining, but they were doing their best.

While they were preparing the food, Josh and Jenny and Roger were sniffing around the common room. A slight smell, new and unrelated to the unshowered state of affairs, had developed—something like egg salad, but intensified egg salad—and they couldn't find where it was coming from, other than somewhere in the common room.

Smell or no smell—nobody was able to track it down—the party started in the common room in the mid-to-late afternoon. (People watching knew that the Martian day was fairly similar in length to Earth's day, so they understood what *afternoon* meant. They could relate.) Things were reasonably festive. Trixie had strung up some toilet paper that she had dyed—again, through some mysterious source—pink and blue, alternating. There was music on the newly-repaired sound system. Not dance music, exactly—yet, anyway—but baby-themed stuff: Stevie Wonder's "Isn't She Lovely," Maroon 5's "Baby, Oh," Bob Dylan's "Forever Young," The Chicks' "Lullaby," The Supremes' "Baby Love," and so on, plus also Ghost Martians' "Ghost Martians," because why not.

And there were activities.

Nicole clapped her hands together and said, almost angrily, "Okay. Who wants to do a few party games?"

Trixie hollered, and Josh said "Me!" brightly (a little *too* brightly, some viewers thought), and Jenny raised her hand with a smile. Roger said, "Sure," and Stefan looked around the room for more signs of trouble that could occupy him, but then said, "Yes, absolutely," under Nicole's level gaze.

So they began with belly-guessing. They needed Roger's yarn for this, and scissors. The idea was that everybody had to cut a length of yarn that they thought was the current circumference of Jenny's abdomen. However, not everybody was allowed to participate—Trixie already knew fairly precisely how Jenny measured, and Nicole knew because, doctor to doctor, Trixie had already told her. And it was suggested that Josh would have an unfair advantage because he slept with his arm over Jenny every night, and, as for Jenny, she was just supposed to watch and enjoy. So, in the end it was just Roger and Stefan, and both of them overestimated the circumference, but Stefan was off by more than a foot—"Is that how big you think I am?" Jenny said, incredulous—so Roger won. There were no prizes, but Stefan still looked at Roger with troubling hostility afterward. And then he said something about what did it matter how big Jenny was if the habitation unit blew up around them.

The next one broke up some of the tension with a little humor. They all—everybody was included this time—had to tape index cards to their foreheads, and then each person was supposed to draw a picture of what they thought the baby would look like, but on the cards on their own heads. So in the end there was marker on people's faces and the drawings turned out to be these pretty amusing impenetrable scribbles. Though, with all the background anxiety plus risks surrounding being pregnant on Mars, some of the viewers saw dark prophecies in those scribbles.

They had gotten to the game of looking at each other's baby pictures and guessing who was who—not as hard as it sounds, given that Nicole, Jenny, and Trixie were the only people of color there and Trixie's skin was distinctly lighter than Jenny's which was lighter than Nicole's, and also that baby Josh already had the same dark, curly hair he'd brought to Mars—when the egg salad smell suddenly became unbearable. The television screen couldn't convey that, of course, but you could see it on the Marsonauts' expressions, all of which squinched up tight.

"Oh, God," Jenny said. "What even *is* that?"

Trixie covered her face. "That is *rank*, is what it is."

Stefan, who had been sick the most recently, put his head between his knees. "Ohhhhhhh," he said.

Again: the baby shower seemed doomed from the start.

In fact, Josh was just standing up, looking like he was about to suggest that discretion was the better part of valor and that maybe they should cut the party short or at least postpone it until after Home Sweet was fully under control again, but Nicole, who seemed the least affected by the smell, put her hand up before he could say anything: *Stop right there.* And then she lifted her hand and pointed one finger in the air, as if to say, *I'm about to say something decisive.*

Which indeed she did. "Spacesuits," she said.

Everybody looked around. Spacesuits did have their own life support systems. They made their own air.

"But is our air supply in actual trouble?" Jenny said.

Nicole looked at Stefan.

He pulled out his tablet and scanned something there. Then he went over to one of the vents and consulted the tablet again. And then he went to a couple of other machines and came back.

"I don't think it's a significant problem," he said. "Things look good as far as breathable air goes."

Nicole nodded. "Spacesuits," she said.

"Am I even going to *fit* into one?" Jenny asked. She hadn't left the habitation unit recently because of the possibility that she'd outgrown the suits.

Josh put his arm around her. "Let's find out," he said.

And so they all got into their spacesuits—Jenny uncomfortably but still manageably—and found that, after a couple of minutes, the suits had cleaned out any and all of the rank air they had brought with them on their bodies, in their lungs.

Some viewers cheered. This was the kind of resilience everybody wanted to see in a Marsonaut. And, for the record, once the shower was over, Stefan found a way to stop the smell, and nobody died.

Interestingly, though, the rest of the episode, which stayed with the shower until it was finished, struck not a triumphant tone but something instead more poignant.

The audience knew from previous episodes that the suits were all fitted with internal microphones and cameras, which allowed the producers to share voices and show faces even when the Marsonauts were outside the walls of Home Sweet, out on Mars itself. And they did use the microphones as the group sat suited in the middle of their common space—their living room, in the language of some of the audience. The viewers got to hear their voices as the group finished up the baby picture game, and also as they each wrote secret wishes for the baby on slips of paper that were then sealed—awkwardly, with big puffy suit-hands—in an envelope that would be shared with the baby when the baby was old enough to read them. Their voices came through clearly as the party culminated in the giving of gifts.

But the editors—and this was the really interesting artistic choice—never looked inside the helmets. There was not one shot from inside the helmets. There were no faces. And so there were just these people—indistinguishable from one another, really—sitting in a circle on their *chaises longues*, breathing clearly, and handing between them: two pairs of hand-knitted booties; a tablet showing a newly assembled playlist of all the popular music of the last twenty-some years that it was essential for the baby to know; another tablet that pulled up a carefully curated photo album of everyone who lived on Mars—especially the parents but also everyone else—living their lives and showing off who they were in all the ways that people do that; even a little handmade wind-up toy that did flips in place. It was beautiful, really, and the way they shot it, from outside, made it all the more beautiful because it was so understated and it seemed so very far away from the planet that was watching it. And then there were gifts between the two parents-to-be, but—this was remarkable—the editors didn't even let the viewers see the gifts. All you could see was the puffy suits. One suited parent said "Oh, Jenny." The other said "Oh, Josh." With lots of different feelings in their voices. Really it was an incredible moment. It was a moment that promised some possibility of elevation, of redemption.

And then . . . all the lights suddenly went out. The common room went pitch black.

After a long moment, Trixie's voice came out of the dark. "Oh, scrotum," she said.

In this way, another T-shirt was born.

The Phenomenon of Event Horizon Recurrence

Purpose of document:

Trixie and Nicole have advised me to outline a "birth plan." The concept was new to me, but it turns out these are common among mothers-to-be (on Earth) and it's particularly sensible in my circumstances, given the unknowns, variables, etc., on Mars. Josh, when he heard the recommendation, seized on it. Continues to be very concerned about the "impending birth," though tries to hide it. Does not realize that words like "impending" give him away.

I continue to be more concerned about what comes after.

In any case, here is a birth plan (constructed by a person who never, ever planned to be giving birth):

Settled (or nearly settled) questions:

The nature of our situation on this planet means that certain decisions are out of my hands.

Epidural injections for pain	Unavailable.
Vaginal birth vs. C-section	Neither Nicole nor Trixie is interested in performing a C-section unless absolutely necessary.

Water birth	Impractical. We lack a sufficiently large tub, and it's in any case not an efficient use of water. Also sounds odd to me. Am not a cetacean.
Birth ball (also a new concept)	Unavailable. And also odd-sounding.
Vacuum extraction	Thankfully, given the mental image I have of it, unavailable.

Medical procedures checklist:

I am open to the following medical interventions:

✓ Induction of labor
✓ Pain medications (aside from the epidurals we don't have)
✓ Alternative pain-reduction methods (e.g., visualizations, breathing exercises, etc.)
✓ Artificial rupture of membranes (if water does not break naturally)
✓ External fetal monitoring (basically, "stetho-ing")
✓ Use of IV/catheter if necessary
✓ Episiotomies (please no "natural" tearing)

Overall, when in doubt, intervene; science, after all, has gotten me this far. Only exception: Forceps. Outside of total emergencies I want to avoid anything that could damage the newborn's skull/brain. There's enough to be worried about as concerns the brain already.

Labor atmosphere:

Location	Presumably, I will be giving birth in the common room; not much room in the bunk dome. And personal privacy is not a priority on Mars. (Also, *chaises longues* actually really comfortable.)
Eating/drinking during labor	If okay with my doctors, okay with me.
Getting up, walking around during labor	Sure.
Allowing photos or videos	Moot question? *Destination Mars!* will be filming the whole thing regardless of my birth plan.
Specific birthing positions	See attached diagrams.
Personalizing the environment:	
Music	i) Trixie has recommended upbeat music, but am not sure I can handle music as upbeat as she's imagining. On the other hand, this is probably not the time for pieces from my personal collection. Karlheinz Stockhausen's "*Helicopter String Quartet,*" etc. ii) Nicole's choral music?

	iii) Cello music? Zoë Keating might be nice. Or Sheku Kanneh-Mason? iv) Josh humming?
Lighting	Dim? I don't have a strong opinion. Josh wants bright, so that Trixie/Nicole can see well.
Smells	The noxious air freshener mix supplied by *Destination Mars!* should be turned *off*.

Personnel:

I would like the following people to be present during labor/delivery:

1) Josh: Birth coach and general support, at least when he's not panicking about the birth.

2) Nicole and Trixie: for obvious reasons, and also to keep Josh calm.

3) The birth plans I found online tend to mention biological family—does the mother want her parents, siblings, etc., to attend?
   a) Of course for me this is impossible, for multiple reasons.
      i) But, what *about* my sister, if she were alive and we were on the same planet? Would I want her here? My sister was my sister. But she was also, to use a tired metaphor, in some ways like a black hole—an irresistible and dangerous center of gravity. The only escape from which is distance. To be beyond the event horizon. And there's so much distance between us

now; far more than the distance between Mars and Earth. Is it enough?

    ii) And although the infinitude of my sister's distance makes my parents' seem almost manageable—I could, after all, have them watch (on delay) via video link—I still can't cross that distance. Or, more accurately: I don't want to. It's not my parents' fault. But I have needed to escape the family my sister was born into. Even if it has meant escaping into the emptiness of a planet like this one. Maybe especially into an emptiness like that.

    iii) Though sometimes these days despite myself I do feel a need for something. Something.

  b) And Josh will be here. Josh is my family. I would not want the world to be empty of him.

  c) And this baby will be family, too. Whoever this baby will be.

  d) Which is to say that to leave one event horizon may be to reach another.

4) Others: Nicole says that if the six of us here on Mars (soon to be seven?) are *not* a family then we'll be nothing. In other words, empty planet. So what about the others? Do I want them there if the alternative is for them to be strangers?

  a) Roger: Probably neither harmful nor helpful in a birthing situation. Optional.

  b) Stefan: Potentially harmful? Josh believes Stefan is more than the angry man he seems to be, the man who hurt Roger when we first got here and who still walks around looking at everyone like something that needs to be run over with the rover.

    i) Is Josh right? I don't understand Stefan.

    ii) But . . . is there a significant difference between wanting to escape and wanting to run people over?

      (1) Obviously yes.

      (2) Also simultaneously possibly somewhat no.

    iii) *Do* I understand Stefan?

  c) Conclusion: I think I might want something rather than nothing. It just . . . it just depends on what the something is.

I of course reserve the right to change my mind about any of this at any time.

Also, Trixie and Nicole tell me that the most important priority in constructing any birth plan is to avoid setting your heart on it. Because that's one thing that rarely comes to pass: the ideal.

The Patterns

YOU'RE STILL HERE. We weren't sure whether you were temporary or permanent, and of course we can't know for sure—these days we basically don't know *what's* going to happen—but it's starting to look more like permanent. Which is a kind of stability, some of us point out. But then others say that you can't be stable if you're the opposite of that.

You can see how forward and backward we are.

We think you would use the word bickering?

Sometimes when it's all too much we go to the edge between where there is something and where there is basically nothing. Well, we're always there, and we're always here, because we're always all around everywhere, but we go *more* to that edge. We go because it's quieter there. Better. But it doesn't matter. It doesn't change the fact that, since you got here, there are some of us and there are others of us, which was never the case before, and it doesn't change the fact that we're hot and we're cold and we bicker now. About you.

Do you have some of you and others of you? If you do, how do you handle that? How can you be multiple Patterns and also one Pattern? That's our bigger question these days. But is that something you even try to work out?

Speaking of which, some of us have been studying you. Taking peeks inside. Listening. Maybe even communicating, is what it seems like. Or almost. And so some of us say that there's a lot we could learn from you, if we could just find a way all the way in. We could learn heaps, is what gets said.

Others of us are pretty sure: we don't need you for anything.

Which just restarts everything again. It's not the best.

And so before we get too remote and proximal we shift more toward the edge and try to count the lights in the basically nothing or we shift to the down and look at temperature Patterns underground or we just think about better times. Anything and anywhere that it's a little quieter.

Or we try to solve this.

We think we need to solve this. Which is to say we think we need to solve you. Except we're pretty sure that isn't exactly the word we're looking for. Do you know what we mean?

There has been some progress, at least from our end. From your end, we don't know what progress would even look like. But on our end we've found that some of the things you brought with you and that make water happen and different kinds of air happen and so on—we've found that those things can be changed, because we're partly inside those things. Tampered with, really. And that tampering seems to make you move quickly this way and that way, and manipulate those things to try to make them the way they used to be—fix?—and there's even more noise. It's unpleasant. But we call this progress because maybe this is a way to get faster to the endpoint we're looking for? The point when the chaos is Repatterned?

Oh, right—now we remember. The word we're looking for is dead. Or kill? Something like that.

Not all of us want that. Definitely not. But at the same time some of us for sure want that. And we're getting concepts, or maybe ideas, about it.

We're more or less learning the ideas from you.

Because the tampering isn't satisfying. It doesn't get it done. Basically, we don't understand the things you brought with you. And so we can't change them in exactly the way we want to. And usually you just make them the way they used to be. We try, and still there's you afterward.

But *you* probably understand those things you brought. *You* probably know how to change them so that the chaos gets Repatterned. The solving. The dead.

Which is why it's good that some of us have almost found a way in, even if those ones of us weren't looking for it for Repatterning purposes. The others of us who do want Repatterning ask, what if the right opening can be found? A crack.

Is the word crackers related to the word crack? We're specifically wondering about that one. Because we have a specific concept. Idea.

Anyway, so, while some of us study you, others of us also study you. We don't have the same reasons. But the result is going to be the same: we're going to find a way in.

And then everything is going to change.

On Chaotic Terrain

STEFAN WAS NOT keen on there being a child on Mars. It was already crowded enough.

You wouldn't think a group of six people would make a planet crowded, but it did, particularly if they all lived in one fairly compact set of domes together, which were surrounded by open land that you couldn't live on and air that you couldn't breathe. If they slept in one small dome together, with no walls between them; if they ate at one small table together. And those six people made a planet noisy, as well, between Trixie's snoring at night and weeping in her unproductive lab during the day, when there was also endless chatter between Jenny and Josh, and all the various recorded music people liked—Nicole's choral music, Jenny's experimental classical oddities, Trixie's Top-40 pop—and Roger's nervous throat-clearing and Josh's smacking his lips at meals, for example. Six people made it messy, too. There were tablets all about the place, and rocks that Roger had brought out from his lab for some reason and then forgotten, and sand tracked in from outside and never swept up. Sometimes Stefan felt that there were electrodes stimulating all his senses at every moment.

He was not keen on adding a child—a squalling, pooping, needy child—to the pre-existing commotion.

Sitting in the front passenger seat of the rover as it grumbled along, Stefan was thinking about children on Mars because, well, because he was always thinking about it those days. It was hard not to, with Jenny so baby-enlarged that she finally couldn't fit in her spacesuit any longer and had to spend all her time in the habitation center, waddling around belly-first, grousing about this or that. And he was also thinking about it because Nicole, breaking a lengthy, lovely silence in the rover, had just asked him about it.

Specifically: "Jenny's getting close. It's exciting, isn't it?"

She was behind the wheel, her lucky Mardi Gras beads hanging off the dash between them, the two of them finishing up a trip to gather supplies from the lander that had touched down the day before. The rover was jammed full of boxes—trunk, back seat. There was even a box under Stefan's boots, so that his knees were up awkwardly. And this wasn't even all the supplies—the autopiloted rockets didn't come very often, so each one always carried a lot of supplies. They had checked the manifest, knew what was there, and they would get the rest in the next trip, which could happen in no particular hurry. The big thing was that, as everyone had expected, the people at *Destination Mars!* had used the rocket to take a small measure of revenge for the pregnancy. Specifically, HQ had elected not to send any freeze-dried ice cream this time. Also, they'd included a snappish note—handwritten—on one of the food boxes that said, *Shouldn't you be growing more of your own food by now?*

Contemplating peevishly the possibility of new life on Mars, Stefan looked at the rough and craggy landscape in front of them, which was dimming in the late Martian afternoon, the orange graying as the sun went down to their right. They could see the habitation center ahead of them by then—Stefan realized he was dreading going back in there—which was not a unified center so much as, again, a cluster of sort-of-shiny domes that didn't at all fit into the general topography, even with the other abandoned landers and rovers scattered about from missions that happened long before the current one. They passed one called the *Prakt*. Swedish, Stefan thought with a kind of internal Danish-nationalist sneer.

Nicole looked over at him. Conversations on Mars were slow, but Stefan had definitely crossed over into ignoring-the-question territory by this point. And Stefan was aware that Nicole already viewed him with suspicion. She was always checking him for signs of trouble, her military eyes narrow in the breadth of her face, her buzz cut almost bristling.

In point of fact the child had already added itself to the commotion. Because monotony and calm used to be the norms on this planet. Once they'd gotten past the excitement of landing and surviving, they'd gradually settled into a slower and slower routine. But Jenny's pregnancy had sped everyone up again. Had energized the lot of them—aside, Stefan knew, from Stefan. Even the people at *Destination Mars!*, for all their official disapproval, were excited. Specifically, they had started filming again; the aggravating reality show was now, with the pregnancy, back on. There were even cameras inside the rover, including one right over Nicole's shoulder. Nicole, who was still looking at him. They went over a significant bump.

Jenny getting close—was it exciting? Well, to be sure, *exciting* was an evaluatively neutral term that merely described an elevation in activation or energy level as compared to baseline. Animals felt it when they were mating or killing something or being chased.

"Quite exciting," he said, quite honestly.

Nicole continued to eye him. The camera presumably did, too.

As they pulled up to the habitation center, Stefan saw that the others were suited up and waiting for them, having tracked their progress back from the lander. Well, three others were there; Jenny, spacesuit-less, was indoors. Still it was a crowd, as three necessarily would be. Stefan sighed, and then, like Nicole, put his own helmet back on so that they could unseal the doors.

A good deal of bustling ensued, everyone tripping over one another—tripping over Stefan, certainly—to help with the boxes. And Trixie whistled as she worked. Into her microphone, which was on, so that everyone heard the whistling. She had always been peppy, a trait that Stefan attributed to her Australian character. But the pregnancy had amplified it to a fever pitch, at least when she wasn't in the workroom staring at her endlessly sterile water samples.

When everything was in the airlock, which had been designed to comfortably hold perhaps three or four people at a time, they closed off the outer door and all took their suits off in the tiny space, jostling and accidentally elbowing. There was some laughing and general good-mood noise; it was as though Stefan and Nicole had just come back successful from a hunt whose spoils had been awaited by a desperate tribe.

"Good work," Josh said, clapping Stefan on the back. The effect of the pregnancy on Josh, the father, had been to make him occasionally hearty in a goofy way—heartier and goofier, in fact, as the pregnancy had progressed. He smiled with bright teeth and an open mouth, and the curls of his brown, curly hair seemed to be springier than they used to be.

Stefan picked up a box and opened the inner door to the rest of the habitation center. And was greeted by some species of bouncy Top-40-type music coming from all the speakers. Loud. Which was again Trixie.

"I thought it'd give us a boost," she said, coming right past him with a box, her dyed-maroon hair down past her shoulders. Stefan gathered from her Japanese ancestry—and her eyebrows—that her natural hair color was black, which would have been easier on the eyes. But she kept it dyed different hot colors. "An unloading boost."

"Or a headache," Stefan said.

"Oh, you wowser," she said, taking her cargo back to the kitchen. Almost skipping.

Stefan sniffed the air. A few weeks earlier at the baby shower a terrible smell had cropped up in the common room for no discernible reason except that everything was going sort of wrong with the electricity and plumbing and so on in the habitation—and then everything had gone back to normal, also for no discernible reason. The air now smelled only like the usual air freshener mixture. The fresheners had been designed to smell like all the astronauts' hometowns simultaneously—like flowers blended with car exhaust and asphalt in the summer and also maple syrup. It was not pleasant, but not like terrible spoiled eggs and mayonnaise, anyway.

And then there was Jenny on one of the *chaises longues* in the common room, looking mountainous and guilty for not having been able to suit up, surrounded by snack food wrappers and saying, "Well, I might be able to help for this part," as she struggled to get off the *chaise*. Her bathrobe was open and her shirt was not quite managing to cover her belly entirely.

Josh and Nicole looked at one another with affectionate disapproval. The look said *There goes that Jenny again*. Nicole said, "Not advisable. You know you really shouldn't do any heavy lifting the rest of the way." Josh nodded.

Roger accidentally bumped Stefan on the way past him to the workroom. In combination with the thumping, bouncing music and the loose socks on the floor and the fact that Stefan just didn't like Roger, this almost made Stefan smack the box out of his hands. Maybe he would have done precisely that, had his own hands not been full. Instead he glared at Roger's back.

"I know what!" Trixie said as she bounced back to the airlock for more. "We should have a dance party tonight."

"Pardon me?" Stefan said. The cameras in the corners of the ceiling glinted down.

"That's a fun kind of idea," Josh said.

"Oh, ripper! We never have a dance party!" Trixie said, almost screaming. "You could chair-dance," she said to Jenny in a slightly more reasonable voice. "Small, gentle movements."

"Um," Stefan said. He still hadn't taken his box where it needed to go.

Jenny smiled. Josh did, too. Roger smiled shyly. Even Nicole did. In her case it was like a bear smiling.

. . . .

Back in the rover, this time behind the wheel and driving, Stefan wondered what he ought to do with himself. He had just told everyone that he was restless and wanted to make one more run to the lander to get some more things. Trixie had called him a *wowser* again, as she often did—he gathered it was Australian for *party-pooper*—but nobody had tried very hard to get him to stay, or even to convince him that someone should go with him, as was the standard practice, especially on night trips. Stefan was not an expert on human behavior, but he had managed to intuit the fact that the others didn't particularly like him.

The rocky landscape was definitely darkening now, and the moons, when they were in the sky, were too remote and little to illuminate anything. Stefan therefore navigated by headlights and drove slowly so that he wouldn't bumble into any rocks or pits that the rover couldn't handle. In any case he preferred when things moved slowly.

Bumping along on rocks the rover *could* handle, Stefan was quite done with the whole situation. With Home Sweet, which was what they called the habitation center. And it was going to get much worse when Jenny finally popped.

The stoic adventurer struck out on his own, Stefan thought, narrating himself for a moment.

But actually he was only going to the lander.

Stefan had applied to the *Destination Mars!* program with the conscious intention of spreading civilization beyond Earth to other worlds. He'd said something to that effect in his application video. But then, once they'd arrived on this wide-open planet, he realized that his secret motivation had honestly been to get *away* from civilization, and he'd for a short time become an anarchist. Unsuccessfully. And since then he'd been gradually realizing that he wasn't an anarchist so much as a person who found other people difficult and who therefore sometimes boiled over and tried to break their fingers, which he was expressly not allowed to do. They had made a rule about it.

In sum, the situation was that he was a misanthrope who had traveled eighty million kilometers to get away from anthropes, but had foolishly brought five anthropes with him. Who were now about to become six.

"Stefan?" someone said from right behind him.

He swerved and stomped on the brakes.

Fully stopped now, he looked over his shoulder, where there was, of course, nobody at all. He looked all about the rover: nobody. He checked his radio, even though it hadn't been a familiar voice. "Did anybody call me?"

After a minute, Roger, with the sound of a dance beat behind him: "We didn't, Stefan. Is everything okay?"

Stefan didn't answer. He turned off his radio and glanced over at one of the cameras. The possibilities were grim: either the people at *Destination Mars!* were messing with him, or he was hearing things.

"Lovely," he said to himself. And perhaps to others.

The lander was pretty close by *Destination Mars!* standards—five kilometers away from Home Sweet, as the crow flew, or ten kilometers as the rover traveled—which meant a trip of about an hour. During that time, Stefan thought about other planets. What if he could somehow re-engineer the rocket that had brought them here? Though it was not designed to be able to take off from Mars, with its different atmosphere and gravity and uneven surface, and there wasn't anything like enough fuel to do it, and Stefan would need Jenny's help to calculate the trajectory to go anywhere. And there was nowhere to go. Jupiter was 555 million kilometers away, and composed of gas; Venus was 120 million kilometers away but averaged 460 degrees Celsius and rained sulfuric acid; Earth was much closer than Jupiter or Venus, but was covered with people. You couldn't get away from them, on Earth.

Stefan had mused his way through these considerations quite a few times already.

The lander was a little more than half full at this point. Stefan, out of the rover, the lander door open, shined his helmet-cam around at all the remaining boxes. There was nothing here that they needed at the habitation center right away—backup food for the food they'd already unloaded, spare parts, backup clothes for the clothes they were already wearing, a replacement *chaise longue*, extra towels they didn't need, a new carbon dioxide splitter/oxygenator in case the current one were to give out, a couple of spare mini solar panels, and so on. The baby bottles and diapers and baby clothes—Stefan shuddered—were already back at Home Sweet.

He turned on the lander's interior light that *Destination Mars!* had put in for no mechanically defensible reason and climbed up into the space. It was actually somewhat roomy—you could stand up, and there was enough width to lie down, too, if you wanted to.

As a compromise between standing and lying down, Stefan sat and leaned against one wall. He closed the lander door, which made the lander airtight. They had designed it that way, ridiculously, mainly to give the included goldfish a chance to survive, though, despite that thoughtfulness as well as the little warming unit that had come with it, the two unfortunates had frozen solid in their tank, of course. No goldfish had ever survived any of the supply trips. Still they kept sending them.

In any case, it was very quiet in the lander. Very, very quiet. Heavenly.

Oh.

Stefan looked over at the extra carbon dioxide splitter, which was one of the things you used for making breathable air. He looked at the airtight lander door. He looked over at the food boxes. He looked up at the overhead light and thought about the solar panels on the top of the lander. He thought about the spare parts and the parts back at the habitation center that he could use to generate water from some of the stuff scattered as ice crystals through the soil. There was even a window, again for no good reason, in case you wanted to look out at orange Mars. It wasn't as roomy as the rocket that had brought them all here, but it was at a much better distance—that is, farther—from Home Sweet.

The lander, the placid little lander, had almost everything Stefan needed.

Everyone was asleep by the time Stefan got back. Trixie snored deafeningly, but she wasn't the only one sawing away, which suggested to Stefan that alcohol had been present at the dance party. He could, in fact, smell alcohol, over the unpleasant background air freshener mix.

Stefan had only brought a few useless things back with him—some clothes and some kitchen appliance parts, mainly, removed from the lander to make more space in there—and now he loaded the rover up with various equipment and tools and water and personal items. It was nothing that the rest of them couldn't spare. Backup things.

Then he drove back to the lander and unloaded.

Then he drove back to the habitation center to drop off the rover so that nobody would know where he was, though he did leave a vague note. In its entirety, it read: *Everything's lovely.*

Then he walked back to the lander, which was not a great deal slower than driving there.

Then he took everything out of the lander that still needed to come out to make room, and he set it all on the ground outside, and he climbed inside, unrolled his bedroll, and, still in his spacesuit because naturally he hadn't yet had time to set up the splitter properly, he looked around at the calm little space one more time, turned off the interior light, and he slept.

He only woke up once in the night, when he once again heard someone call out "Stefan?" Or really it was more like *Stefan?* Because it sounded like it came from right next to him, and it also sounded like it came from inside his head. He sat quite upright in his bedding, half-asleep and spluttering, "Yes! It's Stefan!" But of course there was no one there. After a moment he put his head back down. The night was entirely peaceful thereafter.

In the morning, Stefan did get some radio calls, which he ignored.

"Um," said Roger while Stefan was eating a breakfast of rye bread paste and cheese paste through his helmet tube. "Are you . . . where are you?"

"Hey, Stefan," Josh said later that morning, while Stefan was integrating the carbon dioxide splitter into the lander's circuitry. "We're all wondering about you. Could you just give us a heads-up so we know you're all right?"

"Stefan," Nicole said that afternoon as he was testing the splitter. "We need your position and status."

He tried to turn the volume down on the radio, but you could only do that in non-emergency situations, and apparently someone had designated the situation an emergency situation. There was nothing that forced him to respond, however. In any case, it was a considerable relief when the space heater was plugged in and the splitter and some other pieces had started generating breathable air so that he could remove the helmet and not hear from anyone any more.

At the end of the day, Stefan looked around again. It had been very easy to make the space minimally livable, and he could start on the rest tomorrow—laying out and connecting additional solar panels, building an ice extractor and melter. No problem. The lander seemed ready to be converted, with its strange ports and outlets and sealable door and so on. It was almost as though the people at *Destination Mars!* had wanted this to happen.

Stefan looked around again sharply. Were there cameras in here? Certainly there were in his helmet and spacesuit. He made sure to disable those before he turned in for the second night. The organization had made a practice of messing with him in the past.

But now he was alone.

Over the next few days, Stefan fixed up the place. He did attach the solar panels, and he set up a little box for silverware and plates and another one for clothes. A high-tech chamberpot that had been built for the rover. He built the water extractor, the mini-desalinator. He crafted a tiny squeeze of an airlock out of stretchy but super-strong plastic, so that he didn't have to reoxygenate the lander each time he went in or out. He even, miraculously, revived the goldfish, which he and Nicole had left behind in the box marked *new gold-fish* when they saw that the tank water was frozen, but it turned out that the experience had just been a kind of accidental cryogenic experiment, and they started wiggling around as soon as the water in the tank had thawed. There were two of them, presumably male and female. Stefan refrained from naming them, in much the same way that you wouldn't name flowers in a flower arrangement, but he enjoyed them and left them as the room's only decoration.

During meals he took out his tablet and watched *What We Become* and *When Animals Dream* and *Under the Surface* and other old Danish films. Anything where a town was being destroyed or the world was ending. Or he tried to read Kierkegaard and then gave up, as he had done many other times. Or he put on his spacesuit and went for a walk, eating from tubes, which was not as bad as one would have expected. Or he sat quietly in the lander, looking at the goldfish, or out through the little window at Mars. It was a chaotic surface—on some parts of the planet, it was literally called *chaotic terrain*, a geological term for, as he understood it, giant mismatched rocks all about, though here the landscape was chaotic only in a colloquial sense, as the rocks were littler. If Roger had been there, he could have explained the terms more exactly, and Stefan was pleased that Roger was not there.

The days went like that—engineering work during the day, plus meals, and then a mostly relaxing sleep at night. That voice did very occasionally pop up—once in the third evening while he was eating and twice since then in the middle of the night, waking him up in the middle of odd dreams of fluorescent light and hazy forms. Again, he didn't recognize the voice, and again all it said was *Stefan*. Now these were statements rather than questions. Stefan looked this up on his tablet, and found that it didn't count as hearing voices, in a psychiatric sense, if what you heard was someone calling your name. Egocentrism being a normal human state, apparently.

He had checked the lander many times, and had yet to find a camera or microphone. Let alone a speaker. Still—he didn't put it past *Destination Mars!* to find a way to needle him from across the solar system.

Stefan considered trying to read Kierkegaard's *Three Discourses on Imagined Occasions*, but then he didn't try to read it.

All the while, the lander was warm, the food was plentiful, and the air was perfectly good and odorless. Odorless, that was, aside from Stefan's increasingly unbathed status—he didn't know what he was going to do about showering or cleaning his clothes, as a matter of fact. Perhaps he would get used to his own sharpening smell, as his distant ancestors must have done with theirs. It would be different, he felt, when it was your own smell and not someone else's. He didn't know what the plan would be when he ran out of food, either, but that was a while off. There were some other minor problems—he wasn't producing all that much potable water, for one thing, and so was very slowly working his way through what he'd borrowed from the others. Also, the solar panels required a good deal of regular dusting. And the radiation shielding was, he realized, probably thinner here than it was at Home Sweet. Meanwhile, when he had his suit on, he occasionally got a voice through the radio, wondering where he was and if he was going to come back—"Come on, you crackers boy, you big sook," Trixie said once. "Enough of the sulk."—but he continued to ignore those, as well as all of the other concerns.

One night the voice added *Hello* to *Stefan*.

About a week in, he woke up hazy from a more elaborate dream—the forms were more definite, though definite in a way he couldn't have described when he woke up—to the sound of a relatively elaborate utterance. From right next to him, from inside him. Could it really be *inside* him? Could *Destination Mars!* have put a chip inside him or . . . no, they couldn't have, could they?

Stefan, the voice said again. *Stefan*. And then, with some apparent effort: *Repattern the chaos.*

The next morning he named the goldfish. Guld and Fisk. Gold and Fish.

That wasn't exactly what we meant, Stefan, the voice said next time.

Was Stefan bored? Only some of the time. Generally there was work to be done to get the various life-sustaining machines and devices in finer fettle. And in any case there was nothing the matter with boredom.

Was Stefan concerned about the voice? Only some of the time. One night it said *They make a mess, Stefan.* "Yes, they certainly do," he said in return, somehow knowing that the voice meant the people back at Home Sweet. By this point, he was starting to doubt that this was *Destination Mars!* talking, which was not reassuring, given that it had clearly progressed beyond the simple use of his name that his tablet had assured him was within normal parameters—but he also knew that one of the traditions of hermits was to be a bit mad.

The wise hermit slowly grew eccentric, he narrated about himself. Was Stefan happy? Some of the time, definitely.

Repattern the chaos, he was again told one night. *We think you're the one who can do it.*

Did Stefan ever wonder if this living situation was what he actually wanted, or if this reclusion, like his anarchist period, was something of a red herring? Perhaps yes, perhaps no.

And then, one night, while he was in the middle of eating some freeze-dried and reheated fish cakes, the voice that was next to him or in his head or somewhere said something at considerable length and which left him pondering at even more considerable length.

Now, why is it that you have to make do in this little lander while those other twits get the whole habitation center to their messy selves? We think you would use the word twits.

He wasn't entirely surprised that they came and found him, knocking on the lander door late one morning the following week, but Stefan was so keyed up from the voices that he did jump a bit.

The window wasn't right on the door. Nonetheless, he peered through it and could see the rover parked outside, and the edge of at least one person in a puffy spacesuit.

He sighed and put on his helmet. "You found me," he said into the radio. His voice cracked a little from lack of use.

Josh said, "We actually pretty much knew where you were right away. Like, within a day."

"You did?"

"Bootprints."

"Oh."

"We'd like to come in," Nicole said. Everything she said sounded to him like a command. Stefan supposed it was her Air Force background. Or being a medical doctor; doctors did get bossy sometimes. Or maybe it was only the fact that he was slightly frightened of her.

Stefan glanced at Guld and Fisk as though for support. "It's a bit tight in here," he said into his radio.

"Or you could come out," Nicole said. Also a command.

"Is it just the two of you?" Stefan said.

"Just the two of us," Josh said. "Jenny's back at Home Sweet, of course, and Trixie's there because someone doctor-y ought to be there with Jenny just in case, which I should be, too, honestly, but here I am."

"And Roger?"

"He was reluctant to come."

Stefan could understand that. It was Roger's fingers he had once broken, for, he had to admit, no good reason.

He sighed again. If he didn't give in, perhaps Nicole would rip the door right off the lander. "Let's try indoors."

They came in one at a time, using the stretchy one-person airlock Stefan had rigged up. Josh was duly impressed as he squinched his way through. "Pretty slick," he said, showing a big, open-mouthed grin when he took his helmet off. Then, once he was all the way in, Nicole took her turn with the airlock—if she was impressed, she didn't say so—and then the lander was fairly full.

"I probably should have come outside," Stefan said.

"Well, here we are," Josh said. The three of them were sitting cross-legged in the space, like kindergarten children or American Indians from the old movies. The lander was, in fact, shaped something like a tepee.

"We're like Indians," Stefan said, chuckling. Nicole gave him a sharp, surveying look and he stopped chuckling. She had shaved her head all the way to the scalp since he'd last seen her. It did not make her more approachable. "Are . . . are you hungry?" he asked.

"We had some tube food en route," Nicole said. She had a look on her face that suggested she was acutely aware of Stefan's long-unwashed smell.

Josh reached out and almost touched Stefan on the knee and then instead withdrew his hand. "How are you, Stefan?" he said.

"Good, good, good," Stefan said, eyebrows high.

"Are you?"

"Oh, yes."

"Hmm," Josh hmmed. "Because it's sort of a big deal, just leaving all of a sudden to live in a U-Haul in the middle of nowhere on Mars."

Stefan looked around again, frowning. He didn't know what a U-Haul was, but it sounded like some perhaps boxy thing that you used for hauling and, to his mind, the space was more like a metal tepee than that.

"We're worried about you," Josh said. His face was soft, and Nicole's was still not. "It was pretty abrupt. And dramatic."

Stefan thought for a minute. At this point there was no harm, so far as he could imagine, in just saying it. "It's madness at Home Sweet. Loud and messy. And it's getting worse."

Josh tilted his head and made an expression that said, *Well, fair point.*

"I don't think anyone really wants me there, in any case," Stefan said. "I am not . . . well-liked."

In response to that, Josh made an implausible *You must be joking* face. "Now, come on," he said. "That's not true."

"Listen," Nicole said, leaning forward in the way she did everything: sharply. The lander's interior light gleamed off her scalp. "This is besides the point. Stefan, as far as I'm concerned, you can live wherever you want to, so long as you don't deprive the rest of us of anything we need." She looked pointedly around at some of the equipment that Stefan had installed in the lander and that was humming quietly and productively behind him.

"These are backups," Stefan said. "Backups of backups." Even the rover chamberpot was a backup.

"*And,*" she continued past him, "among other things, your move has deprived us of an engineer."

Well, and *that* was a fair point.

"Here's the thing," Josh said. "Jenny's really about to go into labor any day now."

"Oh." Stefan felt a surge of anxiety, as though Josh had just said *The giant spiders are crawling in this direction.*

"And the electricity back at Home Sweet," Josh continued, "just started acting up again."

"We need you to come back and look at it," Nicole said.

Stefan blinked.

Then, right at his ear, the voice, rather loud: *Repattern the chaos.*

It was loud enough that, although he'd gotten used to this sort of thing, Stefan spun around to look. Nobody there, of course. And when he turned back, the faces facing him were showing concern. Concern plus varying levels of sympathy.

"So I gather you didn't hear that," Stefan said.

Josh shook his head slowly.

So it was only Stefan on the receiving end. And receiving what, exactly? Repattern the chaos, indeed.

Go with them, the voice said quietly.

"Okay," he said. "I'll come back."

Welcome to Your Machines

(Section 17 of the unofficial *Destination Mars!* handbook, as written by the founder of *Destination Mars!*)

You will, obviously, be surrounded by machines. We mean this literally. The rocket is an enclosing tube composed entirely of machinery; the surface rover is a mechanical, wheeled box; in the habitation center there will be machines on all sides of you; even your spacesuits are essentially machine clothes.

This will take some getting used to, but you won't have much choice: you will have to get used to it. If you take away the machines, the machines that warm things up and produce air pressure and give you oxygen to breathe, Mars will kill you more or less right away. Like, in one or two minutes, is what we're told by our people who calculate that kind of thing as part of their jobs. One of our people says fifteen seconds, but he is known for having something of a dramatic flair. And we were given an estimate of an hour from a person who sometimes wears a "Be Happy" T-shirt to work. To *work*. This is why we take averages, and, all drama and unwarranted optimism aside, your average is: dead very quickly.

So accustom yourselves to technology. And probably you already are at least a little accustomed to it. You've already got technology coming out of your ears (sometimes literally). It's in your homes, in your pockets; it takes you from place to place. (The internal combustion engine may not be the latest thing, but it's still a machine.) Our relationship with technology is already called a "dependent" one by some individuals who hate progress instinctively and write a lot of op-eds online.

Still—your Mars setup does take things to another level. If you were outside wearing a helmet on Earth for some reason, and someone took it off your head, you wouldn't get carbon dioxide poisoning within a few breaths and pass out, right before your organs ruptured and then froze solid. So this is another level of dependency for sure.

What we recommend, as far as getting used to all this, is to expand your idea of what's natural. Because that's the problem. The truth is that we've never, ever been independent, in terms of our survival. Plants, animals, the *sun*—we're leaning on a lot to get through the day. But we call those things natural and tell ourselves, *Hey, I'm self-reliant, just living off the fat of the land.* It's a narrative that doesn't stand up to close investigation, but it sustains us, and we would be foolish to abandon it altogether.

Consider your oxygenator, then, the fat of the land. Consider your nuclear reactor the fruit of the earth.

The fact is, we could go into a pretty lengthy critique of the concepts "natural" and "artificial," and early drafts of this chapter did go into that pretty lengthy critique—the thumbnail version is that these concepts aren't so black and white (if a person puts a bed under a willow tree, is that living naturally? if a bird makes a nest in a radio tower, using gum wrappers found on the ground, is that artificial?)—but in the end the detour did seem self-indulgent.

The point is that your life is built around the things you live with, and you will be living with things that were built by human hands and, actually, other machines, and that run on electric power. This will by necessity become your new natural. We recommend you do whatever it takes to adapt.

Adaptation may involve developing personal relationships with the technology that will surround you. Not in the sense of anthropomorphization—none of the machines around you will have souls, per se—but something closer to the way people regard household pets. Naming the HVAC system will make it seem like a minor member of the family; using gender-specific pronouns to refer to the rover (which could easily be *called* Rover) will help you bond. *He's a little sluggish today*, you might say, or *Rover? He's always ready for some adventure!* Military pilots do this kind of thing all the time, though we understand that they usually think of their vehicles as "shes" rather than "hes." It's the same for sailors and boats. But we have no intention of dictating the gender of any of your equipment; that's strictly your choice. And in fact it might be a good idea to think of their gender in more fluid terms.

Better yet, consider embracing this technology as part of yourselves. That's how intimate the relationship will be. As the philosopher Donna Haraway wrote, "By the late twentieth century, our time, a mythic time, we are all chimeras, theorized and fabricated hybrids of machine and organism; in short, we are cyborgs." And that was decades ago. The twentieth century. We didn't even have cell phones when she wrote that.

To the end of helping you into this crucial intimacy, this chapter will introduce you to the machinery that will surround you, and prepare you for maintenance and repair. It's not going to be as profound as the more metaphysical material that we cut out of our early drafts, but we acknowledge that it might be more immediately useful. And it will probably keep you from dying in an untimely way.

- First, a general note: We've included separate, individual manuals for the maintenance and repair of every machine you've got—even the blender. And rest assured that these are not the kind of manuals you're used to from Earth, written first in Slovenian or Korean or Afrikaans and then translated into English by an underpaid and undereducated person distracted by debt and the family problems that come from debt. Nor are they the kind written in English by well-meaning but purely pragmatic engineers. These manuals were written by people who first spent significant time interacting with, even living with, these devices *and* the people who designed them, only after which, when they were fully satisfied, did they begin composing the instructions and troubleshooting guides. In our opinion, these manuals are worth reading for their own sake, even when the machines are working just fine.

- You will also have at least one engineer among you, very intentionally. When in doubt—say, for example, you've encountered an exhilarating but enigmatic passage in one of the repair manuals—turn to your engineers. They know their stuff backward and for-ward. Ideally you'll all pay good attention while they're working so that everyone can learn the basics of maintenance and repair—the responsibility falls on all shoulders—but it has been said more than once that engineers are born, not made.

- That said, plenty of things can go wrong with engi-neers, too, which is why we include the manuals.

- Again speaking generally, the keys to a good rela-tionship with a machine aren't all that different from the keys to a good relationship with a human, or with your own body: sensitivity and attention. A devoted caretaker will know when an engine is overheating before any warning lights start flashing, will be able to gauge the health of a water pump based on tiny changes in pitch, will sense problematic moisture levels in a server even before the server knows it. And then that caretaker brings to the machine what the machine needs, knowingly making things right—a retuned dial, a new transistor, a period of rest, whatever it takes—before things go very wrong. Be that caretaker.

- The most important machine in your lives will be the nuclear reactor. Sometimes people hear those words—*nuclear reactor*—and get nervous. They think Rajasthan or Fukushima, or, if they know their history, they think Chernobyl and Three Mile Island. That kind of thinking is, of course, outdated. This is a small and safe nuclear reactor, and all of your energy for everything you do is going to come through it. Well, we've thrown in a couple of solar panels because of pressure from certain quarters, but they'll probably be covered by dust most of the time, and, unless you want to spend your lives on the roof, dusting, your best bet is probably to ignore them. Basically you're going to be getting your power from the nuclear reactor, which is fine. Just put it a little distance from the habitation center and you'll be fine.

- We have eliminated the clock function on the microwave, because we find that those are always resetting at odd moments and you end up never knowing what time it is. Your other clocks should be fine.

- For the most part, you should find the kitchen equipment pretty familiar. The oven runs a little hot, so you might want to set it cooler than any recipes suggest. (Also, the boiling point of water is a *lot* lower on Mars,

FYI. See Section 21 for more information on running a productive and fun Martian kitchen.) But most of the devices—fridge, microwave, blender, coffee bean grinder—are the ones you're used to from home. We chose them partly because there's no reason to reinvent the wheel, and partly because the kitchen is the true center of any home, and so it's a good place to indulge in some occasional and well-earned nostalgia.

- The HVAC system should allow you to control the temperature of your living space fairly precisely. You can even choose different temperatures for different rooms. For example, maybe you'd want the bathroom a little warmer for people to be comfortable in just before they step into the shower. But then you'd lose that delicious feeling of transitioning from a chilly space into a steamy one. It's a tough call, and we leave it to your discretion. Just know that you have the option. As for the inevitable conflicts over choosing the ideal temperature for a room, we have no advice at all.

- The air produced by the carbon dioxide splitter will probably not smell exactly the same, will probably not taste exactly the same in your mouth, as the air you're used to from Earth. Air is a lot more than oxygen plus some inert gases, and we've been struck by the level of emotion people associate with the various smell-able bits and pieces that get caught up in the stuff we breathe. People get to the mountains and they say, *Oh, just smell this mountain air,* or they catch a whiff of the Delaware River through an open car window as they cross the Benjamin Franklin Bridge into

Philadelphia and they think, *Home*. We're not going to try to argue against this kind of sentimentality. As a matter of fact, we've included a number of plug-in air fresheners in your Communal Resource Stockpile (see Section 11), and we've loaded each one with a mixture of all the scents from your various hometowns. There should be plenty of electrical outlets to use the fresheners if you like. We're not sure that the different hometown odors sit all that well together—some of the people in the focus group actively disliked the combination—but we didn't want to prioritize any one person's olfactory experience over anyone else's, so the combination is what you've got.

- When a machine breaks down once and for all, it will need to be replaced. We can send many of these on supply rockets (see Section 13), and we will do our best to replace the original with something at least equally good. Maybe the new one will even be better than the original. Still there will be an adjustment period. You'll have to get used to the new noises, the new lights, the new hum of a different motor. Things will not be the same as they were. In this way, the machines serve as metaphors for many other things.

- At some point in the future, you may start building machines of your own. This will be a big step, and the thought blows our minds, really. We're probably talking about a while into the future, here—you'd have to start refining metals and so on before you could get into it. But then again maybe you'd start sooner, by repurposing the things you already have, or by combining things. Maybe you'd make Rover smart enough to do some exploring on her own, or you could swipe some stuff from the rocket so that Rover could jet around a bit faster. That all sounds like fun to us. Maybe you'd take the sunlamps out of the greenhouse and attach them to your bunks to make tanning beds. We don't recommend it, but we understand that you could. In any case, the larger point is that someday you may go beyond combining things to create entirely new machines. This is something that is within the power of humans to do—to make something that never existed and that is capable of functions never before imagined. Just reflect on that a moment: it's quite something; it's godlike power. What would these machines even be? We don't know. The truth is, we don't have any advice about how to handle these new acts of creation, so this bullet point is not going to advise you on that. We just thought it would be good to invite you to pause and take in the magnitude of the moment.

• None of your current machines are intelligent, in the Artificial Intelligence sense of the word. This is partly because we don't yet know how to make that kind of machine, and partly because we've seen all the relevant movies (*2001*, *The Terminator*, *Completion*, *War Games*, etc.), and so we know how things can get out of hand once machines start thinking for themselves. Right now your machines are completely yours, but in no time at all *you* can become *their* humans. We hope you've seen these movies, too. They are certainly available for viewing on your tablets. And they really hold up. Sometimes we think about what would happen if we crossed that line into artificial intelligence, and we feel a delicious tremor of excitement at the possibilities. But excitement can be good and it can also be bad. We know that. We haven't crossed the line. If you do make intelligent machines, we suggest that you at the very least don't make them any smarter than yourselves.

- If you do create something new, just be sure to write a manual for it. You'd be surprised to see how easy it is to forget how things work. And then where will you be?

- Oh—another key to a good relationship is dependability. Showing up. Being there when you're needed. Because it's a relationship that goes in both directions. You need them, of course—you'd be dead within a minute or two without them—but they need you, too. Without you, *they* would die (if a machine can be thought of as alive or dead), and then you would die. Be, therefore, the person who shows up.

- You will be in possession of a number of machines designed to produce drinking water for you. (This water will also probably not taste like the water you remember from home, but that distinctive taste was largely due to unsafe things, so it's best to let go of it.) You've got the ice-melter, the desalinator, the dehumidifier, and a drill to try to get at subsurface liquid water. You have purifiers to reclaim wastewater. With all of these different pieces of equipment, you should be covered as far as hydration is concerned. But don't let the abundance lull you into any kind of complacency. It doesn't mean, for example, that you can choose a favorite water-making machine and use it exclusively, ignoring the rest, hoping that your favorite will last forever. It will not. And then you will die of thirst.

- Back to reactors for a moment: the real danger is not a meltdown; the real danger is the reactor *stopping*. Don't let that happen. Mars without electricity is a dead planet.

- You may be detecting a central tension in this section of the handbook, and you are right to detect it. On the one hand, the machines we're giving you and the machines you'll go on to create are amazing, awe-inspiring. You're going to want to sit back and just admire them. On the other hand, they are machines, which can break, and then you'll be dead. Although perhaps that just enhances the awe; we don't know. You could argue that, either way, the effect is the same. Whether or not we here on Earth are currently cyborgs, you certainly will be, in the sense of not being able to walk away from the technology that surrounds you, of being in a relationship on which everything absolutely depends. If something goes right, wow. If something goes wrong, wow.

- If it becomes relevant, please see Section 35: *Dealing with Death on Mars*.

To Think About Something

OUTSIDE THE LANDER, Josh and Nicole more or less placed Stefan in the rover's back seat, almost like someone being taken in a police car. Nicole held his helmet in her lap, as though setting precautions against an escape.

On the way, the rocky way, Josh chattered updates that Stefan didn't want. Jenny was nesting—she had rearranged the furniture in the common room and had made Josh set up the bassinet that *Destination Mars!* had sent. Jenny was also still eating a lot of strange foods together. Orange juice over breakfast cereal, etc. Oh—and the baby had "dropped," whatever that meant. Stefan gathered that it didn't mean anything bad for the pregnancy, which, he had to admit to himself, was emotionally complicated for him. Not that he wanted anything to happen to the baby, exactly. But not that he didn't want anything to happen to the baby, either. Well, of *course* he didn't. But if it happened naturally? Of course nobody would *root* for an outcome such as that, but—and Nicole told him about the electricity, which had gotten back to flickering again.

"Did you read the manuals?" he asked, still a bit distracted.

"The manuals don't make a huge amount of sense," Josh said.

"The manuals are horseshit," Nicole said.

Stefan knew that that was correct. "Okay," he said. "I'll take a look."

Oh, you'll take a look, all right, said the voice. Stefan kept that to himself.

. . . .

Back at Home Sweet, he was greeted by a rearranged common room, with all the *chaises longues* bunched on one side of the room, and by music—some recording of an oud piece?—and also by awkwardness. Trixie made a big "Hallooooo" at him as he came in, but it felt even more forced than usual. Roger was on the far side of the common room, looking down at the floor. And Jenny sat on the couch glowering. Or, well, sat there until she managed to lever herself up and waddle over to Stefan and stand about three inches from his face. He flinched—he was also a little frightened of Jenny, even though she was perhaps twenty-five centimeters shorter than him.

"No," she said, through her teeth. "You don't get to just wander off like that. You don't get to make things dangerous."

He saw on her round face—as much as he could see, from this way-too-close perspective—that her most ferociously protective maternal instincts were fully awake. And aimed at him. Her breath, on his face, was sour.

Just then, the lights flickered.

"That," Nicole said. "That was it."

"I should probably check into that," he said. Jenny was still there, staring right into his face.

Outside, at the nuclear reactor, Stefan grumbled silently to himself. And he pictured punching Jenny in her mouth. Or—this picture came and went in a flash—in her belly.

That thought left him open-mouthed with shock. He never would, of course. A pregnant belly was a great deal beyond fingers.

There wasn't even any real reason to be at the nuclear reactor; there wasn't much chance that it was the source of the problem. But you had to check, and, more importantly, it got him away from the others. Or mostly. Presumably the *Destination Mars!* cameras were all going. And Nicole was also suited up and standing ten meters off, keeping an eye on him, her arms folded across her chest.

She's a twit, said the voice.

"Exactly," Stefan said.

"What was that?" came Nicole's voice over the radio. "Did you find something?"

"Give me a minute," Stefan said. "I have to make some checks."

He made some checks.

After that, he climbed up on top of the domes and gave the solar panels a good sweeping, even though there wasn't much chance that they were the source of the problem. But you had to check, and it got him more away, in a sense, than the reactor had. Nicole stood at the bottom of the ladder, but he couldn't see her from up there.

You could show her a right thing or two, the voice said.

Stefan nodded. He could.

Then, having dawdled on the roof as much as he could get away with, he came down and took readings on all the lines, which he knew would probably be fine, and which they were.

Finally, he checked the service conductors, which is where he knew the problem would probably be, and which is where it was. He had to replace the insulation on all the wires, and he had to replace some of the wiring, too. While he did all this, he put Home Sweet on backup power, so that they wouldn't die.

Interesting, said the voice. *You know*, said the voice, *if you were alone on Mars, you could do pretty much whatever you wanted to do.*

Stefan could feel Nicole watching him. *Now, just hold on*, he thought to himself, sweating a little.

Just a notion, the voice said.

It was true that you could think about something without actually doing something.

· · · · · · · · · ·

When Stefan was finished, the lights were steady and they stayed steady. It had not been a complicated problem. As a matter of fact, he was even able to explain it to the rest of them afterward, which was something Nicole insisted he do. He supposed that she was planning for the possibility of him not being there anymore at some point. Either because he left again, or because she killed him.

Dinner that evening was a continuation of the earlier awkwardness. First of all, Roger had put on this irritatingly soothing New Age music and his gaze darted between his soup and Stefan's face. Meanwhile, Nicole and Jenny eyed Stefan grimly, and Josh and Trixie attempted to make hearty conversation. Three years into this experience, conversation over the dinner table had become a spotty thing at best, and it was not at all common to hear things like, "Well, *you* had quite the walkabout!" in loud Australian, or "It's nice, huh, being together?" in earnest group-therapy-ese.

Meanwhile the cameras in the corners of the ceiling glinted down.

Nobody objected when, shortly afterward, Stefan said, "Well, I think I'll go in early for a bit of sleep."

And then he lay on his bunk among all the other bunks and stared up at the ceiling and listened to voices that talked about what it would be like if everyone else was no longer there.

At first, he argued strenuously. *This takes things quite a bit too far*, he thought to himself.

But *Does it?* came the voice.

We're talking about human beings, he said.

Is that . . . an important consideration?

He still hadn't figured out exactly where this was coming from. It no longer seemed at all plausible that it could be *Destination Mars!* messing with him, because it happened even when his helmet was off, and nobody else could hear anything. And also the things the voice was suggesting were . . . a bit much for even the folks running the reality show. And it wasn't someone standing next to him, obviously, because then they would still be there when he turned to look. Stefan had to assume that this was an inner voice, some long-latent internal compass that had stepped forward in order to guide him through difficult times. Or possibly he was deranged. Because if that was his internal compass. . . .

And then there was one other explanation, which made Stefan feel even more bonkers.

Trixie hadn't found any signs of life in her searches. Not in the air, not in the soil, not in the water, not in the deeper water. But what if Stefan now had? And, if so, *what* had he found, exactly?

You should probably stay on topic, the voice said. *These human beings are the worst.*

But they are <u>people</u>, Stefan thought. <u>Living people</u>.

They make an awful mess of things. And they don't like you.

Even if they don't, Stefan said.

They don't.

Even if they don't! That's no justification—

You broke that one people's fingers, came the voice.

Once. A long time ago. And they were only fingers. And just because I get angry sometimes doesn't mean—

They don't want you here.

I know they don't, Stefan thought.

Listen. The voice sounded a little different, like it was changing tone. *Let's just do the thought experiment. Just as an experiment.*

Thought experiment?

Yeah. It'll make you a better engineer. Imagining the scenarios. The—what's the word? The what-ifs.

The what-ifs.

Or maybe you're just not able to figure it out. Maybe it's too complicated.

That's not true at all, Stefan thought.

The easiest approach would come down to the carbon dioxide

splitter/oxygenator, obviously. As it stood, the machine was busily taking carbon dioxide—CO_2, which was ninety-five percent of the Martian atmosphere—and dividing it into O_2, which you could breathe, and C, which was released back into the atmosphere. But if you adjusted the machine so that it split the molecules into O and CO, well, then, you'd be making carbon monoxide, and you could allow that to fill up Home Sweet, having already removed all the spacesuits while everyone was sleeping and having gone off to wait in the rover. And then, when enough time had passed, you could restore the splitter's original settings, and wait for it to make everything right again, and go in and just deal with the—

He pictured the bodies. Clapped a hand to his mouth.

Now, don't think about that, the voice said.

Stefan didn't have his tablet with him, but he had the feeling that he was operating well outside the normal range in taking this line of thought.

Really? the voice said. *What does "normal" mean, anyway?*

It was a long time before anybody else turned in, which gave Stefan far too much time to think, and to listen to the voice that kept going nearly all the time now. *It's only a thought exercise,* the voice said. *Only a thought exercise.*

Sometimes the voice got on his nerves a little.

Eventually everyone else did make their way to the bunkroom and went to sleep. Everyone except Jenny, who Stefan knew had been sleeping on one of the *chaises longues* in the common room recently. As they all came in, Stefan kept his eyes closed and played the part of the resting angel as best he could. All the same, Nicole hovered over him for quite a while before she was somehow satisfied, and then she did something to his sleepsack—he felt her tug on it—and she finally settled into her own bunk.

The habitation center was then entirely dark. After a time, the night sounds started. Above the HVAC system—obliterating it, really—were the sounds of Trixie's snoring. Nicole snored, too, but it was more of a purr, actually, and nothing like Trixie's wood chipper. Stefan could only hear Nicole between Trixie's giant and not-quite-rhythmic snarls, and in those same intervals he also heard some mumbling from Josh. Josh talked in his sleep not infrequently, though Stefan could never make out what he was saying. The man sleep-mumbled.

Together, an anti-symphony. Roger, at least, was habitually quiet.

Wide awake with no chance of passing out now, Stefan continued to think things through. He also checked his sleepsack, where Nicole had clipped a little motion sensor for which they had not ever found a use. Until this night. Stefan was its first use. And it was going a bit far, he thought—at his age he did get up multiple times in a night to use the lavatory, and doing so under these circumstances would have raised a clamor. He unclipped the device angrily but gently—engineer's hands—and, again with some deft use of engineer's hands, he disabled the thing, and in the dark, too.

Nice. You are good at this sort of thing.

Thanks, Stefan thought in return, still seething a bit about the motion sensor. They really did have it in for him.

Want to take a look at that carbon dioxide splitter?

Stefan thought, *Why would I—*

Listen, the voice said. *There's no harm in <u>looking</u> at it.*

As he slipped out of the bunkroom toward the common room, the voice delivered a little speech. *Things would be so orderly if it were only you*, it said. *Just saying. So neat and tidy and quiet. Everything in its place. Everything predictable. Everything would finally be in a Pattern again.*

Stefan paused in his tracks, his hand on the metal corridor wall, standing in the darkness, and he thought something back. *Wait—*

how do you know there isn't already a Pattern? It was something Stefan had occasionally wondered—what if his fellow Marsonauts weren't chaos but instead some more complicated machine of a thing that he hadn't yet figured out?

There was a pause in return. And then, a voice that sounded a bit different: *Yeah. We thought of that. It's a head-scraper for sure. We think you would say head-scraper.*

Head-scratcher, Stefan thought.

Anyway, said the original voice, *better safe than sorry, as we think you say.*

Maybe, came the different voice. It was almost like a separate speaker.

Stefan, old legume, the original voice said. *These people would get rid of you if they could.*

Would they? he thought.

It's just a thought experiment. Unless you think your idea wouldn't work.

The common room was dark, too, the only light coming from a few tiny indicator bulbs on one wall, so that Stefan wasn't exactly sure how to proceed; Jenny had rearranged the furniture. He stood there and listened to the silence—Jenny made no sound when she slept. He waited for his eyes to respond to those few lumens in the room. When he had a very imperfect sense of where the main objects were, he took a few slow steps toward the airlock dome, and then a few more, and then he was across the room and out the other side.

At which point he stopped. Because there, in front of him, was Roger, sitting with his back against the airlock door. Eyes wide open.

Stefan shook his head. This was unexpected.

Roger stood up, and Stefan could see in the slightly better light of this room that he was holding two rather large rocks, one in each hand. "You're not going out there," Roger said, in a characteristically soft but unprecedentedly firm voice.

This is the one whose fingers you broke? came one of the voices.

"Yup," Stefan said.

Well, the voice said, *there's a bit of nice symmetry there.*

Roger had not moved or reacted to Stefan's *Yup.*

"You're going to hit me in the head with those rocks if I try to go out there," Stefan said.

"I'm going to hit you in the head with these rocks if you try to go out there," Roger agreed. Then he added, more quietly: "Also, I've been studying martial arts for a year."

"What?" Stefan was at a loss.

"Well, I had to learn to protect myself," he said pointedly.

Stefan could feel himself flushing a little with embarrassment, which was not a common experience for him. "When did you learn without anyone noticing?"

Roger shrugged. "People generally don't come into the greenhouse."

"Huh." After a minute of taking all this in, he sat down on the floor opposite Roger, who also sat down again.

"Are people taking shifts trying to keep me from leaving?"

Roger shook his balding head. "Just me."

"Just you," Stefan said. "Wow."

They sat like that, opposite each other, silently, for several minutes. It was a period of uncertainty, but also calm. Even the voices were quiet.

Then Roger said, "You know, I'm anxious about the baby coming, too. Nervous, I mean."

Stefan blinked in surprise. Roger had spent the last month making baby food and booties and jumpers for the baby. "But you've spent the last month making baby food and booties and jumpers for the baby."

Roger took a deep breath and exhaled it slowly. "Well, I guess you have to do something with the nervous energy."

"Nervous energy," Stefan said.

Roger nodded. "I'm not actually really a people person. I was born and raised in the Yukon, and even that felt crowded some-times," he said. "Why do you think I came to Mars?"

Stefan gaped.

"And it's already so busy here. It's only going to get busier."

This is pretty interesting, a voice said. The second, different one. *It's as though you're the same, in a way.*

"It *is* going to get crazier," Stefan said. "It's going to be lunacy. It's going to be chaos. Total chaos."

Oh, we don't like that, said a voice that was more like the original voice.

"You're both damn idiots," came another voice. But Stefan recognized this one.

The lights snapped on, and—Stefan blinked in the lights—Jenny was standing at the door to the airlock dome, leaning against the jamb. Her curly black hair wild all around her face.

Are we going to do this thing or not? said the original voice, a little whinier than usual.

Let's just see where this goes first, said the newer voice.

But....

"Oh—hi," Stefan said.

"Thank you for keeping watch, Roger," Jenny said. One of her eyebrows went up. "Martial arts?"

Roger nodded shyly.

"For a year?"

He nodded again.

"Hm." Jenny turned her attention to Stefan. "You realize you can't go anywhere."

Stefan was still processing the new Roger he was learning about, full of discipline and resolve, but he caught up to what Jenny was saying and retorted, "I can do what I want to do."

"Not when it's dangerous," she said.

This was the same argument they'd all had after Stefan had broken Roger's fingers. He felt everybody could do whatever they wanted—in retrospect, he realized he had mainly been interested in his being able to do what *he* wanted, if he could only figure out what that was—and they disagreed. He'd lost the point that time.

But you don't have to lose the point, this time, said the original voice. With a definite whine.

Shhh, said the other.

"You'll be fine," he said to Jenny. Though, he realized, they obviously would *not* be if he had done the thing at the splitter that he had been thought-experimenting about.

"*We'll* be fine?" Jenny said. "Maybe. Maybe. But what about you?"

Wait—what?

"Do you have any idea what the radiation levels are out there? You *know* that lander isn't shielded in the way that Home Sweet is. And food and water? Stefan—you dumbass—it's not safe!"

"Wait," Stefan said.

Wait, a voice said.

"You're worried about *me*?"

Jenny exhaled an exasperated exhalation and threw her hands in the air. "Of *course* I'm worried about you. I'm worried about everybody. The baby, me, Josh, Roger—" she gestured at Roger—"everybody. Of *course* you!"

Huh, said the second voice.

Stefan had no idea what to do with this.

Us neither, honestly, came a mixture of the voices. *That's another head-scratcher.*

"I don't understand it myself. It's as though I'm becoming the prototypical Earth mother," she said, almost to herself, trying to tie her bathrobe over her considerable belly. "Mars mother. Whatever."

Stefan glanced at Roger, who shrugged an *I don't know* shrug.

"Is it hormones?" Stefan said.

"No, you dumbass," Jenny snapped. "Well, perhaps somewhat. But it's also because—do you know why I called you *idiots*?"

Stefan almost suggested hormones again, but then didn't.

That's a good call, came the second voice.

"Because this isn't chaos," she said, swirling her arm around in the light, indicating sort of everything. "You two are scientists. I would expect you to know better. This isn't chaos."

"It isn't?" Roger asked in his tremulous voice.

Jenny threw her hands in the air, turned, and retreated into the common room, where she sat down on a *chaise longue.* And then, when the two men failed to follow her, she gestured impatiently, and they both got up and went in there. They sat together on a *chaise longue* right next to hers.

"*This*—" she swirled her hand around again—"is a very particular structure."

Ooh, said the combined voice. *We like the sound of that.*

"Like a machine?" Stefan asked hopefully.

"No. Nicole said it first." Jenny eyed both of the men. "This is a *family.*"

A family? the voice said. *A family.*

"Didn't you two have *childhoods?* Families?" Jenny said. "This is how families are . . . loud, ridiculous, and on your nerves." She looked off to the side and added, almost to herself, "And some are worse than that." She turned back. "Some are a lot worse than this," she said. "Do you know how damn fortunate you are?"

Stefan and Roger were more or less speechless.

"Do you?" Jenny leaned closer to them. "And you know what the thing is about *this* family? *Nobody gets to opt out.*"

Stefan was reeling to the point where all he could do was repeat things that Jenny said. "Nobody gets to opt out?"

"No," she said.

There are rules here, the newer one said.

Could you guys leave me alone? Stefan thought to himself.

Hey, the original voice said. *This is skully stuff for us, too. Or maybe you would say heady?*

"Guys?" Jenny said.

"Guys? Oh," Stefan said. "I'm just thinking."

Her face softened. "I'm aware that things are crazy around here. And, like you said, the baby is going to make things much crazier."

Stefan felt a pulse of anxiety at that statement.

Jenny put one hand on Stefan's arm and another on Roger's arm. "But maybe you could go back in your greenhouse to get some alone time when you need it," she said to Roger, and then, squeezing Stefan's arm, "and you could take walks, and perhaps the lander could be a kind of meditation studio that you could go to sometimes."

Stefan thought about Guld and Fisk waiting back in the lander. Smiled.

"And perhaps we could have quiet hours, and less music," Jenny said. "It gets on my nerves, too, sometimes."

Stefan was absolutely gobsmacked. "And maybe people could pick up their socks?" he said. "And their rocks?"

Roger and Jenny both nodded. "That seems fairly reasonable," she said. "The point is, if this is a family, your needs matter, too."

"Our needs matter, too," Stefan said.

"Okay," Roger said.

"This Mars mother thing is . . . remarkable," Stefan said.

Jenny laughed, and then Roger laughed, and Stefan chuckled a little. And then they all sat quietly together for a few moments.

"Do me a favor," she said, and she took both men's hands and placed them on her belly, where there was movement. This was remarkable in its own right. She looked at her belly and spoke to it. "This is your badass uncle Roger," she said. Roger visibly blushed. "And this is your cranky uncle Stefan."

"Cranky uncle," Stefan said.

"Everyone needs a cranky uncle," Roger said. "Mine was named Albert. Albert from Quebec."

Maybe it was the voices getting less inciting, or maybe it was the fact that the two men were apparently both misanthropes, but right then Stefan didn't want to hit Roger for saying that.

Maybe we need to take a little more time and think about things, said the newer voice.

You could think about something *without* doing something.

Ugh, said the original one, but in a tone of resignation.

The baby moved under Stefan's hands. He looked up and he and Jenny stared into each other's eyes for a minute. Movement, movement, movement. It wasn't *so* bad, right then. Plus Stefan would have his meditation studio. Without the pressure of the voices, it *was* seeming increasingly extreme—deranged, in point of fact—the thought experiment he'd been thought-experimenting a surprisingly short time ago. He shuddered when he thought of it. But then he absorbed this movement under his hand and let go of that derangement.

Because thoughts were just thoughts, and actions were something else.

And then something seismic happened in Jenny's belly, and the men let go and her face went very *WOW*.

"What was that?" Roger said, sitting back.

"That," Jenny said, "was a contraction. I think that was a contraction."

"A contraction?" Stefan repeated.

"Get Josh," she said. "Get Trixie and Nicole."

"Get Josh," Stefan said. "Get Trixie and Nicole."

"*Get them*," Jenny said with some intensity.

And then Stefan and Roger were up and going, racing down the corridor. If he had been able to stop and reflect, Stefan would have realized that he was definitely excited, with all the complexity that a word like that contains.

Well, a unified voice said, sounding curious. *Here we go.*

What You Can't Do (Part Two)

(Section 4 of the unofficial *Destination Mars!* handbook, as written by the founder of *Destination Mars!*)

Subsection 4:2: Biological Issues

Of course the social issues surrounding sex are only the beginning. The biological issues, at least in the case of heterosexual intercourse, are scarier still. (We considered sending only LGBTQ astronauts to Mars, but sexuality can be pretty fluid, so ultimately it seemed pointless.) You will, as you know, be submitting to operations intended to make it impossible to reproduce, but we know that no procedure is entirely infallible, and even the remote possibility of a pregnancy is so concerning that we need to take every precaution to avoid it. We detail the medical risks below, but they boil down to this: sex may feel good now, but it's probably going to feel terrible later, when a deformed baby is produced—and when it dies, along with the mother, in childbirth.

More specifically:

- Do you know how much radiation is going to be hitting you?
  - On the trip through space it's going to be a lot. A LOT. Not that you're going to be unsafe; we can protect grownups. (NOTE that this is not a legal guarantee.) Fetuses, on the other

hand? We make no claims about fetus safety at all. Radiation is basically a nightmare when a human is under construction. Think failure to implant; think cell destruction; organ destruction; limits to fetal growth; miscarriage; malformations; major post-natal neurological and motor deficits. Think cancer; think death.

o So that's the rocket, which is very, very dangerous. But even on the planet, which has an atmosphere to block some of the radiation, you're still getting a lot more than you would on Earth. Maybe not capital letters a lot, but still too much. So the same concerns basically apply.

o In other words, are you a big fan of birth defects? Or death?

- Do you ever think about bone density and how it's lower in places with lower gravity, such as a certain red planet we could easily name? Well, you *should* think about it. Adults can handle this okay with proper exercise and milk and vitamin supplements and so on (see Section 22 on keeping fit), but what about babies? Nobody knows. But we can speculate: if you have a baby, you might end up having a baby with fragile little bird bones. This sounds cute. It isn't cute.

- Plus, some scientists say that low gravity is bad for stem cells, which are important enough to be called *stem* cells.

- Have you ever heard of fluid distribution? As in, you're supposed to have your bodily fluids distributed in a good way throughout your body? Well, gravity plays

202 - DAVID EBENBACH

a role there, too. Imagine a baby with very awkward fluid distribution. Maybe all of the fluid is to the left, or maybe in one leg. This is your baby.

- And what about the mother? What if the fetus sets up shop in your Fallopian tubes instead of your uterus? Or right over the cervix, blocking the way out? And how will you handle eclampsia during the pregnancy? How about hemorrhaging during the birth? Infections after? Pulmonary embolisms? Other complications we haven't even thought about? You will not have the supplies you need to save the birthing mother if something goes horribly wrong. And—just to be clear—when you don't save her, she *dies*.

- To summarize in another way: If you try to have a baby on Mars, we don't know what will happen to you, and we certainly don't know what will come out of you.

Apples

THIS IS HOW Jenny gives birth on Mars.

First of all, it starts at night, while I'm asleep in the bunk dome.

When Stefan wakes me—Stefan and Roger heard her first and woke the rest of us, yelling "*The baby—the baby's coming*"—I look around for something that I couldn't name or identify if I saw it, and then, abandoning that something, I zip on out to Jenny. Who is sitting on a *chaise longue* in the common room and not looking the way I expected her to look. I expected her round face to be sweating, a drop of sweat at the tip of her nose, another at the tip of her chin. But she looks the same as she did when we all went to bed. Too big for her shirt to handle, and disheveled in her open bathrobe, her hair all over the place, but not like a person rolling a boulder uphill at all.

"Are you—?" I say, pulling up short a few feet from her and losing track of the adjective or noun I wanted.

"I just had a contraction," she says.

A little bit I feel like I've been hit in the head with a frying pan. I was dreaming something very hazy and fluorescent and now here I am in front of my Jenny, who has had a contraction. *Contraction*, I think. *Contraction, contraction, contraction.* It's like the hazy fluorescence has followed me into the room.

Trixie, because she is one of our medical doctors—we have other, less relevant kinds of doctors, too, including me—slips past me in a

flash of dyed-maroon hair, almost blood-colored, and starts checking on things. First she looks on and under the *chaise*. "Looks like
your water hasn't broken yet, eh?" she says.

Jenny shakes her head no. "Not that I know of," she says.

"Oh, you'd know, babe," Trixie says. "You get a pop, and then it's
here comes the flood."

Nicole, all seriousness, says, "How long ago was the contraction?"

Jenny frowns in a thoughtful way. "Right," she says. "I should have
made a point of looking at the time. Well, a minute, give or take."

"Okay," Nicole says.

Roger and Stefan and I stand there dumbly, in the sense of stupid
as well as in the sense of mute. And then I go all the way over to
Jenny, who is obviously not surrounded by a forcefield, and I sit
next to her and hold her hand. "Are you okay?" I ask.

"This is it," Jenny says with widened eyes.

"Wow," I say. This is a wow situation.

"Well," Nicole says.

"There's probably going to be a bit of a wait, Mum," Trixie says.
She has a tablet out to keep track of the time. I can see the numbers
accumulating already.

My mother used to make up stories about my birth. She told the
stork one when I was very little, although we didn't live in a house
with a chimney. She told something like the Moses one when I was
a little older and had been to some family Passover Seders, and in
fact we did live near a river that I suppose I could have floated down,
if we'd had a seaworthy basket. She told one where she found me
in a cave—"A nice cave," she would say. "Not one of the run-down
ones." When I was a teenager and being difficult she downgraded
the quality of the cave. My mother also told a story of me being very
tiny at first, like a seed, and just blowing in through an open window
one spring day. And it's true, anyway, that I was an April baby.

But my favorite family birth story wasn't mine—it was the one I was told by Lil, my fiancée on Earth until . . . well, it was the one her mother had told her, and Lil described it to me. Her mother said she'd grown Lil in her garden. Next to the carrots. That, when it was time, also on a nice spring day, she'd taken hold of the greens that showed above ground and that were attached to Lil's head underground, and she'd yanked her daughter right out of there. And until she saw Lil's face she'd expected her to be a carrot herself, or at least a turnip.

Mostly Lil's mother grew flowers, apparently, not vegetables. But it was still a nice story—for Lil, and then for me.

Actual births are of course not this magical. There are no baskets to float in, and no babies waiting to be lifted from the soil.

The contractions are eighteen minutes apart at first, which they tell me is a normal amount to be apart when things are just getting started.

"The best thing for now is to distract yourselves," Nicole advises us, as though it's both of us giving birth. "Things won't really get started until there's about five minutes between contractions. They'll be more intense, then, too." And then she looks at Trixie and the others. "And *we* probably ought to get back to our bunks. There's going to be plenty to do soon enough."

Trixie gets an *aww* face, like a kid told that she has to wait until after dinner before she can have dessert. I know she's particularly invested in this birth. But then she gets a hold of herself and nods. "Too right," she says. Meanwhile, Roger scratches the pale strands on his balding head in a dazed sort of way, and Stefan looks scared, as though Jenny might suddenly explode.

"Wait," I say. "So, this is all based on how people give birth on *Earth*, right?"

Nicole nods and makes a face that says she sees where I'm going with this. "Well, yes," she says. "But as far as we know everything's working the same way as it does on Earth."

"Okay," I say.

Trixie squats down to our level. Her maroon hair is somehow more jarring than the bright hair she usually has, but somehow her vivid goodwill is steadying. "Guys, what we're expecting is that the contractions are going to get closer together over time, and longer, and more intense. It could take hours. If anything different happens instead of what I just described, anything at all, wake us up."

"Okay. It could take hours," I say. "Martian hours, right?"

Jenny gives my hand a communicative squeeze. The truth is that Martian hours are only a little bit longer than Earth hours, technically. How long they feel is a different question.

When they've all gone back to the bunk dome, Trixie walking out backward as though she can't stand to take her eyes off Jenny, saying things like "Take a spin around the room, watch a movie, cuddle a bit," then it's just me and Jenny.

"It's just you and me," I say, trying to affect a calm voice.

"Plus one," she says, pointing at her belly.

"Well, almost," I say.

The people at *Destination Mars!* included an extensive and strange electronic handbook on each of our tablets, with chapters on all kinds of things—how to cook on Mars, for example, and ideas on how to decorate the habitation center, and how to handle radiation exposure, and what comes in the communal stockpile, what kind of people shouldn't even apply to go to Mars, and why we aren't supposed to have sex here. That section—Section 4—is a hard one to reconcile with Section 34, which is about how to not get bored on Mars. Especially when one of the people with you on Mars is Jenny, and she's sitting right there, being Jenny right in front of you. But it's there, and even though the handbook is labeled "unofficial"—it was apparently written as a sort of pet project by the eccentric person who founded *Destination Mars!*, and who in my opinion has a touch of a God complex—we really weren't supposed to have sex. The section says, *sex may feel good now, but it's probably going to feel terrible later, when a deformed baby is produced—and when it dies, along with the mother, in childbirth.* It's one of the most strongly worded sections of the handbook.

Jenny and I spend the next little while walking around the common room. She leans on me a little, which is nice. I don't even think she really needs the support so much as she likes it, which is even more nice. Still, I'm pretty tense.

It's not a big common room, so after a few laps we expand to include the dining room and kitchen, and also the workroom in back and the greenhouse. Still it's not very big, but it's bigger than the common room by itself. The scenery also changes more. We look at *chaises longues* and orange side tables, and we look at our circular dining room table that can be reshaped into whatever shape we want it to be, though we've never actually reshaped it, and we stop in the bathroom for Jenny to pee, and then we look at our microwave and our fridge, and we look out the windows at Mars, which is dark right now, and we look at Stefan's station in the workroom, which is orderly, with one small machine open on his table, ready to be studied, and we look at Trixie's station, with its mini-fridge and its vials of water samples and soil samples and gas samples, all of which have come up sterile, every single time—it's not easy for Trixie, whatever a person might think from watching her bop around—and we stop in the greenhouse and stand in the rich and humid air, heady with oxygen.

The room that reminds me of Lil, who grew gardens like her mother.

Jenny keeps having her infrequent contractions.

After a while of walking, we sit down again, and we watch a movie on the common room screen. Here on Mars we have every movie ever made in the history of the human species, up through and including movies released this last Friday, but we watch *All of Me* for some reason, which is a decades-old movie about soul possession, but comedic. Steve Martin and Lily Tomlin.

Jenny leans on me on our *chaise longue* and we watch. It's pretty funny. And every once in a while she has a contraction—she gets to the point where they're about twelve minutes apart—and those are kind of intense, but when those aren't happening sometimes I doze, and sometimes she dozes, and every once in a while one of us says something like, "Well. Isn't this something?" And we mean all kinds of things by that.

According to my father, there was a lot of blood when I was born. My mother's blood. According to him, the doctors became concerned. They became concerned that I was going to die, sure, but also that my mother was going to die. Well, not really, in that they would have probably saved her—but they were worried, I guess, that they would *have* to save her.

My birth came out fine for everyone. But things don't always come out fine.

After *All of Me* we do more walking, and we eat a snack or two, and then we get on a Steve Martin kick and watch *The Jerk*, which is hilarious, though again we do each fall asleep briefly through various parts of it, only because we're already very tired. And then we walk some more, and take pee breaks, and snack breaks, and there are contractions, in which Jenny leans on me for actual support and I wonder acutely if everything's okay, and then the light slowly comes up outside the windows on Mars, and the others start to wake up back in the bunk dome.

Trixie is up first, bouncing into the common room like someone from that manic Australian kids' show *The Wiggles* that she sometimes watches for nostalgic reasons. "How's the Jenny?" she says.

Jenny, still leaning on me a bit, gives Trixie a dutiful thumbs-up, and then we do a full check-in: time between contractions (ten minutes at this point), baby's heart rate (130, fine), dilation (progressing nicely), et cetera. Everything's fine, it seems. Assuming that Earth measurements are relevant here. At all.

And then Nicole's out with us, and Roger and Stefan peek shyly in, too. Roger's eyebrows seem permanently raised in astonishment. And Stefan looks basically freaked.

"Hey, Stefan," Jenny says to him. "Do you want to listen to the heartbeat?"

After a moment of hesitation, he nods silently. And Trixie hooks him up, and he gets to hear it.

"It's like a metronome," he says, stunned. "Like a fast little metronome."

Jenny pats him on the arm. I don't know how she always knows what to do, but she does always know what to do.

The day goes on from there in a sort of normal and sort of very abnormal fashion. As in, there's breakfast, in which we pretty much sit at our circular dining room table and where most folks eat their normal thing—Stefan his rye bread and cheese, Trixie her sugar cereal, Roger his Cream of Wheat, et cetera—but Jenny's not hungry for the moment and only has a single scrambled egg, and that at Nicole's insistence. After that, Roger and Stefan go off to work—Stefan has some electrical stuff still to do, I guess, because our lights have been flickering again over the last few days, though there seems to be a sudden reprieve today—and Nicole and Trixie try to focus on whatever they're supposed to be focused on. Jenny is clearly the big game in town, but everybody does manage to give us some space, which is not easy, let me tell you, in a Martian habitation center.

It'd be nice to go outside for a walk, but Jenny can't fit into any of the spacesuits, which I know has been making her a little bit bonkers for the last trimester. So instead of going outside we sit on the couch and watch *Dead Men Don't Wear Plaid*, which is funny but maybe not as funny as some of Steve Martin's other movies. Though perhaps more artistically ambitious. We debate about that a little. Also, at one point, Jenny says, "What kind of person do you think we've made?" which would be a sweet question from most people, but in Jenny's case is a frightened question, because Jenny's sister was not well. And bipolar disorder *is* somewhat heritable.

Jenny's not worried about the birth the way I am; she's worried about what the birth will produce. And then we're both worried about whether it's right of us to bring a life into the world if the world is Mars. Between her and me, we have all the possible worries covered.

Eventually, at lunch, Jenny and I have whatever we have—it's hard to even know what we're eating—and all the others have what they have. We try to talk about normal things, but mostly it's about contractions. Jenny's down to seven minutes between. I do not love the contractions. Jenny says they feel like squeezes; from my perspective they look like pretty tight squeezes.

"Seven minutes? Aces," Trixie says. And she supports that assertion with a thumbs-up.

"It's coming," I said.

Trixie smiles. "Sure is, Dad."

It's really coming—like headlights coming at us.

Then everybody goes back to whatever they were doing, and we turn on *Three Amigos!* and then turn it off again, and try *Roxanne* instead, which is pretty good, as far as I can tell through my preoccupation. At one point, Jenny, who is still leaning on me and is currently between contractions, thank God, sits up and turns to me.

"Hey," she says. "What are you thinking about?"

I go blank. What I *had* been thinking about, I don't want to say: Lil. "What are *you* thinking about?" I ask her instead.

"I'm thinking that we're about to become a real family," she says, tearing up a little. "And I hope we're going to be an okay family."

Which means she's thinking about her sister again. I stroke Jenny's hair, look into her silver-gray eyes. "We're going to be fine," I say. "We're going to be fine."

When Jenny turns back to the TV, I try very hard to breathe calmly.

At some point that afternoon, when everybody's more or less hovering, Stefan points out something that we all already know but that we don't always think about. "They're filming this whole thing," he says, pointing up at one of the cameras in the corner of the ceiling.

We look up at the camera. Jenny is in labor and that's going to be edited into an hour-long-segment format, and Earth is going to get to watch the first baby ever born on Mars—if everything goes well.

"Hey," Trixie says. "You know what I'm thinking about?"

And we know, because she has a certain look on her face that we recognize.

"I wonder how this is playing back on the old blue planet," she says.

Sometimes we do follow the way we're talked about back on Earth; *Destination Mars!* warns against the practice because they feel it could, in the words of the handbook, *affect your mental well-being. It can be disconcerting to see one's life turned, through editing—and, dare we say, manipulation—into a narrative. And even more to see how people react to that narrative.* Which is a fair point. Trixie once came across a reference to herself as "a fun supporting character" and "a bit of color," and she was pouty for days. That was what first got her talking in my office, and which opened the door to deeper things; nobody sees herself as a supporting character in her own life. Plus that "color" comment was *probably* mainly about her hair and all her colloquialisms, but it might have also been a little bit racist; hard to say for sure. Anyway, similarly, Nicole didn't enjoy discovering that she was seen by one entertainment blog as "a strange mix of house manager and military police." Never mind that Trixie was popular in Australia and the generator of many great memes throughout the internet or that science-minded black children all over the world had posters of Nicole in their bedrooms—still those stray unflattering comments stung. I had that in mind when Roger learned that on Earth he was called, surprisingly frequently, a nebbish; I, as the closest thing to a local Yiddish authority, made some editorial adjustments and told him that meant "nice guy." But I don't think he believed me. From the look of him, he's been working out a lot lately. Stefan and Jenny, meanwhile, have almost completely avoided reading about themselves, and I mostly have, too. Not because *Destination Mars!* told me to, and not even really because I'm afraid to find out what they're saying, but because Earth is very far away—I left it behind on purpose, after all—and it's hard to care a lot about what anyone there is thinking.

Trixie, in any case, is scanning her tablet now. Despite the "supporting character" thing, which has actually come up more than once, she's always been the most addicted to what's going on back home. She looks at Jenny and me. "This pregnancy is big," she says. "People are rooting for you and Josh, though they think you're a bit passive and flip-floppy—" she says this to me, and then turns to Jenny— "and nobody ever knows how you really feel about anything." Trixie winces a little as she says it. "Anyway, there are also heaps of probability tables—sex of the baby, health of the baby— and betting pools. Wow—one place is taking odds on there being *antennae*! And what name the baby's going to have, and weight and length, survival—" She breaks off and claps a hand over her mouth, just too late.

Just then, Jenny has a contraction, and it's a long one. It's an intense squeeze. With my heart going very, very quickly, I hold Jenny's hands and we do some mindfulness. I tell her to imagine a lake, a very still lake. We haven't seen a lake of any kind for several years now, except on video screens. But luckily you don't forget about them. She holds my hands and keeps her eyes closed and tries to picture that lake.

When the contraction is over, I notice that Trixie's tablet is away, and that nobody brings up the reality show anymore. Which is more the point. We're here; us. This is what matters, where everything that matters goes one way or another.

In the late afternoon we watch *Parenthood*. It's a movie from Steve Martin's transitional period, between silly and serious. It seems like it's going to be right on the nose for our situation, but mostly it's about how to not screw your kids up on a planet we haven't touched in years. Maybe it feels more relevant from Jenny's perspective. Me, I can barely follow it right now.

In fact, neither of us can; Jenny is having contractions often. There's pain and imagining lakes and panic that I try to keep to myself.

I am dimly aware of Keanu Reeves bopping through his scenes. He was a young person once.

Then Jenny's water breaks. I don't hear the pop, but there's the flood.

Lil and I did talk about having kids, of course. You don't agree to get married without having talked about that. Or you shouldn't, anyway. We called them our "future kids." We almost believed in them, like they were already real.

Which the car accident demonstrated they were not.

. . . .

Now that her water has broken, Jenny's labor is more for real. Contractions are five minutes apart and Trixie and Nicole are paying closer attention to things. In a worried way? Just in a here-the-baby-comes kind of way? I can't tell.

"Everything's okay, right?" I ask them, as I sit there with Jenny.

"She's apples, Dad," Trixie says to me. That means she's doing fine, which may or may not be truthful, and it's also an example of the bit of color Trixie adds. The colloquialisms and her hair. I try to focus on that.

"We'll let you know if there's anything to be concerned about," Nicole says. Then she pulls her lucky Mardi Gras beads from her pocket and puts them around my neck.

I try to be reassured.

As we get further in, and Jenny's actually starting to push, trying different positions on the *chaise longue*, I'm aware that Jenny is sort of receding from me. She's going inside. She's having to concentrate a lot on getting through labor, and so she has her eyes closed a lot of the time, especially when another wave hits, and, even when they're open, her eyes are a little unfocused when they look at me, almost like, *Hey, you—I feel like I'm supposed to know you, and you seem kind of nice, but I'm not so good with names right now. . . .*

Dinner comes and goes. I think I eat something, sitting with Jenny. Jenny doesn't eat anything.

There's a movie playing, at least for a while, but it's hard to know what it even is.

. . . .

I've had dreams about the birth, definitely. Usually I don't remember my dreams, but I remember a lot of them about the birth. They are not hard to interpret. Sometimes it turns out Jenny was never pregnant at all—just bloating—and sometimes she gives birth and the baby is invisible or it flies away before I can see it, or it's a chicken cutlet on a plate, uncooked.

And sometimes Jenny dies.

The pushing goes on for a long while, into the night. By now, Jenny definitely looks the way I would expect her to—but of course it's not in any way a relief to see her look the way I would expect her to look: her face sweaty, curls of her hair sticking to her forehead, her light brown eyes shaky some of the time. I can't tell exactly what's happening for her. She moans and sometimes howls. But overall she's further and further inside. Trixie and Nicole keep track of everything, and Jenny pushes. If I didn't know she was giving birth, I would think something terrible was happening to her. And of course maybe something terrible is happening to her.

"You okay, Dad?" Trixie says to me, her eyes concerned. Her maroon hair is a little sweaty, too.

"Is it supposed to be like this?" I ask, clutching the beads around my neck.

She and Nicole both tell me not to worry, but then I realize once again—in this moment it *really* hits me—that neither one of these are OB/GYN doctors. *Destination Mars!* didn't send any of those, because we weren't supposed to need any of those.

"Have you ever been at a birth before?" I ask.

"Of course," Nicole says, but I know she means that she was at one or two, maybe, during her rotations.

"Relax, Dad," Trixie says to me, and then she makes significant eyes and points her head back at Jenny. As in, *Don't upset her.* "Let's keep it upbeat," she says.

Okay, I think to myself. *Okay.*

I step up. I get Jenny cool, wet *Destination Mars!* washcloths to put on her neck, and I hold her hand, and I talk to her about calm things. And inside I imagine her vanishing. No baby and no Jenny.

It's like I'm being reminded of Lil, but I realize that it's actually the precariousness and fragility of everything, not Lil, that I'm being reminded of. Because what's terrible about that, right now, is that that precariousness is all around and inside and through Jenny. Jenny who is brilliant and her eyes see everything and she's beautiful to such an extent that she makes it hard to think about anything else when she's around and who may be the most astounding fact about the universe, and this is coming from a person who's seen more of that universe than a lot of other people. It's *that* Jenny who's in danger—and also this baby, who is still the future and not real yet. But, as hard as I've tried to stop myself, I have secretly started to believe in this future family. This endangered future family that isn't real yet.

There is some blood. There are *Destination Mars!* towels that aren't very absorbent because of the enormous logos. I feel dizzy and uncertain and like I don't know where I am. I glance at the windows and see how dark it is outside. Outside could be anyplace.

"Ohhhhh . . ." Jenny says, a soft and plaintive moan. "It's so difficult," she says. "What am I doing?"

Trixie and Nicole don't manage a response, as they are working very hard on the situation, I can see. Moving quickly around Jenny, checking things, consulting with one another. They're in motion.

So I make sure that Jenny's hand is in mine, and I try to make myself be completely with her, though I really, really want to fly away to somewhere where I never think about any possible futures at all. "We're all here together," I tell Jenny.

Jenny's eyes open. She squeezes my hand. This is a short moment between contractions, which are coming very frequently now. I see Jenny's eyes, which are looking into mine. "Is that what you're thinking?" she says. "That we're all here together?"

"Yes," I say, which is true. I'm crying as I say it.

And then a contraction hits, hits hard, and she's all about pushing and making it through. She squeezes my hand very hard.

When it passes, we are both crying, and our hands are almost one hand, all together.

I am in the presence of the most precious everything that can be. And it's an impossibility—it *can't* be—and I know it.

I turn to Trixie and whisper into her ear. I say, "Can we stop this? Can we just go back to before this?"

Trixie takes my head in both of her hands, looks at me very close. "Shut up, you drongo," she says. But I see that there are tears in her eyes.

After the next push, Nicole says, "Do we have a mirror?"

I'm wondering what's gone wrong, and Stefan, who must be nearby, runs off and grabs a mirror. Later it will turn out that he'd ripped it right out of the bathroom wall and we'll have to bolt it back up. But he comes back with the mirror.

"Hold it there," Nicole directs him.

"What's going on?" I ask. I yell it.

Stefan's eyes widen as he sees directly what we're now seeing in the mirror.

"*What's happening?*" I say. Because what *is* happening? I see blood and, in my mind, headlights. And in a whisper, I ask again, "Can we stop?"

"This is called crowning," Nicole says. "This is your baby. This is the top of your baby's head."

Wait. I can't tell what I'm seeing at all. "That's the baby's head?"

The doctors nod.

"You mean nothing's wrong?" I say.

"Focus," Trixie says, giving me a little smack on the shoulder. There are tears in her eyes—but they're—I think they're *happy* ones? "You're about to become a father." She points.

Wait.

I see it. What Nicole said—I see the dome of the baby's head. Really? I am crying very profusely now. Jenny is, too. And I'm almost understanding what's going on.

Right now, at Jenny's side, holding her, staring into the mirror, I can just begin to see what's crowning.

A voice in my head says, *Well—would you look at that.*

"I think everything's okay," I say to Jenny, in enormous astonishment. "Oh, my God. I love you."

"It's okay?" she asks. "You love me?"

I nod. "I think we're having a child."

At that, everybody around laughs. Everyone is happy. And, catching up, Jenny laughs, too—a big one.

Which turns out to be enough to do it.

Laughter is enough, at least today, at least here, to complete this labor. To bring, with a sudden movement, a world into a world. To make something both old and new. To make the entire universe a garden—a new one, seen countless times in the past and also never seen before, a garden fruitful and forgiving—and to hold us together in it.

What You Can't Do (Part Three)
(Section 4 of the unofficial *Destination Mars!* handbook, as written by the founder of *Destination Mars!*)

Subsection 4:3: Post-Natal Concerns

But let's just say that the baby manages to get born, and that the mother doesn't die in the process, and that the baby is reasonably healthy. And that you haven't destroyed your mini-community in the process. That combination of outcomes is obviously unlikely, but let's say it all manages to happen somehow. Well, guess what? Your problems are just beginning.

- To state the obvious: we will not be there to help with all the challenges—medical, developmental, social— that will inevitably come up throughout childhood. You will be on your own, for that and for everything else. You will by necessity be making this parenting thing up as you go, with inadequate training, help, or supplies. What will your child need? Will you have it? Who knows?

- And then there's the evolutionary question. Just consider for a minute the fact that we, as a species, evolved on Earth. Evolution being a system where babies are born (on Earth) and then subjected to environmental conditions (on Earth) and then the ones who are most fit to thrive (on Earth) reproduce, producing babies that are also likely to thrive (on Earth) and so on.

- o If you make a baby on Mars, it will be on a planet it wasn't designed to be on. Of course, you weren't designed for it, either, but at least you had a choice. And we chose you. And you trained for it. If Darwin was right about survival of the fittest, just how fit will this baby be?

- o Furthermore, if the child *does* find a way to adapt, it will be adapting to the environment of Mars. This isn't dangerous, precisely—it will actually be pretty impressive—but it raises big questions. Like, what if this baby grows up and has more babies with other Mars-adapted people? This will send evolution in an entirely new direction: humans who are more fit for Mars than for Earth. Real Martians. That's a big deal, and one *we* aren't ready for. We doubt you are, either. Playing God may sound like fun, but is it? God's telling silence over the past several millennia suggests a very different conclusion.

- Even Elton John thinks it's a bad idea. ("Rocket Man," anyone?)

- Anyway, assuming the baby *is* healthy and *stays* healthy, it will probably outlive you. And although we hope to send more people after you, what if we can't make that happen? The baby—now an adult— will be alone on Mars. Can you imagine being alone on Mars? Well, maybe you can, a little. But *entirely* alone? It won't be an easy thing, being on your own on a dangerous planet without guidance or support. In other words, what kind of life are you bringing this baby into?

We do realize that many of the concerns listed in the subsections above—social dynamics, biological risks, the enormous issues that come up in raising a child—also apply on Earth. It's a big deal, making a baby, no matter where you are. And in some sense there's never enough help even on Earth. In some sense you're always on your own. We don't deny that this is the fundamental condition of being in the universe: trying to figure out what to do, on your own.

But maybe you can escape that on Mars, if you just do what we tell you to do. And if you *don't* do what we tell you *not* to do. After all, the stakes are higher than ever.

The Block Universe Theory of Newborns

Observations: Her

- APGAR score: 10 (out of 10)

- length: 19.25 inches

- weight: 2.7 pounds, which terrified me until I remembered that that was Mars weight; she would be 7.2 pounds on Earth

- Fingers and toes: all of them

- Overall:
  (if I could describe her in some sufficient way I would)

Observation: Planets

Earth:	Mars:
Still spinning.	Still spinning.

Observations

- Her face.

- Josh's face.

Observation: Family
Is.

Observation: Abandonment
Life—making life, living life—*is* an abandonment. It means leaving life in the hands of life.

Observation: Probability
Unknowable. Which means you can't know that things will go wrong.

Observation: Knowledge

%

■ What I know about the universe   ■ What I absolutely do not

Observations: Time

Relativistic Physics is correct; time *is*.

- The past is still present. Which does not mean that the present *is* the past.

- We can't see the future, but there apparently is one.

They Called Her Able

AMABLE (from the Spanish for *lovable*) was born on Mars and then she grew up on Mars.

She was the first child to do either of those things.

Lots of people thought it was impossible—thought she couldn't get born, couldn't live, couldn't grow up. But she managed all of it pretty easily, or as easily as any of us do in our own circumstances.

The child first rolled over on a rug made out of a space-age polymer that could feel like almost any woven textile you wanted it to. She learned to walk on the smooth floors of a habitation center that had been built by robots before any people were on that planet at all. She made her first crayon marks on that floor, too, using run-of-the-mill crayons that had been sent in a supply rocket. And she learned to walk outside, in a mini-spacesuit sent from Earth, over very uneven ground. Learning to walk in a spacesuit is no easy thing, either; it's like you're using your own body to get a puppet to walk. But she did that. And she learned to eat solid foods and then to feed herself sitting at a table in a dining dome, a moldable table that the adults remolded so that part of it was at her level and had a lip on it for spills. Children on Mars spill just like children on Earth.

The child's first word was *mama*. Because what did you expect?

Her first pets were two goldfish that had accidentally been frozen solid on the way to Mars but had swum right back to life when they were accidentally thawed. Sometimes things happen like that.

And maybe it's that rebirth of the goldfish that explains the child's optimism, which developed early and stayed with her all along. Or maybe it was being born into the role of a pioneer. Or maybe it was the lower gravity. Or maybe something else altogether; it would be foolish to believe anyone who claimed to understand these things completely.

People said that the child would be abnormal. And in some sense she was, by definition. There was no statistical precedent for her. But essentially she was the same type of creature as the creatures that have been born from humans for two hundred thousand years now. She emerged incomplete, like the rest of us, and she entered into a vast but similarly incomplete universe like the rest of us, and she stood and walked as soon as she could, and she went off in pursuit of completion from that point on.

Of course, the child had help. She had two parents and there were four other adults besides, which is a small social circle—one of the smallest in human history, surely—but not an empty one.

Also there were those goldfish, and, soon enough, the offspring of goldfish.

The adults had been hand-chosen. Not for parenthood or for watching over children at all—in fact, as they had been chosen for a one-way mission, they were chosen mainly for their technical skills and for their self-sufficiency, for their tendency not to need anyone new or perhaps even to know what to do with them if they appeared. They were all quite limited. Still they rose to the occasion, as people sometimes will. One of the adults taught the child to drive the rover, and another taught her how to take a person's temperature and blood pressure, and another taught her how to disable a person by punching that person in the throat, and another taught her how to make a plant grow from a seed. These adults taught her to read and write, to cook, to repair circuit panels and the tread of space boots. They taught her biology and physics and astronomy and chemistry and geology and engineering and the workings of the human mind.

The child was, it's true, abnormally clever. Her mind was very quick, and also very deep, a combination quite unlike a metaphorical river. You could fill it and fill it and still it would move briskly along.

One example: she was the first person to demonstrate definitively that Mars was alive, and in a way that you couldn't find in a water sample, or see or hear at all with your normal senses. The way that Mars is alive remains hard to describe to this day. But the humans and the Martians have found each other, and they mostly get along pretty well, and that's what counts.

The adults around her grew older, too, as adults will. Her parents never did have another child but they had no regrets, either, which is not nothing for adults. They were Mars' first family, and knew it, and they celebrated it, with many special occasions and special food that they made for those occasions and special thoughts the rest of the time and special looks on their faces, too. It could have been otherwise. The father had been worried that none of this would ever come to pass, and the mother worried that something would go bad once it did happen. Both reveled in their wrongness. It was, they felt, the greatest wrongness that had ever been.

They and the others continued their work on Mars, which was work they had sometimes forgotten to do before the child was born. But they got back to it. They studied the stars and they studied the soil; they built machines and they repaired them and one another, as necessary and in various ways. The engineer among them, using materials sent on supply rockets and materials taken from the planet itself, did over time build new domes so that they might each have private spaces—he was always a bit of a loner—but the domes were all clustered so that the people could come together, too, which was something they persistently did. Even sometimes the engineer.

The child became a teenager, in the way that children do. Except in her case it technically took both longer and shorter than it had all the other humans in human history. Longer because it took more than twenty-four Earth years before the child's age, in Martian years, had *teen* at the end of it. And shorter because she was already behaving like an Earth teenager by the time she was, in Martian years, six.

The people of two planets realized that numbers were just numbers.

By this point there were other adults on Mars—Earth had sent more—and there were other habitation centers, and people were doing things to warm the planet up a little, in a nice way, and shift the air just a bit toward breathable, and soon people didn't even all live in the same place on the planet, and eventually there were other children being born. But this first child would always be the first child. And the first adults knew one another best, and they continued to live close together.

By now there were generations of goldfish—bountiful, seemingly endless.

And then one day the child—she was a young woman by then—came to Earth. When the colony started on Mars, the rule was that it would be a one-way trip because nobody had the technology to go both ways. But the child motivated people—they wanted to bring her to Earth—and her growing up gave them a few years to think their way through solutions.

She and her parents got on a rocket that was the first rocket to ever leave Mars for Earth. It felt the way rockets do, which was not something the young woman knew about from personal experience.

During the trip, which despite technological advances was still several months long, the family floated in the lack of gravity, which was disconcerting at first, but they got used to it—the parents for the second time—and they told one another all the stories.

When the rocket arrived, everyone on Earth called it a homecoming, and there were crowds and balloons and all the usual things that people make and do when they're greeting a hero. As the young woman stepped out, she was understandably overwhelmed—video representations can't prepare you for this sort of thing, the sound, the sight, the motion, the great clamor that we specialize in here. And obviously this wasn't a homecoming; she'd never been to the planet before. She was, unless there's something we don't know, the first human to become an adult before seeing the Earth.

The young woman honestly found it a heavy place; she was used to much less gravity. Her parents, too, were shocked by the difference, especially after those months floating in the rocket—but nostalgia kicked in for them, and it was okay. They saw the things they had once seen, and were even reunited with some people they had left behind. There were tearful family reunions that salved places that needed salving.

The young woman, for her part, never quite felt fully upright on Earth. Nor did she get used to the clamor, which was indeed dramatic and more so all the time. Not just because of her, but because that's the way we've always gone—toward more clamor. Nor did she even get used to the colors, which were, she thought, too vivid and too many. She was accustomed to a uniform red-orange and, as it turned out, she preferred it. Though there were Earth things she liked—the sensation of wind on her face, and the feel of a cat's fur under her hand. A real bagel.

Over the next few months, there were many speeches and many ceremonies in her honor. Her parents accompanied her to each one and they felt a pride in their child that had never been felt in the universe before, and that had also been felt billions of times already. The young woman endured it all with grace and difficulty.

We had never thought about what Earth would look like to a stranger. Earth being the cradle of the species, the garden of our evolution. It was our great given.

The people of Earth realized that nothing was a given.

Then, as soon as it was possible—it took almost two years—she got herself back on a rocket and went home again. Her parents gladly went with her, and they brought a cat along, though her father was slightly allergic. There were pills for that.

In space, between Earth and Mars, they floated. The mother floated and the father floated, and so did the young woman, and even the cat floated. It was disconcerting at first, especially for the cat, who was about to be the first cat on Mars.

By the time they got there, Mars would already be starting to edge toward green, new patterns spreading across the planet. Things were changing. But slowly. In measured steps.

Meanwhile, those of us still on Earth felt another change. It was palpable, in the wake of the departing rocket taking that young woman away again: gravity, for all of us, was rapidly losing its hold.

HOW TO USE THIS HANDBOOK
(Section 36 of the unofficial *Destination Mars!* handbook, as written by the founder of *Destination Mars!*)

First of all, count yourselves very lucky indeed that you even have this handbook. Did the Apollo astronauts have a handbook? Did the astronauts on the International Space Station have a handbook? We're not sure, actually, but, if any of those folks did have handbooks, in any case they weren't like this one. And so you are fortunate people, who can make your way into the universe with some assistance, assistance we have been very glad to provide.

That said, your success in your new life does depend somewhat on how *well* you use this handbook. Which is why this section exists. Read on.

- In our time, people are reputed to have short attention spans, and we are told that texts need to be a very particular length if they are to be accessible to contemporary readers. This handbook was not designed with these facts in mind. Or, rather, it *was* designed with these facts in mind, but with the intention of upsetting those short spans of attention. Some sections will be too long, and you will have to stay with them; others will be too short, and you will be left with idle time on your hands. We will be interested to see how well you handle the situation, and what becomes of you.

- We will not be using this section to summarize the other sections of this handbook. You can read those other sections for yourselves. And perhaps you already have, and then we'd be wasting everyone's time.

- A word to the wise: it would probably be better to familiarize yourselves with the contents of this handbook *before* you need them, instead of waiting until you need them very desperately. Desperate readers may not be level-headed readers. Also, considering the handbook's ideas out of context might lead to new and creative connections that nobody could foresee. Like paging through a cookbook while you're very full; you might suddenly imagine yourselves with a future in color photography, or you might wonder why some fruits are sweet and others are spicy or even flavorless. This handbook presumably offers similar opportunities for divergent thinking, and you wouldn't want to miss that.

- Some will choose to read this handbook from front to back—and we did, for sure, put a great deal of effort into deciding the order of the sections. There's a reason why we talk about how to work with your machines before we talk about how to work with other people, or why we discuss boredom before death. There's a reason why this section is the last one in the book. Still—you are free agents, and you will read in whatever way you decide to read. That's the nature of people. And let us be the first to admit that there is a great deal about this handbook that even we don't understand, and so we are not about to try to control your experience.

- Still—it's probably best not to read the entire handbook in one sitting. That would trivialize the work that went into the handbook, which certainly took more than one sitting to write.

- One of the worst things about bad handbooks is the way they quickly become dated. After all, knowledge is always growing, so documenting reality can be a somewhat thankless task. One solution is to update the text from time to time, which has significant downsides, including the amount of work it would require. The other solution, and the one we've adopted, is to focus the text mainly on broad principles (e.g., flexibility, diligence, acceptance of one's fate). Not only are these unlikely to change, but they can be applied to new situations in a way that up-to-the-minute toaster oven instructions cannot. (This is the difference, you understand, between a handbook and a manual.) We've therefore aimed our writing at a level of generality that ought to serve you best and which may, at times, even strike you as profound.

- One of the central questions: is this book a how-to, or is it a what-to or when-to or where-to—or could it even be a *why*-to?

- Note that if you do read this handbook differently than we've anticipated or if you apply our information and guidelines to situations we haven't outlined or in ways we haven't suggested, we cannot be held responsible for the results. Legally or even ethically.

- There is a table of contents in this handbook, but no index. We didn't want to coddle you.

- Nor are there any appendices. An appendix seems to us to be a subordinate, second-class kind of chapter, and we value all our chapters equally. We hope you will do the same.

- No handbook can ever claim to be complete, and the responsible ones refrain from making that claim. We are going to take that discretion a step further by *pro*claiming the *in*completeness of this handbook. Indeed, there are many subjects—even potentially crucial ones—that you will not find covered here. Sometimes this is because there are things we don't know, and sometimes because there are things that we don't know that we *do* know, or that we know but we don't know that you want to know them, if you see what we mean. And sometimes things are missing because we decided to leave them out. It has been observed that, in many aboriginal cultures, craftspeople intentionally build flaws into the textiles and pottery they make, with the understanding that humans are incapable of perfection. We've always found that very compelling.

- When you do encounter a gap in the handbook, don't become panicked. There is meaning in absence just as there is meaning in presence. In fact, there may be more meaning in absence. The only difference is that you have to figure out what it is.

- You can certainly reach out to us whenever you like. Bear in mind, however, that it takes six months for us to get supplies to you. Month to month, in other words, you'll be making do with what you have. But it's even more minute than that. You know, for example, that it takes eleven minutes to get a message from us; by the time you get it, it's already a little bit out of date. Not hugely, but enough to make you feel slightly unsettled when you get that message. *What is this, exactly?* you'll ask. Don't worry; you will get used to these delays, for better and for worse. You will change the way you think about your situation and about us and the connection between the two. We may eventually come to seem very remote, almost unreal, to you. We may come to seem like something you've made up in order to comfort yourselves in times of uncertainty. This is natural, though we're not sure that we will be at our most comforting in those times.

- Which leads us to this: you're on your own. Moment to moment, you'll be the one living this life of yours. And of course this has always been true, though never before in the exact way that it's now true for you. Which has also always been true. This is, in some sense, the human tradition. And the human tradition is yours. It's yours to experience, and it's yours to inhabit, and it's yours to live forward in your own particular and imprecise way.

- Every day is the same question: what will you do with this day, as a free person in a free universe where nobody but you has the power to make that decision for you?

- If this handbook helps you along the way, we will be very glad. But we also know that you will mostly find yourselves in the gaps, where we cannot reach you, and where you cannot reach us. You will make meaning where and how you can.

- We have been told that this is what it means to be alive.

Afterword

I STARTED WRITING this novel in 2015 after reading a stunner of a news story about something called Mars One. This, I discovered, was a company (now bankrupt) that had put out a call for applications; they said they had plans to send twelve people on a one-way trip to Mars. Even crazier, by the time I found about them, they were claiming that 200,000 people had applied. It was hard to tell whether the organization was visionary or deranged or fraudulent, but the idea of going to Mars with no option to come back struck *me* as totally insane, and it got me wondering just who would sign up for such a thing: to leave Earth forever, to never see any other people aside from the other folks sent on the mission, to never feel a breeze or pet a dog or sit under a cherry tree in bloom. Never, ever again.

So, in a state of shock, I wrote a short story—"*Prakt* Means Splendor," now the first chapter of this novel—about a group of people stuck on Mars with no way home, and who had just learned that one of them was pregnant. (Mars One was also famous for its rule that participants would not be allowed to have sex.) Each character had had reason to leave Earth forever. What would happen now that these dead-enders suddenly had to consider the possibility of new life?

The next thing I wrote was a short story called "What You Can't Bring With You," which took the form of rules and instructions from a fictional organization pushing a Mars-One-like mission. I wrote it because I was still stunned by everything these Mars One applicants were willing to leave behind. (I usually write about things I *don't* understand. Doing so helps me understand a little better.) The story also came because I was interested not just in the applicants, but also in the idea of a company willing to play G-d, cheerfully ready to relocate humans from one planet to another.

The stories—soon enough I was thinking of them as chapters— spilled out from there.

Along the way I did a lot of intentional reading, because I hadn't ever written much about space travel. Some of the standouts from the stack of both fiction and non-fiction: Jennifer A. Howard, *You on Mars: Failed Sci-Fi Stories*; Lee Billings, *Five Billion Years of Solitude*; Ray Bradbury, *The Martian Chronicles*; Tom Gauld, *Mooncop*; Anthony Michael Morena, *The Voyager Record*; Stephen Petranek, *How We'll Live on Mars*; Rod Pyle, *Curiosity*; Mary Roach, *Packing for Mars*; and Robert Zubrin, *The Case for Mars*.

I also read books (in most cases these were rereads) to help me think about voice and tone and general absurdism, including several books by Aimee Bender; *The Great Frustration* by Seth Fried; *Pym* by Mat Johnson; *LoveStar* by Andri Snær Magnason; *Two Years Eight Months and Twenty-Eight Nights* by Salman Rushdie; *Blindness* by José Saramago; several books by George Saunders, and *Cat's Cradle* by Kurt Vonnegut. To study novels-in-stories I reread *Welcome to the Goon Squad* by Jennifer Egan (which also helped me think through different formats for prose) as well as the gold standard of novels-in-stories, Allegra Goodman's *The Family Markowitz*.

Anyway, as you can see from the start date, it can take a long time to do all that writing and reading—to finish a novel, in other words. With this one there were many false starts and changes (in early drafts, for example, there were eight Marsonauts and now there are six) and lots and lots of revisions. Writing a book is a *process*. (As a proud Philadelphian, I know instinctively that one has to Trust the Process.)

As for Mars One, it turns out that they may have wildly misrepresented their number of applicants, and maybe some other things, and in any case the whole thing—whether scam or lunacy—has collapsed. But by the time any of that came out, I was already deep into the novel, and wasn't going to stop. Because at that point it was bigger for me than one strange news story. And it wasn't only about what kind of person, with what kind of life, would be willing to go on a trip like this—it was also about what would happen to someone once they were there and still had to face the things they had tried to leave behind.

More than that, this novel was (and is) supposed to be about all of us. Here we are, living not in a manicured paradise but in a vast and complicated universe, seemingly left to our own devices—wrestling with the unknown, trying to figure out what to do with the lives that have been handed to us. Thus *How to Mars* is also supposed to be about how to Earth. How to human. How to be.

David Ebenbach
Washington, DC

Book Group Questions

- If someone offered you a guaranteed-safe one-way journey to Mars, how tempted would you be? What if it was two-way but would take several years to complete?

- Do you relate to any of the characters' motivations to leave planet Earth?

- Do you think there may be intelligent life out there in the universe somewhere? If so, what do you think it might be like? How like/unlike The Patterns might it be?

- The novel's characters are all quite different—in what they want, in the way they think and express themselves and behave. Which character do you relate to the most? Least?

- This is a novel-in-stories—a novel whose chapters are mostly standalone short stories. How does that make this novel different as a reading experience?

- What contribution does humor make to the experience of reading this novel? And in what ways is the book also serious?

- Did *Destination Mars!* send people with the right skill sets to Mars? What kinds of professions and skills do you think would be crucial to living on another planet?

Acknowledgments

THIS IS WHERE I get to express my gratitude. And I'm feeling a lot of it.

First of all, I am grateful to anybody who's reading this. That's a big deal, choosing to read this, as opposed to the many other things you could be doing, and it genuinely means a lot to me. Thank you.

I'm also deeply grateful to Michael Carr, who championed this book so that it could now be in your hands. On top of that, many thanks to the excellent people of Tachyon Publications—Jacob Weisman, Jaymee Goh, Jill Roberts, James DeMaiolo, Rick Klaw, Elizabeth Story, and Rie Langdon, among others—who have devoted great skill and effort to the task of transforming my manuscript into our *book*.

Thanks, too, to the magazines and their editors who first published earlier versions of some of these chapters as stand-alone stories. "Welcome to Your Machines" was published in *Analog Science Fiction and Fact*; "Pregnancy as a Location in Space-Time" first appeared in *Asimov's Science Fiction*; "*Prakt* Means Splendor" first appeared in *The Kenyon Review*; and "Team Orderly Mars" was published in *Not One of Us*.

Of course, the manuscript wouldn't have been ready for publication at all without the wise feedback I got along the way—from Michael Carr, from magazine editors and the editors of Tachyon, and from some brilliant writers in my life. In that last category, I send a big thank you to Angie Chuang, Tania James, Melanie McCabe, Emily Mitchell, West Moss, and David Taylor. (If you've finished reading this book, you should drop everything and go read their books next. You won't regret it.)

And *How to Mars* wouldn't have ever even been ready for feedback if not for the people who have energized and sustained me as a writer for so long. I'm thinking of my family, including my supportive parents and sister, and so many friends who have encouraged me again and again. And above all I'm thinking of my incomparable wife, Rachel, who is (beyond being spectacular in her own right) my most crucial booster and soother and champion and source of wisdom; and of my fantastic son, Reuben, who is my inspiration and, by far, my best reason to have hopes for the future.

Thank you.

BORN AND RAISED in the great city of Philadelphia, David Ebenbach is the author of eight books of fiction, poetry, and non-fiction, including the novel *Miss Portland* and the short story collection *The Guy We Didn't Invite to the Orgy and Other Stories*; his books have won such awards as the Drue Heinz Literature Prize and the Juniper Prize, among others. With a BA in Psychology from Oberlin College, an MFA in Creative Writing from the Vermont College of Fine Arts, and a PhD in Psychology from the University of Wisconsin-Madison, David teaches creative writing, literature, and identity development in Georgetown University's Center for Jewish Civilization and he teaches creativity in Georgetown's MA program in Learning, Design, and Technology. David also works as a project manager for Georgetown's Center for New Designs in Learning and Scholarship, the school's center for teaching and learning. He's taught at George Washington University, Earlham College, Vermont College, Montclair State University, LaSalle University, and the University of Wisconsin-Madison. All this work has required a lot of moving; David has lived in Pennsylvania, Ohio, Wisconsin, New York, New Jersey, and Indiana—and now he lives in Washington, DC, with his wife and son. You can find out more at davidebenbach.com.